CANDLELIGHT REGENCY SPECIAL

CANDLELIGHT REGENCIES

The Enterprising Minx

Marian Lorraine

A CANDLELIGHT REGENCY SPECIAL

Published by
Dell Publishing Co., Inc.
1 Dag Hammarskjold Plaza
New York, New York 10017

Copyright © 1981 by Marian L. Horton

Dell ® TM 681510, Dell Publishing Co., Inc.

ISBN: 0-440-12270-8

Printed in the United States of America

First printing—February 1981

Chapter
ONE

Outside the old Jacobean manor house, which sat serenely on the crest of a rise that overlooked the river Arun, the crescent wind whistled threateningly through the denuded branches of the venerable beeches while a heavy, silent snow fell steadily this early January. The two ladies Ingram remarked aimlessly on the particularly fierce expression of winter's fury as they sat in reasonable comfort before the roaring fire, dressed in their warmest clothes, with a pot of steaming tea and little biscuits to sustain them.

"I wish we were back in Italy," the older woman said pensively as if it had only been a short while since they had visited there, when it had actually been almost three years. "The warm sunshine and bright colours of the flowers and the sea are so uplifting to the spirits. Much as I love England, I cannot admire the generally wet climate and depressing gray skies."

"Now, Mother, that's what I call a curious exercise in self-deception," the young girl chided, cocking her head and smiling affectionately. "I remember very well the many times you were wilting from the heat and shading your eyes from the glare, wishing you were back in Sussex."

"Was I really?" the lady asked in surprise. "Well, perhaps that is true, and I am sorry to be so complaining, but I do so like the warm weather and to be out of doors."

"But, darling, the weather is not often so inclement that you cannot venture out for a few hours. The winter is just beginning, and if you are already dispirited, the days will seem to drag excessively. I shall have to devise some interesting employments for you so you may occupy your mind and pull yourself out of the doldrums."

"Laurel, I beg you will not exert yourself in that direction," Lady Madeline protested hastily, being well acquainted with her daughter's unnaturally inventive mind and not wishing to be drawn into any of her projects. "You know I have no talents and no interest in making a career for myself. I am much too indolent. In fact, it tires me just to see you working incessantly, and it confounds me to have to admit that you have, by some inauspicious quirk of fate, inherited your father's intellect and his energy. It is not seemly that you should spend so much time with your nose buried in those fusty books and drawing ridiculous diagrams and curlicues. And it is certainly injudicious for you to devote all your efforts to helping Jason forward his ambitions, especially when it gets you nowhere. You are twenty-two, much as it pains me to admit it, and should be thinking seriously of establishing yourself in an agreeable, permanent connection instead of unprofitably harbouring false hopes. It is perfectly obvious that he sees you only as a dear friend and associate, although I do truly believe you could easily alter your indifferent status if you made any attempt to show yourself as the beautiful, desirable young woman you are, instead of impersonating a dowdy bluestocking."

"Mother, I wish you will not nag me on that subject again. You are becoming exceedingly vexatious with these repeated importunities," the girl charged with a show of irritation.

"You do not have to be so uncivil," her mother protested, looking offended. "You know I only have your best interests at heart. You are my only child, and I can't bear to see you headed for a life of unhappiness."

"My love, I'm afraid you have a rather narrow view of happiness," Laurel noted with a softened expression. "Be-

8

cause you and Father had such a lovely relationship, you think that is the only kind of existence that could be satisfying."

The older lady, a purely comparative description as Lady Madeline was only forty-two and looked several years younger, showed her skepticism of this aggravatingly unaspiring attitude and attested with some warmth, "My dear Laurel, I may not be as percipient as you are, but I am not feebleminded either, and you will have a hard time convincing me that you would not be happier if you were married to Jason."

"But barring that," her daughter replied with a maddening calm, "I am content as things are."

"And what if things should change? Jason is a handsome, wealthy young man and, unencumbered as he is, is certainly fair game for any young lovely who would set her cap for him. It is not beyond the realm of possibility that he might marry one day and then where will you be?" Lady Madeline demanded ruthlessly.

Since this was an unwelcome thought that occasionally forced itself upon her consciousness and was definitely not a pleasant contemplation, Laurel reacted testily, placing her cup loudly on the table as she submitted, "All right, Mother! I am going to be perfectly frank with you, telling you exactly how I feel and why I carry on as I do, and then I do not want to discuss the subject again. If you will not indulge me in this, we will likely come to cuffs because your hectoring only makes it difficult for me and serves to cast me into a fit of the blue devils. Yes, I love Jason and have ever since I had any inkling of what it meant. I made excuses to be near him, actually directing my capabilities and energies in a direction that gave me an opportunity to work with him, and in doing so, I found that I have a genuine talent for contributing substantially to his endeavours. You ask why I do not try to make him see me in a different light. The answer is that I am afraid. Afraid that if it made him uncomfortable, it might upset this beautiful accord we have now, and I would rather have only this much than risk putting a strain on our friendship. Even if

9

he would respond positively, I could not bear to be loved less than I love because I could not hide my feelings and would likely embarrass him and myself."

"Oh, Laurel, my dear," Lady Madeline said dolefully with tears in her eyes, dismayed by her daughter's intensity, "I am so sorry. I didn't fully realize how deeply you felt. Now I fear for you even more, and I suddenly have a terrible foreboding."

"Dear God!" a sorely pressed young lady exclaimed in exasperation. "Not much can be said for your sensibility when you can predict only disaster."

Her mother dabbed at her eyes and apologized, though she still felt constrained to repeat her warning. "But, Laurel, you must consider the possibility that he could marry someone else."

"Yes, love, I know. I have thought about it, and if it comes to that, I shall just have to bear the blow. I think I have enough strength of mind and character to come about. Not that I wouldn't be miserable, but after the first shock I am convinced I would be able to face up to it, I promise you. And, Mother, you must recognize that I have become extremely accomplished in the work I am doing. My services will be in demand even should it, for some inauspicious reason, become inadmissible to work with Jason. There is much to be said, you know, for developing a talent that can give some purpose to life. I truly enjoy my work, so I do have some resources to fall back on if I am destined to be a spinster."

The distressingly offensive word seemed to have an unfortunate, upsetting effect on the older lady, and she leaned back in her chair with her hand on her head, displaying a look of horror. "How can you be so unnatural as even to think such a thing! Never could I have imagined you an ape-leader. Don't you know how beautiful you are? You could have anyone you wanted if you put your mind to it—even Jason, I am persuaded. But you dress like a prim schoolmistress and wear your hair in that lamentably unattractive fashion, and I have come to recognize it as a deliberate affectation. I can't imagine how you became so deluded!"

"If you are quite finished," Laurel said coldly, losing her patience, "we will conclude this discussion here and now and then consider it done." She looked at her mother with an intense expression and asked feelingly, "Can you imagine how precious these hours that I spend with Jason are to me? I know that he is fond of me, that he admires my talent and depends on me, and I treasure his regard more than anything. I have found a surpassing degree of happiness, Mother, so I wish you will not try to ruin it for me with your constant, plaguesome dissertations!"

In the face of this fervent appeal Lady Madeline realized at last that her daughter could not be induced to follow a more aggressive course and violently resented any interference, well intentioned though it might be, so she submitted with a long-suffering sigh of resignation. "All right, Laurel," she said. "I think you are benighted, but I will not say any more." And she determinedly picked up the lastest fashion magazine to contemplate designs for the several new gowns she would have made for the Season, to which she looked forward with more than her usual, pleasurable anticipation.

Laurel sat back to recover her serenity, staring abstractedly into the fire. She sincerely hoped she had finally persuaded her mother to stop worrying her about her nebulous situation. It was enough that she had her own hidden misgivings and a recurring sense of frustration and unfulfillment. It was too much to have to be pricked time and again because she actually did realize that this state of affairs could not go on forever, and the worst of it was that she really could not decide what to do about it. Sometimes she thought that her mother was right and that she should show Jason a different face. But every time she had summoned enough courage, she suddenly lost her resolution because she could not bear to take the chance of putting him off. She often suspected she might have missed her golden opportunity. There was one beautiful moment that would always remain alive for her, and she treasured

11

it secretly, dwelling on it often. In reality, it was not much to sustain her for a lifetime, and she had a regretful feeling that things might have turned out very differently by now if she had not been so shy and timorous and had trusted her feminine instinct to take advantage.

They were on their way back from Italy. Jason had been assiduously studying Roman and Greek architecture for three years, having left for the Continent immediately after Napoleon's abdication in 1814. He had returned to England twice during that period, remaining for two months or so, but finally was ready to come home to begin his work.

He and Laurel had always been sympathetic companions even though there were six years between them. After her father had died, Jason undertook to appoint himself knight-errant to her and her mother as the families had always been close neighbours and friends. His own father, who was a younger son of the Earl of Dismore and had made a name for himself and reaped his fortune in the Navy, having risen to the rank of admiral, had died after only three years' retirement at the end of Jason's second year away. The young man came back as soon as he received the news and stayed with his mother for two months. It was at this time that he and Laurel had begun to collaborate because he had unwittingly discovered, when he allowed her to examine his notebooks, that she had an inherent artistic sense and an uncanny eye for proportion. He began to teach her how to draft architectural drawings and encouraged her to design decorative moldings, friezes, and mantels and to recognize quality in materials and workmanship. Her surprising aptitude and enthusiasm delighted him because he was unequivocally impressed by her remarkable talent, and he was elated that he had already found an exceptional assistant so conveniently close to home. Laurel couldn't have been happier. At eighteen she had outgrown her adolescent hero worship, having graduated to an advanced state of adoration which soon would blossom into a deep and lasting love, and she avidly devoted all her time and energy to perfecting the skills which would effectively ensure her a prominent and permanent place in Jason's life.

When he was preparing to leave for his last year of study, Jason conceived a sudden inspiration, and he enthusiastically suggested that his mother, Laurel, and her mother might plan to join him in the warm clime of Italy for two or three months the coming winter. Then they would all return to England together. This proposal was met with unanimous approval and anticipation, so Jason immediately commandeered his cousin Philip, who was two years his junior and would soon be graduated from Oxford, to serve as escort. The young man, not having yet formulated any concrete plans for his immediate future, was wholly receptive to the proposition, and in early January 1817, he shepherded his charges across the Channel to Paris, where they spent two extravagant weeks before continuing on through southern France to the Mediterranean. They boarded a ship at Marseilles that took them along the coast past Genoa to Rome, where Jason was waiting for them. Laurel remembered those next few months as the happiest time of her life. Jason bestowed on her a particularly warm welcome, as though he had been waiting with impatience, and eagerly took her to explore, with her sketchbook, the Vatican City and many of the ancient ruins, including the fascinating archaeological excavations at Pompeii and Herculaneum. The whole party obligingly accommodated themselves to several of these excursions, finding other things to amuse them when Jason and Laurel went off to admire and examine with a professional eye dozens of beautifully designed classical buildings in varying states of preservation. Before they left Italy, they took a leisurely tour through the northern provinces, stopping at Florence to examine the fabulous art masterpieces for which the city was renowned. They continued on to Venice to spend a few days before crossing back across the peninsula by way of Verona and Vicenza, where they found the several magnificent houses and public buildings that had been designed in the sixteenth century by the great Italian architect Andrea Palladio, an ardent admirer of the architectural triumphs of the ancients. He followed their concepts of construction conscientiously, preserving his researches in

13

The Four Books of Architecture which had been a Bible to many of the English builders of the previous century. The dedicated tourists then proceeded to Genoa, where they soon boarded a ship which would take them back to England.

It was during this voyage that the magical, unforgettable moment occurred. In the second week of the journey Laurel and Jason were standing alone on deck one late afternoon, as they sailed up the coast of Portugal, in perfect communion as they silently marveled at an especially spectacular sunset on a lightly rolling, shimmering sea. She suddenly felt a light touch on her hair, followed by a soft pressure of lips, which so thrilled and bemused her that she was afraid to move for fear of breaking a spell, though she had an almost uncontrollable desire to turn towards him invitingly. That she did not do so proved to be her great mistake, as she so keenly realized afterwards. She had hoped for a more intense and explicit demonstration of ardour so that she could be positive of his meaning. But it was not forthcoming, and when she did face him, the opportunity to acquaint him with her sentiments had passed. He was looking at her with his usual affectionate expression and a friendly smile which convinced her that he had meant nothing significant and merely had been momentarily moved by the peculiarly uplifting power of the extraordinarily beautiful natural phenomenon. Since that time their relationship had stayed within the bounds of an unreservedly affectionate and intimate, yet platonic, alliance. Laurel resolutely conditioned herself to an accommodation with this less than perfect, but intensely agreeable, state, and it was only when she was forced to analyze the precariousness of her situation by one of her mother's reproaches that she acknowledged the fact of her unsatisfactory and potentially insecure position.

Laurel's musings were interrupted by a banging at the front door. However unlikely it might seem that they would have a visitor in this weather, it appeared that someone had braved the elements. She quickly rose to go to

14

look down on the hall to discover who might be so imprudent.

"Jason! Good heavens!" she exclaimed as she hurried downstairs to greet a gentleman who looked like a personification of Jack Frost. "Whatever are you doing out in this blizzard?"

"Hello, Laurel," an exceptionally well-favoured young man answered with a grin as he turned over his snow-covered greatcoat and beaver to the footman. "I know you have a mind to give me a scold, but I had to come to see you. I was delivered a most untimely summons, and I am going to have to ask you to bail me out."

"What a perfectly unintelligible explanation," Laurel deplored with a doubtful shake of her head. "Do come upstairs to warm yourself by the fire, and you can unravel it for me."

He followed her into the warm parlour with a folder of papers under his arm and teasingly put a cold hand on Lady Madeline's cheek.

"Jason! Oh, that is too bad of you, and just when I had fixed my mind on more pleasant matters," that lady scolded as she pulled her shawl more closely about her. "What can be so important that you should have to venture out in this weather?"

"I have some things for Laurel to work on. I have to go to London early tomorrow, and I had promised to submit some plans to Lord Brathewaite before he leaves for his hunting box. I had almost gotten it put together, but I would rather present him with a finished product than a sketchy draft. Do you think you would have time to tidy it up for me, Laurel?"

"Of course, Jason. When will you be back?"

"In four days, if the weather doesn't hold me up. I admit I'm not exactly enthusiastic about setting out in this storm. In fact, I won't be able to unless it lets up by morning. But the devil of it is that I received a letter from my uncle George's solicitor requesting that I be present for the reading of the will the day after tomorrow at his office in London. I don't understand why my attendance is at all neces-

15

sary. The estate is not extensive and is largely entailed besides, not to mention the fact that my uncle told me some months ago that he did not intend to leave me any money because I didn't need it and Lawrence did. I assured him that such a disposition would not disturb me in the least, so I am at a loss to imagine why my presence is required."

"There is probably some small bequest, Jason," Lady Madeline suggested. "You know Lord Dismore was always exceedingly fond of you. It would be very surprising if he did not remember you at all."

"Yes, that is true, I suppose," Jason agreed, staring absently into the fire. Then, after a moment, he began to open his folder to get to the matter at hand. He knelt to spread the plans on the hearth rug in front of the fire. Laurel joined him on the floor to be shown what alterations he had in mind.

"Lord Brathewaite belatedly decided he would like to have access to the library from his dressing room so that he could wander about as he chose without fear of being accosted by any of the frequent guests that mill about," Jason confided with a laugh. "He has made several pithy observations on the disruptive effects of a large family on one's serenity, and I must say he is especially afflicted, what with being surrounded by half a dozen high-spirited children and a wife who impetuously keeps open house for her all too visible family and friends. Consequently my lord came to the inescapable conclusion that even though this is to be a private wing, he could not rest assured that he would have any guarantee of privacy, since Lady Harriet's apartments would be just across the hall. So he is insisting that we must somehow contrive to install a door between his suite and the library to provide him with a personal sanctum."

"Poor man," Lady Madeline sympathized. "He would be perfectly content if he could retire to some hidden retreat with his books where he could pursue his researches in solitude. Instead, he must constantly suffer the importunities of his lady and their brood."

16

"Yes, but since he fairly acknowledges that he is captive to the extent that he must certainly share the responsibility for his circumstances," Jason remarked with a grin, "he means to settle for a practicable isolation."

Laurel was sitting with her lower lip between her teeth and narrowed eyes as she studied the drawings, and Jason asked quizzingly, "What is it, love? Do you see a problem?"

"Oh, well, not exactly," Laurel replied dubiously. "It's just that everything had worked out according to scale so beautifully. I hate to see the plan thrown out of proportion. It's obvious the way the two rooms adjoin that any opening would have to be off-center."

"Yes, that bothered me, too," Jason agreed. "But then I hit on the idea of making a whole section of shelving into a revolving panel. You see? Here. So that it will be just on the other side of the built-in wardrobe in Lord B.'s dressing room."

"Jason! That's ingenious!" Laurel exclaimed enthusiastically with a frankly admiring expression.

A pleased gentleman smiled and observed teasingly, "Well, I can see you're properly impressed, although you know it is not an original idea. We have seen it done before."

"That's true, but never incorporating bookshelves," Laurel amended. "I see what you want to do, and the alterations can be made without any problem."

"Good," Jason said as he folded up the plans. "I'll leave these with you and will come for them as soon as I get back." He stood up and helped Laurel to her feet, remarking ruefully that he envied them their cozy fire and wished that he did not have to face the prospect of what promised to be one devilishly uncomfortable journey.

"Well, put it out of your mind for a moment," Laurel prompted, "and let me pour a cup of tea for you before you go back home."

Jason sat with them for almost an hour and then reluctantly decided he had best bestir himself since he hoped to make an early start in the morning.

Laurel followed him to the door, but he turned to say, "No, stay here where it's warm. I'll let myself out."

"Jason, you will be careful?" she asked anxiously.

He laughed and promised, "Yes, love, I will. I am taking Jenkins and Smithson with me, so you can be sure we three strong fellows will manage very well." Taking her chin in his hand, he bent to kiss her brow, saying, "Don't worry. I'll see you in just a few days."

When he closed the door, Laurel returned to her chair to pick up the plans and felt her mother's speculative gaze. She looked up to warn threateningly, "Do not say a word."

Lady Madeline meekly lowered her eyes once again to the pages of the *Belle Assemblée*, but not without heaving a deep, expressive sigh, which, as it was intended, could not go unnoticed. Laurel determinedly ignored the dramatics and concentrated on studying the diagrams before her.

The trip to London was not as arduous as Jason had anticipated since the snow had lessened as they neared the city, and by the time they reached the outskirts, it had dissipated almost entirely.

He ordered the carriage to the Clarendon Hotel and bespoke a suite of rooms for two nights for the three of them. Then, after refreshing himself and enjoying an elegant, leisurely dinner, he walked to Brook's, where he spent a companionable evening with a few of his friends who happened to be in town.

The next morning he presented himself a few minutes early at the solicitor's office, where he found his cousin Lawrence, the new Earl of Dismore, waiting in the anteroom.

"Jason, old boy! It's good to see you. You are getting to be a regular hermit that it takes something like this to get you to come to town."

"Not exactly a hermit, Larry. I have been busy, and you know that I have never found London to my taste anyway. You're looking fit," he said, remarking to himself that the earl had lost some weight and was considerably improved in appearance. "How are Helen and the children?"

"Very well. The little ones are healthy, active little rapscallions and keep the household in a bustle, but Helen wields a firm upper hand even though she is just a couple of months or so shy of another confinement."

"Good Lord!" Jason exclaimed. "How many will that be?"

"Seven," his cousin replied sheepishly.

Jason shook his head in amusement and noted, "Well, I can see that this inheritance is going to serve a good purpose."

"Yes," the earl acknowledged with a sigh of relief. "Things have been a little tight, but with this additional income we will manage excellently. In a few weeks I think we will remove to the country because London is not the best place to try to bring up a lively brood. They will do much better at Dismore Hall."

The door to the lawyer's office opened. A bespectacled clerk announced, "Mr. Halliburton is ready for you now," and stood back to let them pass.

"Ah, good morning, gentlemen," a white-haired, spritely elderly man greeted them affably. "I am sorry to have kept you waiting. I have everything in order now, and we can proceed immediately. Will you be seated?"

He unfolded an official-looking document and read off the usual preliminary statements, rapidly progressing to the specific bequests, which included a few small sums to favoured retainers and a modest pension to his housekeeper. And then:

> To my nephew, Lawrence Devereaux, I bequeath all entailed properties and all my wealth, including jewelry and other personal belongings.

Mr. Halliburton paused deliberately and spoke to Jason. "I believe you were aware that Lord Dismore would make such a disposition."

"Yes, so he informed me some months ago," Jason replied, as he smiled reassuringly at his cousin, who was wearing a faintly embarrassed expression, "and it has puzzled me why you required my presence today."

"You will understand when I read the next section," the lawyer advised, and he continued:

> To my other nephew, Jason Devereaux, I bequeath the landed estate in Sussex, including the residence Dismoreland and the surrounding 520 acres.

Once more Mr. Halliburton paused significantly to allow his audience to contemplate this unexpected legacy and was amply gratified by the reaction of the astonished recipient.

Jason looked stunned but managed to ask, "How is that possible? Surely it is irregular, and the property should be included in Larry's portion."

"No, no," the lawyer dissented, "I shall explain. The property was not an original family holding. It was bought by the late earl in anticipation of his marriage some forty years ago. But his betrothed unhappily contracted a fatal fever and died suddenly, a month before the wedding. The young man was consumed with grief, and in an effort to block out the painful memory he closed up the mansion, which he had intended to enlarge and redecorate, and never set foot in it again. When he called me to draw up this will almost a year ago, he recognized that since the house was in an extremely run-down condition from decades of neglect, it would require a considerable amount of work and money to renovate. Even so, with a somewhat peculiar, nostalgic sentiment, he wished to see it refurbished to honour the young girl he had mourned all of his life. However, he did not feel that his heir would have the time, the inclination, or the funds to contract the necessary work and would be tempted to sell the property, possibly for a paltry sum, considering its condition. Therefore, it was his hope that his younger nephew, who had made a career for himself as an architect, would be sufficiently intrigued by the challenge to consider it worth his time and money to restore it to its former elegance."

"My God! I can't believe it. Dismoreland," Jason whispered hoarsely with obvious emotion. "I always thought it was part of the entail, or I would have offered to purchase it long ago. I suppose Uncle George knew I coveted it, but he never gave me any sign that he intended to leave it to me. I say, Larry," he announced, revealing his scruples, "I feel deucedly guilty about this, and I hope you will let me reimburse you for the property."

"Confound it, Jason! Have you lost your wits? How the deuce do you figure you should reimburse me for something that is yours and was never mine? If I didn't know you were barmy because of what you consider your good fortune, though I don't know how anybody can get so worked up over such a ramshackle pile, I would jolly well take exception to the idea that you think me some kind of dashed highwayman," the earl spouted indignantly.

Jason had to laugh at this forthright declaration, which he recognized as a sincere expression of goodwill, and he clasped his cousin's shoulder, saying, "You have a generous heart, Larry."

"Balderdash! Uncle knew what he was about, and I don't doubt you will build a showplace worthy of a queen."

These friendly exchanges were brought to a halt by a significant "Ahem" from the lawyer, who said apologetically, "Gentlemen, I must beg your indulgence for a few more moments because there is still another stipulation."

Both men looked at him in surprise but gave him their attention, and Mr. Halliburton, in the manner of one who enjoys the role of messenger of departed souls and is pleased to affect a dramatic flair in the exercise of his duties, sat back, resting his elbows on the arms of his chair and making a tent with his fingers, as he discoursed, "I believe it would be helpful if I told you of a certain obligation that the late earl honoured which I do not think was generally known. Does the name Lady Danila Wilmington mean anything to either of you?" Noting two blank faces, he said, "No? Well, she is the daughter of the fifth Marquess of Exmoor. He died some ten years ago, and the title passed to his uncle. Lady Danila and her mother lived in

Derbyshire with the sixth marquess, an irascible old bachelor who was a great friend of the late earl, until Lady Caroline died five years ago. The marquess did not wish to have the responsibility of raising a young lady and had no female relatives on whom he might call, so he enrolled the child at a young females' seminary near Bath, where she has been residing ever since. When he also passed to his reward two years ago, your uncle, by prior agreement, assumed guardianship of Lady Danila, who, being the last of her line, is a considerable heiress and has extensive investments to be administered. I am pleased to say that your uncle was content to leave her affairs in my hands, and her holdings have increased substantially. Now," he said, having related this seemingly irrelevant history, "let me continue." He leaned forward once again to resume reading:

> *If I should die before my ward Lady Danila Wilmington reaches her majority, I hereby transfer the office of guardianship to my nephew Jason Devereaux with every confidence that he will exercise this obligation honourably and will protect her interests and make appropriate arrangements to assure that she is suitably established.*

"Good Lord!" Jason exclaimed with a look of shock, for if the first bequest came as a surprise to him, the second exceeded the bounds of credulity. "Guardian to a schoolroom miss! What the devil possessed my uncle to conceive such a lamebrained idea? Surely his heir would have been a more logical choice, being a family man with an established household."

"I believe," Mr. Halliburton advised blandly, "that the late earl thought that Lord Lawrence already had sufficient family responsibilities to occupy his attention fully and that you would have the proper contacts to see to the young lady's happy future."

"Damnation!" Jason exploded. "How old is this girl, and where is she staying?"

"She is eighteen and has actually remained at Miss Eddington's Academy for young females beyond the usual tenure. Your uncle had acknowledged that a new arrangement would have to be made, certainly by the end of this term. But I must tell you that he had not made any progress in devising an acceptable solution. His preoccupation with his ill health the last few months prevented him from giving the matter serious consideration."

Lawrence looked at his cousin sympathetically. "That's a damnable hobble, Jason. If you can postpone any action for a few months, I am sure that Helen and I would be able to offer our assistance."

"Larry, you are a prince," Jason attested gratefully. "But if Uncle George had wanted you to be burdened with this responsibility, he would not have specifically appointed me. I shall have to honour his wish. However, I am certainly not prepared to take on any such assignment at this point. I shall have to take time to consider just what arrangements I will be able to work out. For the present, Mr. Halliburton, I will ask that you continue to act in her behalf as you have been accustomed."

"Of course, Mr. Devereaux, I will be happy to. But may I suggest that you at least send a letter to the young lady to introduce yourself and personally assure her of your solicitude?"

"Yes—yes, I'll see to that," Jason replied impatiently, wishing to postpone any contemplation of this cheerless prospect of an unwanted responsibility so that he might get back to savouring the more exciting novelty of his acquisition of Dismoreland, an overwhelming stroke of fortune which he had not yet had time to assimilate.

With this last bolt from the blue it seemed that Mr. Halliburton had exhausted his tantalizing revelations. He assured the two Devereaux gentlemen that he would expeditiously implement all directions and that they would hear from him in a very short time.

Both men thanked him for services rendered and left to celebrate their good fortune at the earl's residence on Cavendish Square, where Lady Helen and all the new little honourables and ladies waited to be apprised of the results of the morning's conference.

Jason was greeted enthusiastically by a bevy of Devereaux offspring, ranging from age two to ten, who seemed to have done some determined exploring as they popped out of the walls from all sides. He swung the youngest onto his shoulders and threaded his way through the rest of them to embrace Lady Helen affectionately. She soon restored order, sent the youngsters on their way, and invited the two men to join her in the library, where they could have a comfortable coze. The countess was a tall, handsome woman with intelligent eyes, a good-humoured nature, and an air of efficiency and authority who basked in the role of wife and mother. She was a fitting complement to her easygoing, affable husband, and they were a devoted couple who rejoiced in their family life. Jason always found a great deal of pleasure in their company and readily agreed to spend the afternoon with them and to remain for dinner.

"Jason," Lady Helen said with a twinkle in her eye, "I do think it extremely propitious that you are to have Dismoreland. You are the only person I know who could consider it a prize."

He laughed in appreciation of her sally and agreed, "Yes, you are probably right. I shall no doubt have good reason to appreciate the admiral's diligence in seizing all those rich cargo ships, even though I have often had reservations about that particular manner of accumulating a fortune."

"Lord, it's a good thing he did," Lord Lawrence contended. "With your scruples, if it had been left to you to make your bundle, you wouldn't have a feather to fly with."

Jason burst out laughing but protested, "No, Larry, that's coming it a little strong. I do profit considerably from my architectural commissions, you know."

"Really? Become expensive, have you?"

"Rather," Jason replied with a grin. "But thank goodness I have nothing scheduled in the immediate future and can concentrate on Dismoreland. It's been years since Laurel and I climbed in a broken window and spent hours exploring the interior, but I remember it clearly. It has sensational possibilities. It will need alteration, of course, but the basic design is classically simple, giving us a lot of flexibility. I can't wait to tell Laurel. She will be in transports."

The earl and his wife exchanged quizzical looks. Lady Helen asked casually, "How is Laurel? I haven't seen her for ages."

"Very well. I depend on her implicitly. In fact, I left her to finish up some sketches for Lord Brathewaite," Jason answered matter-of-factly.

Concealing her disappointment at this unpromising remark, the countess asked curiously, "What are you going to do about your ward?"

"My ward? Oh, my God!" Jason groaned expressively. "I forgot about that already. At least I have a few months' grace. Maybe a solution will present itself by then."

Lady Helen voiced her willingness to lend her assistance in the matter and then excused herself to see to her other duties, saying she would rejoin them at dinner.

The two men spent a companionable afternoon catching up with each other's activities since they had last met, and then, after a hearty but simple meal and a somewhat boisterous session with the children, who were permitted to join the grown-ups for an hour or so, Jason returned to the hotel to prepare for an early departure the next morning.

The weather remained cold but there was no precipitation, and a bright sun helped to clear the more traveled roads so that they arrived at Devereaux House by midafternoon.

Jason went immediately to his room to change from his traveling clothes. He then sought out his mother, whom he found in her usual hideaway on an elegant blue velvet chaise in front of a window in her boudoir.

"Jason, my dear. I thought I heard you return. Do come in and tell me how things went in London."

The young man grinned and leaned to kiss her cheek as he privately gave thanks that she seemed to be in one of her more receptive moods.

Mrs. Theodosia Devereaux was a pretty, plump little lady who often lived in a fantasy world—not an irrational one, but merely in one devoted to abstract musings and philosophy. Having been consigned to a lonely married life because of her husband's occupation as an officer in the Navy and possessing an unusually sensitive nature, she unwittingly discovered an outlet for her emotions in literature, developing through the years a reputation as a highly respected poetess. And because of the lamentably self-centered outlook of persons afflicted by artistic inclination, she generally tried to avoid any contemplation of practical matters, retreating at every possible opportunity to her own special world.

"Well, my love," Jason told her, "it seems that all had not been as routine as I had supposed. I have unexpectedly assumed two new responsibilities."

"What do you mean, dearest?" she asked, showing an unusual interest.

"First of all, I shall tell you the good news, which is that Uncle George has bequeathed me Dismoreland."

"Jason! How could he?" his mother asked in surprise.

Jason explained and then added, "But along with this prize he saw fit to exact a certain penalty. I am unhappily obliged to tell you that he has saddled me with the guardianship of his ward."

"I didn't know he had one!" Mrs. Devereaux exclaimed. "Who is he?"

"Not he—she: Lady Danila Wilmington, who has been residing at Miss Eddington's Academy in Bath for the past five years and is now eighteen."

"Wilmington—would that be a relation of the Marquess of Exmoor?"

"Daughter of the fifth, niece of the sixth, and now sole survivor of the family," Jason said dryly.

"But why you? Whatever can he have been thinking of?"

"He evidently decided that Lawrence had too many responsibilities of his own and that I was a suitably unfettered candidate."

"Jason," a suddenly apprehensive lady ventured, "I hope you are not going to ask me to take her under my wing. You know that I would be wholly inadequate to the task."

"Don't worry, love. Such a solution never entered my mind," Jason assured her ruefully as he thought about the rather indifferent relationship he had always had with his parents. But for his intimate association with the Ingrams and his cousin Philip's household he would have enjoyed very little family life.

"Well, my dear," his mother said abruptly, showing signs of boredom with these mundane discussions, "I know you are pleased with your new estate, and I hope you can find some acceptable solution for Lady Danila. Do keep me informed of your progress in both matters."

"Of course, Mother," Jason promised, accepting the fact of his obvious dismissal placidly. With a sense of duty done, he left her to her aesthetic meditations, which would no doubt culminate in some lofty verse extolling the virtues of a simple existence undisturbed by wordly considerations.

It was already five o'clock and nearly dark, so, as much as he wished to tell Laurel of the news, Jason decided to put off his visit until the morning, when they would have more time to contemplate their good fortune and would be able to ride over to the mansion, which was only five miles away, to make their first estimates of what a complete renovation would involve.

Chapter
TWO

Jason slept soundly but wakened early and rose immediately, for he could hardly wait to begin exploring his new property. Only by a concentrated effort was he able to refrain from shocking the Ingram household by appearing at the door at the crack of dawn. As it was, he did create a mild sensation by an eight o'clock call but was admitted and directed to the morning room, where Laurel had just sat down to breakfast.

"Good morning, Jason. Have you eaten?"

"Yes, but I'll have some coffee. I must say," he remarked in mock disapproval, "that you are remarkably unmoved by my appearance. One would think you were accustomed to entertaining a gentleman at eight o'clock in the morning."

She giggled and went to the sideboard to fill her plate as she admitted, "I saw you riding across the fields."

"Well, my dear girl, put down that plate and give me your undivided attention," he said commandingly.

She raised her brows but did as he asked and was immediately swung off her feet by a rash young man who waltzed her around the room recklessly as he prompted, "Laurel, you will never guess what has transpired." And he placed her back on her feet, keeping his arms around her waist, teasing her with an uncommonly jubilant expression.

Laurel realized she was supposed to say something but was having difficulty getting her wits together, for while theirs was a mildly affectionate relationship, Jason had never been quite so demonstrative, and she was thoroughly unsettled. She finally managed to ask, "Jason, whatever has put you in such high feather?"

He laughed delightedly and released her as he announced dramatically, "My dear Laurel, I am supremely happy to inform you that you are now looking at the master of Dismoreland."

"Oh! Oh, Jason! Truly? But how? I mean—oh, dear!" And she surprised both of them by bursting into tears. "I'm sorry, Jason. I don't know what has come over me. It's just that I know how pleased you must be, and I am so happy for you."

"Sit down, love," he said with an indulgent smile, "and I'll bring you your breakfast. Then I will tell you all about it."

He sat across from her and explained how this unexpected beneficence was received. Then he remarked on his visit with the new earl and his family. "Helen asked about you, and I must tell you," he added with a crooked grin, "I was shocked to learn that she is increasing again and in a couple of months will add to her collection."

"You need not pretend to be so censorious," Laurel said reprovingly. "I'm sure she is very happy. She and Larry are just the sort of people who should have children, for they love them and enjoy them and share the responsibility for their upbringing."

"Um-m-m," Jason agreed abstractedly, and Laurel was surprised to see a little frown creasing his brow.

"What is disturbing your thoughts?" she asked anxiously.

"That wasn't the only unexpected legacy from my rascally uncle," Jason told her with a wry expression. "He also transferred one of his obligations to me. I now find myself saddled with a ward who is, of all things, an eighteen-year-old heiress."

Laurel stared at him in disbelief and then burst out

laughing at his obvious disgust, saying, "That is one of the drollest things I have ever heard. Where is she now?"

"At a young ladies' seminary. It seems I have a temporary reprieve. I won't have to concern myself actively until the end of the school term, so I am determined to not let the pesky matter interfere with our setting to work immediately on Dismoreland. And, my dear girl, I am chafing at the bit. I beg you to go put on a riding habit, and we will storm the gates."

"You foolish man. I can see that this boon has addled your wits." Laurel rose and, turning to him shyly, said, "Jason, I am very pleased that you have asked me to go with you the first time."

He smiled affectionately and teased, "I wouldn't have dared to go without you." He gave her a little shove and reminded, "Dress warmly."

"Jason, what fun it will be—to do your very own house exactly as you want it."

"Yes," he agreed with a satisfied sigh. "We will make it a showplace, as Larry predicted."

The sun had just emerged from the clouds as they approached the shuttered mansion, and there was a peculiarly melancholy atmosphere surrounding the center block structure with its two partially completed wings. Bare twigs and vines formed a sort of latticed screen, disguising the classical façade, but it was obvious that the original builder had been an admirer of the Palladian school. The simplicity of design would always, even in the present run-down state, present an appearance of elegance.

Jason and Laurel dismounted and went up the steps to the columned portico. He said humourously, "I have a key, so we won't have to climb in a window this time." He inserted it in the lock and bowed gallantly, motioning Laurel to precede him. She curtsied and smiled as she stepped in. Lighting the oil lamp he had brought with him, Jason followed her and closed the door. They passed through a fair-sized reception salon, which had doorways leading to the wings and an angled stairway on one side providing access to the upper floor, to a circular hall of immense proportions with a marble floor and marble columns that supported a clerestory balcony beneath a shallow painted dome. After admiring this impressive room for some moments, they moved slowly through the other rooms almost with reverence and were especially struck by their large size.

Laurel said in an awed voice, "Jason, just think what it would cost to duplicate this now."

"Yes. Appalling, isn't it?" he replied. "The place is in much better condition than I had expected." They continued to examine the upper rooms, but the old musty smell was becoming oppressive, and Jason said, "Let's make this a short tour today. I will have some of the villagers come to clean out one of the fireplaces so we can set up shop and work here on the premises some of the time."

After they locked up, they walked about the grounds, admiring the setting, for the house was situated at the top of a hill, overlooking a small spring-fed lake.

"Aren't you excited, Jason?"

"Yes, Laurel, I am. Actually, I know it is sheer folly to expend a lot of money to restore and finish this place because this sort of extravagant domicile is truly going out of style, but I don't think I am going to be able to resist the temptation."

"Can you make any estimate of the cost?"

"Not yet, but it will be staggering." Amused at her doubtful expression, he assured her with a grin, "Don't worry. We'll do it up right. I can afford it."

After one last leisurely promenade they returned to their horses and rode back to tell Lady Madeline of the astonishing news. They found her still in her morning wrapper just finishing her coffee. Upon seeing their laughing, happy faces, she experienced a sudden hope which prompted her to ask leadingly, "What have you two been up to so early in the day?"

"Oh, Mother, you won't believe!" Laurel said excitedly. "Jason is now owner of Dismoreland! Isn't that the most famous thing!"

Trying not to show her disappointment, Lady Madeline

congratulated him and then began to experience distressing misgivings as she listened to the two of them extolling the magnificence of the mansion and its possibilities, and she firmly decided that enough was enough. It would take a year or more to set the place in order, and they both would be so wrapped up in the details and supervision that they would never break out of this ridiculous pattern they had locked themselves into. Somehow or other she would force Laurel to accompany her to London for the Season, and she would turn her into a fashionable young woman in spite of herself. If she could just separate them for a while, perhaps Jason would come to his senses.

She was brought to attention again as she heard Laurel addressing her. "Mother, do stop woolgathering. You did not hear what I just told you!"

"I'm sorry, my dear. I'm afraid that I cannot pretend a deep interest in such dreary matters."

"I know, love, but you would be extremely entertained by my last remark." She repeated, "Jason's uncle transferred the guardianship of his ward to him, and he is fit to be tied because his new responsibility is a Lady Danila Wilmington."

"Good heavens! How bizarre! I haven't heard of her for years," Lady Madeline said unexpectedly. "She must be—eighteen."

"Do you know her?" Laurel asked in surprise.

"Well, yes, but I haven't seen her since she was a small child. I knew her parents, however, and I remember now that I had news of Caroline's death several years ago. How in the world did this obligation get passed on to you, Jason?"

He related Mr. Halliburton's narrative and then remarked that he still thought it would have been more proper and logical to have appointed Lawrence. "Thank goodness I have time to consider what to do about her. I am sure I will be able to make some suitable arrangement. However, we have more pressing matters at the moment," he said, dismissing the subject. "Did you finish the work for Lord Brathewaite, Laurel?"

"Yes, the plans are in the library. I'll get them."

She came back shortly, and he glanced over her drawings approvingly. "Very good, love. I'll take these with me and ask Master Corcoran to begin the work. Then I'll stop by the village to hire a crew to start cleaning up the debris around Dismoreland and also to check out and repair the fireplaces so that we can dry out some of the dampness. Tomorrow we will go over to begin measuring."

"All right, Jason. I'll be ready early," Laurel replied with enthusiasm.

The next few weeks Laurel and Jason became totally immersed in making a detailed scaled drawing of the entire house. They concentrated on one room at a time, making occasional notations about possible alterations or additions.

Lady Madeline was becoming exceedingly vexed because she could not make any headway in forwarding her design and, in fact, was fortunate even to get two minutes of her daughter's attention except at dinner. She facetiously resorted to calling on the Fates to show her the way. In later weeks she would remember this flight of whimsey and wonder if there had been something in it after all.

However, for the moment things continued unpromisingly, and nothing could distract the two dedicated architects from their project until the day Jason came to them one early morning to request their advice. He had received a letter from Mr. Halliburton, bringing him up to date on Lady Danila's affairs and finishing with a mild, but recognizable, reprimand. Jason read this portion to Laurel and her mother:

> . . . *I have just returned from a business trip to Bath, and I took the time to call at Miss Eddington's Academy to acquaint myself with Lady Danila, whom I had not met before. I was surprised to learn that she had not yet received any communication from you, and she was anxious to be informed what arrangements you might be contemplating for her removal from the school. I told her you had no doubt been deeply involved with your own affairs but that I*

would write to remind you of your commitment
which you made at our earlier conference. I trust you
will not take offense at my presumptions. I offer you
my best wishes in your endeavours at Dismoreland. I
remain your devoted servant. . . .

"Oh, dear, he did rap your fingers, didn't he?" Laurel said in amusement. "He would have made an admirable schoolmaster."

"Yes, and I can't truly cut up stiff because I *have* been remiss in not acknowledging my responsibility. I shall have to write something. What the devil shall I say? I haven't the faintest notion what I will be able to work out for her." He looked at Lady Madeline with a pleading expression.

"Jason, I don't know how to advise you except that I think for the moment you may just write a formal letter to introduce yourself and to assure her of your good faith."

The young man grinned sheepishly and admitted, "That sounds simple enough. I should be able to handle that. I'll post a letter tomorrow." And then, as usual, he and Laurel disappeared for the rest of the day.

A few days later Lady Danila Wilmington, in the private parlour of Miss Elizabeth Eddington, owner and head-mistress of the fashionable young ladies' academy (which designation belied its actual function, for it did not make any pretense to a purpose of elevating the mind and was really merely an elegant finishing school for the daughters of the aristocracy) eagerly tore open a letter that she had been impatiently expecting ever since she had artfully cajoled that puckish Mr. Halliburton into acting as her go-between.

She hastily scanned the few lines, which required a mere ten seconds, and then in vexation threw it into her companion's lap as she exploded, "Well! If that isn't the poorest excuse for a letter I have ever seen in my life! I cannot believe I have landed another pompous ass for a guardian." She flopped ungracefully in a chair and frowned darkly, declaring, "I tell you, Eddy, this is the last straw! Oh, if only I were of age, I could tell them all to go to the devil!"

"My dear Danila," a handsome, regal-looking middle-aged woman chided with a twinkle in her eye, "if you persist in flying into these passions, I am persuaded I will have to fear for the reputation of my establishment. In fact, unless it specifically is brought to light, I wish you will refrain from mentioning that you spent several years under my mantle."

This whimsical set-down brought a bubble of laughter from a slightly built, dark-haired girl with lively eyes and vivacious manners, and she admonished, "Eddy, it is perfectly horrid of you to ruin my temper tantrum with your nonsense. Now I shall have to work myself up all over again. Give me back the letter!"

The older woman handed the offensive missive back to her young charge, but the girl's dark mood had passed, and she could only threaten, "Well, Mr. Devereaux, if you think that I am going to stand for that indifferent treatment, you are in for a surprise! You may not realize it, but this contemptible little letter is going to be my billet to the fashionable world. I do not mean to be a perennial schoolroom miss, and you can just jolly well come up with some other idea!"

"Danila, for heaven's sake! Do leave off with the dramatics," Miss Eddington said quellingly and then asked with a dubious expression, "Just how do you propose to force his hand?"

"Well, for a start, now that I have his direction, I am going to write an odiously plaintive letter asking him to please see to my immediate removal from school."

"Good Lord! He will imagine you to be ill treated. Do be discreet, I beg you."

"Don't be goosish, Eddy. I shall merely tell him that I am too old and should not have remained this long. You know, it is not that I wish to leave you, but—"

"I understand, darling. You do not have to try to explain. I quite agree with you. You should be given the opportunity to take your rightful place in society, and so I will tell Mr. Devereaux when he deigns to make an appearance."

"Good," an impish young lady applauded. "I am pleased to see you are showing the proper spirit. Now I will go to compose a letter. I will let you read it before I post it."

"I hope you will not," a cowardly mentor demurred quickly. "I have a feeling that I would not wish to have to admit to any connection with it."

"Faintheart!" a laughing Danila accused as she swept out of the room.

And so it was, later in the week, that Jason found the fateful letter among his other correspondence when he and Laurel were working one afternoon in his study. He glanced curiously at the several messages and then singled out the unfamiliar, decidedly feminine missive. He remarked wryly, "Well, it seems my ward has something to say." He opened the envelope, soon discovering that she had quite a lot to say, and he became increasingly discomfited as he read the unwelcome representations. "I should have known this was not going to be easy and that I would have to pay the piper," he said pessimistically as he handed the letter to Laurel.

She looked at him questioningly but accepted the sheets and read:

> Dear Mr. Devereaux,
> I was extremely gratified to have received your communication, which I have been anticipating for several weeks. I understand that you have also acquired another responsibility, which has no doubt occupied your immediate attention, so I have tried to be patient. However, now since you have so kindly assured me of your good offices, I felt persuaded it would not be improper for me to address you personally to apprise you of my own aspirations.
> I have been dissatisfied with my situation for quite some time, but in deference to my former guardian's moribund condition I refrained from making any importunities for changing my present circumstances.
> I hope I shall find you receptive to providing me

36

*with a change of residence, for I must tell you that I
have long since outgrown this pose of schoolroom
miss. I have dutifully acquired all female accomplishments offered at Miss Eddington's Academy, in varying degrees of efficiency, some indifferent, to be truth-
ful, but I am sure that you will understand that
capability is a determining factor in all endeavours
and one cannot be expected to excel in everything.
Nevertheless, I am confident you will agree that I am
creditably educated in those areas considered appropriate for young ladies of quality. In addition, I have,
through the special interest of my good friend Miss
Eddington, also devoted some considerable time to a
study of useful and mind-improving academic subjects.*

*I perceive from your letter that you intend to post-
pone any consideration of terminating my residence at
the academy until the end of the school term. I feel I
must, respectfully, take unequivocal exception to such
a position. By then I shall be nineteen and totally out
of place in this environment. It is not as though I am
destined to remain on as a teacher, for while I am not
generally thought to be of a toplofty disposition, the
fact remains that I am the daughter of a peer and a
wealthy heiress besides. I am persuaded my fate lies
somewhere beyond Miss Eddington's Academy.*

*No doubt you will envisage me as an encroaching
female with a lamentable lack of sensibility, but I felt
impelled to state my case with you and hope you will
interest yourself in my behalf with a little more enthusiasm.*

*Now that I have strongly revealed my pent-up re-
sentments, having felt deplorably misused by the turns
of Fate that have left me dependent on total strangers
for the ordering of my life, I feel much better for it,
and I will beg your pardon if I have misread your
intentions. I shall be hoping to receive an early reply,
advising me of any new ideas you may be inclined to
invent on my behalf.*

With all proper respect and appreciation of your consideration, I remain your dutiful ward.

Lady Danila Wilmington

By the time Laurel had finished this extremely forthright, hard-hitting composition, she was laughing so hard that tears were running down her cheeks.

Jason looked at her in reproach and noted sardonically, "Not exactly a schoolroom miss, wouldn't you say?"

"Hardly," Laurel agreed. "Or a not particularly dutiful ward either, I suspect, if she doesn't get some action. Oh, Jason," she said, bursting into laughter again, "poor Miss Eddington must have been led a merry chase these last few years."

"Yes, it's obvious the blasted girl is not just going to sit there and wait my pleasure," Jason deplored with a resigned sigh. "I suppose I had better go to see her to find out exactly what she has in mind, or I shall likely discover an unwanted female on my doorstep one day."

"Jason, I think it's rather obvious what she wants," Laurel told him quizzically.

"It is? How the devil can you tell? I didn't detect one positive suggestion, in spite of her promise to 'apprise me of her aspirations.' "

"Well, if I read between the lines correctly, I have to assume that she naturally wants what most young girls of her station want at this time of their lives," Laurel hinted ruefully.

Jason looked at her with a horrified expression. "Laurel, you are not trying to tell me that she wishes to be presented?"

"I'm afraid so."

"My God!" Jason groaned, putting his head in his hands. "How the devil am I going to contrive that? My self-serving, unsympathetic mother has already expressed a total disinclination to exert herself in any fashion in behalf of Lady Danila, believing herself to be, as she so pungently put it, 'totally inadequate'."

38

Laurel giggled and said, "And so she would be, when it comes to that."

Jason grinned and remarked, "If only Helen were not going to be indisposed, I know she would serve as sponsor, but I'm afraid that's out for this year. Besides that, of all times for my uncle and aunt to decide to make the Grand Tour, I must say that this is decidedly the least propitious, at least from my viewpoint. There is no telling when they'll get back, so I suppose I shall have to cross them off the list. And that," he judged regretfully, "exhausts the possibilities as far as I can see."

"When did you last hear from Philip?"

"Almost a month ago. He had been leading his mother and father over the same ground we had traveled earlier and seemed to be enjoying his role as tour guide, but I have no idea where they are now."

"Jason," Laurel said tentatively, "I've been thinking. You know I never had a Season because the year my mother had set her sights on for my come-out we went to Italy instead. By the time we returned, it was too late. And afterwards I really had no interest in the ritual and refused to be bullied into parading myself before society. I'm afraid Mama has never forgiven me."

"I know she hasn't, Laurel," Jason said gently, "and I'm aware that she lays the blame at my door for involving you in my affairs."

"Well, perhaps," the girl admitted. "But she always goes to town for the Season, and she has already invited Cousin Mary to stay with me for those months. I wonder if she would consider sponsoring Lady Danila—especially since she has been acquainted with her family?"

"I don't know why she should, Laurel," Jason demurred. You know she enjoys a full social schedule and would hardly be pleased to be encumbered with a determined little chit, who," he added wryly, "obviously is going to require a vigilant chaperone."

"I shall ask her anyway," Laurel decided. "But you need not worry that she will think you had any intention of imposing on her, for I will tell her that the inspiration was my own. May I take the letter to show to her? The perfectly outrageous manner of Lady Danila's expressing herself might intrigue Mama. The girl certainly means to cut a dash and no doubt will be a sensation."

Jason looked at her quizzingly. "How can you make such an arbitrary judgment? For all you know she might be a hopeless wallflower."

"Really, Jason," Laurel admonished with a disgusted expression, "sometimes I think you live in that other world with your mother. A girl who has no pleasing personal attributes to recommend her would not have developed the enterprise or self-confidence to have taken the offensive in that shocking manner. It's plain as a pikestaff that she is used to getting her own way. I don't know if she is a beauty, but she is certainly a charmer, and I like her very well already."

"Well then," Jason said with a laugh, "let us hope Lady Madeline will feel similarly well disposed and take a notion to present her. It would certainly solve my immediate problem."

Laurel approached her mother that very evening after dinner, when they had settled themselves comfortably in the library, where Laurel usually worked on her drawings.

This evening she sat across from Lady Madeline before the fire and took Lady Danila's letter from the pocket of her skirt.

"Mother, I have the most amusing story for you. Jason posted a letter to his ward, as you suggested, and I am very much afraid that seemingly innocent and proper execution served to put him in a 'hobble," she informed her parent sternly.

"Laurel, whatever do you mean?" a faintly apprehensive lady asked with raised brows.

"Well, my dear, here is what came of it," her daughter replied gaily and handed her the sheets.

Lady Madeline began to read. When she had finished, she looked up in dismay. "Oh, dear, that perfectly outrageous child!"

"Yes, only I doubt very much if she would appreciate that particular representation," Laurel advised.

"No, I suspect you are right," her mother agreed with a smile. "Poor Jason. What does he mean to do? It is obvious she wants him to arrange for her debut."

"So I told him, and it gave him quite a turn," Laurel said with a giggle. "But he is at a nonplus because Helen is almost at term, and Philip and his parents are on the Continent."

"What about his mother?"

"Mama, you know that Theo would be completely useless. She would always be off in one of her reveries. Besides, she has already informed Jason that she does not wish to be involved."

"That woman exasperates me beyond belief. If she were not one of my oldest friends, I am sure I would sever all connection with her!" Lady Madeline expounded ill-humouredly.

"Mama," Laurel said with a tender smile, "you know she is just different. Theo is a wholly delightful lady in her own way, and you are extremely fond of her. But the fact remains that she will not interest herself, and so—I wondered if you might consider sponsoring Lady Danila."

"I?" Lady Madeline exclaimed with a wide-eyed expression.

"Yes, Mama. It suddenly came to me that it might amuse you, and I told Jason I would approach you on the matter. He is of the opinion that you would not wish to be encumbered with what promises to be a marvelous challenge if the girl is half the minx she seems, but—would you?"

Lady Madeline looked at her daughter's pleading expression and experienced a faint glimmering of an idea that she wished to take time to contemplate. She looked at Laurel speculatively and responded, "My love, at first impulse I am inclined to say no, but I will think on it and give you an answer tomorrow night."

"All right, Mother. Thank you," the girl said gratefully

41

and went to embrace her before going over to her worktable.

The next evening Laurel eyed her mother anxiously at dinner and asked, "Mama, have you decided about sponsoring Lady Danila?"

"Yes, darling, I have, but it is not a simple yes or no conclusion, so we will speak of it after dinner," Lady Madeline replied enigmatically.

Laurel noticed her faintly reserved expression and wondered what scheme she was hatching. Over the years the girl had had numerous occasions to appreciate her mother's artfulness, particularly in dealing with her husband, so it was with a certain wariness that she prepared herself for their tête-à-tête.

When they had retired to the library, Laurel remarked bluntly, "All right, Mama, you need not bother to play a deep game. I know you have something up your sleeve, and you may as well put your cards on the table."

"Laurel, I do wish you could learn to dissemble just a little. Your forthright manner is exceedingly unladylike, to say nothing of disconcerting to a person of delicate sensibility," her mother chided lightly with a pained expression.

The girl waved her hand impatiently and prompted, "Please, Mama, get on with it."

Lady Madeline sighed but presented her argument. "Laurel, I regret that I feel I must resort to such unworthy measures, but I have been praying for some kind of outside instrumentality to come to my assistance, and now that it has been presented to me, I cannot fail to take advantage of it. I will present Lady Danila if you will accompany us to town and participate in the proceedings."

"Unworthy is precisely correct," Laurel charged bitingly. "However, I began to expect as much when I remembered your devious propensities."

Lady Madeline refused to rise to the bait but waited anxiously to learn if her ploy would meet with success.

"Mother," Laurel began pleadingly, "surely you do not envision me as a debutante. It would be too gauche. I am much beyond such youthful festivities and would appear perfectly ridiculous."

"It would not be a formal presentation, my love. But if you went as a companion to Lady Danila, you would naturally be drawn into all of the celebrations and would enjoy as much exposure as the younger girls."

"And of course, that is what I should wish above all things," Laurel observed sarcastically.

"My love, I do wish you will at least consider the suggestion. It would be for only two months—or perhaps a little longer because both of you will have to be provided with a proper wardrobe. The clothes you wear around here are totally unsuitable, and the thought of finally dressing you properly has sent me into transports. I have been imagining all sorts of lovely things—silvery spider gauzes to accent your lovely corn silk hair, sapphire blue to match your eyes, and—"

"Mother, stop fantasizing, I implore you!" Laurel declared quellingly. "You know very well I will not be a party to this scheme, and I think it very shabby of you to put it to me in that perfectly reprehensible manner. I thought you had given up on that particular design long ago."

"Well, now you know that I have not nor ever will," Lady Madeline avowed uncompromisingly with a set face.

Both similarly determined ladies looked at each other stonily. Finally Laurel tried once more. "Mother, can't you take this on as an act of benevolence? Lady Danila, it seems, has no champions, and it is a pity that such an obviously spirited girl should be treated so unsympathetically."

A gleam of appreciation appeared in the older lady's eye, but she countered, "I think you might practice what you preach, my love. It is your choice, and I feel compelled to inform you unequivocally that you had best accept the fact that this offer is not negotiable. It will be my way or not at all."

"Then the matter is closed," Laurel conceded in defeat. "I cannot possibly go to London even if I should wish to, and I do not. We are progressing fantastically on the plans for Dismoreland, and I am wholly caught up in the excitement of it. I will tell Jason of your refusal."

"Do not take a pet, my love," Lady Madeline admonished gently. "I refuse to be apologetic for a laudable, if fruitless, effort."

"Mama, you know I will come around in a few minutes. I am aware I cannot expect you to jump just because I ask you to. We are neither of us the other's cat's-paw after all," Laurel remarked with a little smile, retiring to her corner to apply herself to her work once again.

The next morning, when she and Jason had settled themselves in the studio they had set up in the future library at the mansion, Laurel told him indignantly, "Jason, I'm afraid Mama is determined to behave badly."

The young man looked up in amusement at this resentfully phrased statement. "I presume she refused you?" he asked with an unruffled manner, having expected nothing else.

"Well, yes and no," Laurel said peevishly and then related the unsatisfactory conversation.

Jason did not make any comment for a moment, then ventured hesitantly, "My love, I wonder if you should not indulge her in this proposal. It would please her so much."

"Jason! How can you suggest such a thing! We are going along swimmingly, and I do not want to take time off now."

"That's just it, Laurel. You never do. But we have no set schedule here, so we could arrange some sort of moratorium in certain areas if necessary."

Laurel tried to put down the lump in her throat as she said expressionlessly, "Well, of course, if you do not need me, I suppose I have no valid reason to refuse—except that I do not wish to go."

Jason realized she was hurt and, for a not immediately fathomable reason, was especially elated that she did not appreciate his noble gesture. He took her hand in his and comforted, "I did not say I did not need you, love. You know very well we are inseparable partners. I would be at a loss without your quintessential perception—truly, I promise you. I just thought I should make some effort to play the honourable gentleman, but I confess the words almost stuck in my throat for fear you might feel inclined to act on my suggestion."

"Oh, Jason," Laurel responded with a happy laugh. "Whatever would I do in London? All the while I would be on pins and needles wondering what you were doing here behind my back, and I would not enjoy myself for a moment!"

Jason grinned and declared with satisfaction, "Well, that is settled. I shall think of something else to amuse my ward, but I suppose I will at least have to go to see her. We will get some things organized here, and then perhaps I can leave for a few days next week."

"Jason," Laurel asked hesitantly, "are you sure you wouldn't prefer that I succumb to my mother's blandishments so that you did not have to worry about Lady Danila?"

"Yes, my dear, I am," Jason said firmly, "so do not tease yourself about it."

Chapter
THREE

Eight days later Jason began a reluctant journey in a cold mist to introduce himself to a troublesome charge situated at Miss Eddington's Academy just outside Bath. He had brought some of his work with him and studied the plans in the comfort of the traveling carriage as he, his coachman, and his valet headed in a northwesterly direction towards Newbury, a historical town important because of its peculiar position at the cross-point of well-traveled north-south and east-west turnpikes, where they would stay overnight. This first stage would cover more than half the journey. The second day they would pick up the Bath Road, which was a major thoroughfare, and make excellent time the rest of the way.

Following this simple and uninterrupted schedule, they arrived at the White Hart Inn in the old Roman town in the late afternoon. Jason immediately sent a message to Miss Eddington, advising that he would call on her and Lady Danila the next morning at eleven o'clock.

When this unexpected, but thoroughly enlivening, note was read by two aggressively minded females, they immediately put their heads together to concoct convincing arguments for Lady Danila's position should the gentleman prove to be of a recalcitrant inclination and to form helpful suggestions should he show himself lacking in imagination.

These deliberations went on well into the night. It was with some sense of satisfaction that they finally settled on a line of attack, agreeing that it would be only sporting to allow Mr. Devereaux the opportunity to make some acceptable proposal to initiate the negotiations which they would receive with proper civility but act on accordingly, an unworthy, patronizing conclusion which made it obvious that their expectations were not high.

After asking directions of the hotel porter, Jason and his coachman drove to the school, which proved to be the primary building on a modest estate about three miles out of town.

A resigned gentleman presented himself at the door and was escorted to Miss Eddington's office. When he was admitted to that lady's presence, her composure was put to a severe test, for she had certainly not expected to deal with an exceptionally personable young man of pleasing countenance and obvious means. She immediately began to revise her strategy.

"Good morning, Mr. Devereaux. I am very pleased to meet you. Please be seated, and I will send for Danila," she said as she motioned to the servant to execute this commission.

"Thank you, Miss Eddington. May I say that I am greatly impressed with the appearance of your academy? It is a lovely piece of property, and I perceive that this building was formerly a residence."

"Yes, it has belonged to my family for many generations," she replied easily.

"I see," he commented thoughtfully, as he realized this handsome woman was obviously a Lady of Quality who was obliged to earn her living. She was no doubt eminently qualified to teach her charges the intricacies of social etiquette, along with the other routine accomplishments that were expected of fashionable young ladies.

At this moment there was a knock, and Miss Eddington called lightly, "Come in, Danila."

The door opened, and a hesitant young lady, dressed demurely in white, stepped inside with her head lowered and hands folded before her, a pose that nearly put Jason out of countenance. There was no way that such an apparently meek creature could have composed so militant a letter.

"Do come forward, Danila," Miss Eddington prompted, "and present yourself to Mr. Devereaux."

The girl moved slowly to stand a few feet from Jason. Raising her eyes, she was so startled that immediately all pretensions were thrown to the wind. She looked in dismay at her friend and groaned expressively. "Oh, no! *He* can't be my guardian!"

"Danila, please show some conduct," Miss Eddington admonished, trying to contain her amusement. "I know that Mr. Devereaux is not what we expected, but that does not give you license to be uncivil."

"No, do not scold her," Jason said with a laugh, "for I have to confess that when the prospect was put to me, I experienced exactly the same sentiment."

Danila looked at him almost malevolently and asked bluntly, "How old are you?"

"Twenty-eight," Jason answered affably.

"Are you married?"

"No."

With a gesture of vexation she demanded, "Then how the devil are you going to—" and then stopped abruptly, remembering that the matter had yet to come up for discussion.

But Jason indicated he understood and countered with a wry grin. "Precisely. How am I?"

"Don't you have any sisters?"

"No, I'm afraid not."

"And no other female relatives?" Danila asked pessimistically.

"A cousin who is about to have her seventh child, an aunt who is traveling on the Continent, and a mother who is a poetess and rather uncooperative," he answered apologetically.

"Lord Dismore must have had a deplorably whimsical turn of mind," Danila assessed darkly. "This situation is positively ridiculous."

"The timing is certainly unfortunate," Jason admitted. "But my uncle had no knowledge things would work out like this. He made his will over a year ago. I cannot hold him to account too severely because he did treat me handsomely, and I am certain that he had no malicious intent."

"Well, Mr. Devereaux, pray tell me just how you propose we go on from here," the girl said pointedly, trying to follow the planned program, giving the gentleman first chance.

"Lady Danila," Jason began patiently, "I could not fail to understand from the tone of your letter that you were desirous of leaving the school with the prospect of making your debut. But I must tell you that my circumstances quite preclude any such venture at this time. I have no female connections who could lend me their services, and for obvious reasons I cannot take you into my own establishment. Therefore, I was hoping to convince you to remain as you are until I am able to make some suitable arrangement. By next year, or even by the pre-Christmas Season, some solution will surely present itself."

"Mr. Devereaux," the headmistress broke in, "Lady Danila will be nineteen in early April. Next year, it follows, she will be twenty. I'm sure you are not well primed in these matters, having a dearth of females in your family, but there is a certain convention that is generally recognized. I'm afraid twenty is an advanced age for a debut."

"But surely not inadmissible?" Jason pressed with an unacceptably unsympathetic attitude.

"Well, *I* consider it inadmissible!" Danila declared vehemently. "I have been finding it exceedingly tiresome to watch my friends leave one by one every year to be presented and take their places in society while I remain behind. When we were all schoolgirls together, I would be invited to their homes for occasional visits. But once they left for good, I would hear from them rarely. And I can tell you, it was no great favour at that, for I found their patronizing letters nauseating to a degree, though one could hardly expect them to have much in common with a perennial schoolgirl."

The girl's self-assured manner nettled Jason, but he saw a glimmer of hope in this fervent speech. He asked, "Are any of your friends going to be presented this spring?"

"Yes. Sally Armistead and that odious Pamela Farrington."

Jason thought that was a strange designation for one's friend, but he ignored the discrepancy and turned to the other lady. "Miss Eddington, would it be possible to ask one of the ladies to sponsor Lady Danila as well as her own daughter?"

"I'm afraid not, Mr. Devereaux," Miss Eddington replied unpromisingly and then addressed the girl. "Danila, I think that Mr. Devereaux and I will progress more satisfactorily in these conversations if we could dispense with your impetuous pronouncements. Since I see no way of assuring your silence, I ask that you leave us in private. I will come to your room when we have finished."

To Jason's surprise the girl made no objection but merely bade him good day with a pretty curtsy and quietly left the room.

Miss Eddington noticed his faintly skeptical expression, and she said humourously, "You see, she does know how to conduct herself properly. It's just that she has very high spirits and has developed rather a crotchet about this matter."

"May I ask why you were so adamant in your reply a moment ago?" Jason asked suspiciously, wondering if the girl had committed some solecism which rendered her totally unacceptable to society, a not unimaginable circumstance given her abominable behaviour so far.

"Well, as I'm sure you have perceived there is no love lost between her and Pamela Farrington, who, I have to agree, is of a singularly unpleasant and overweening disposition. And Lady Sarah of no fault of her own, being a true daughter of her family, is an insipid, ill-favoured little creature. It is not at all likely that her mother would consider placing her in the shadow of such a lovely, vivacious girl as Danila."

50

"I see," Jason said regretfully. "And you have no other suggestions?"

"Not for the moment," the lady replied obscurely. "May I offer you some refreshment, Mr. Devereaux? I think it would be of some merit if we would just speak conversationally for a few moments. I should very much like to know something of your circumstances. You see, I have become very attached to Danila the last few years, and I do have a special interest in what happens to her."

"Of course. I can see that she has been fortunate insofar as she has had your affection and counsel. And no, thank you, I do not care for anything. What do you wish to know?"

Miss Eddington favoured him with one of her warm, friendly smiles and said, "Well, I wondered about your background and how you occupy yourself. I was intrigued by your statement that your mother was a poetess, and I perceived that she must be the celebrated Theodosia Devereaux. I have read some of her works."

"Have you? I hope you understand them, for I'm sure I don't," Jason commented dryly.

"Sometimes it is not a matter of understanding but one of feeling," Miss Eddington instructed helpfully.

"Thank you. I shall try to remember that if ever I am tempted to bury myself in one of her tomes again."

"And what do you do?" a persistent lady probed, ignoring what had unintentionally come off sounding like a proper setdown.

"I am an architect, Miss Eddington. In fact, I am presently deeply involved in an extensive project, and I cannot appreciate this interruption in my work. I have had to leave my assistant to manage alone, and I am impatient to return. I do hope we can come to an early decision regarding Lady Danila's position. There is just so much Laurel can do without my help," he said with an air of abstraction.

"Laurel?" the lady asked interestedly.

"Yes, Laurel Ingram, my assistant," Jason advised, coming to attention.

"That seems rather an unusual occupation for a woman," Miss Eddington noted, trying to divine the tenor of his relationship with this uncommon female.

"So it is. But she is extraordinarily talented, and we work together extremely well. Now there is really no more to tell, Miss Eddington. I do not lead a social life and am generally considered to be an unexceptionable gentleman by even the most severe critics." He rose to leave and remarked, "I hope these revelations will relieve your apprehensions concerning my suitability as a guardian, for it is not my character, but my disinclination, which presents the difficulty. However, I will do what I can, which at this particular point in time is not much."

"I meant no offense, Mr. Devereaux," the lady said soothingly, realizing she had set his hackles up. "I will speak with Danila this afternoon. If you will call on us again at the same time tomorrow morning, perhaps we will have some constructive suggestions."

"All right, Miss Eddington. I, too, will make an effort to find some resolution," Jason replied and gratefully made his escape from an interview that he had found somewhat unnerving. He directed his coachman to drive back to the hotel, where he satisfied himself with a hearty lunch. Then he went off to explore the town, which held a particular fascination for a person of his occupation, being surely one of the most architecturally beautiful towns in England, if not in the world.

Danila joined Elizabeth Eddington in her private parlour for a review of the day's proceedings and found the conclusions singularly depressing.

"You made no headway at all?" Danila bemoaned.

"I'm afraid not, my dear. Mr. Devereaux has no interest in this matter whatsoever and obviously appeared here only from a sense of duty. If there are any positive results to be obtained from this meeting, I'm afraid they will have to be devised by our side."

"Well, I hope *you* have some ingenious idea because *I*

am flummoxed!" the girl declared with a dismal expression.

Miss Eddington eyed her charge speculatively and asked casually, "Do you not think Mr. Devereaux an unusually attractive gentleman?"

"Oh," Danila replied, with little interest, "I suppose he is well enough if one is impressed with regular features and an elegant bearing. But he is so serious and—and rather indifferent."

"Yes, so he is. I'm afraid that his being an architect may account for it."

"An architect!" Danila exclaimed in surprise.

"Yes, he is the son of a younger son and naturally was obligated to take up some occupation, although I have the impression that he is not exactly down in the world, especially if, as I suspect, the special project he is working on is the Dismoreland estate that Mr. Halliburton told us he had inherited. It would take an exorbitant amount of money to renovate such a mausoleum. As ill luck would have it, he is apparently totally preoccupied with the undertaking. I do not think he is going to be at all receptive to any scheme that would require him to absent himself from the premises for any length of time. So there is only one answer—that he should take you to Sussex. And the only way he can do that is if you are betrothed," Miss Eddington announced matter-of-factly, as though she were mouthing the merest commonplace.

"Betrothed!" Danila squealed inelegantly. "Who?"

"You and Mr. Devereaux."

"Eddy! Have you taken leave of your senses? I haven't the least ambition to be betrothed—to Mr. Devereaux or anyone else. I want to be presented!"

"Yes, my love, I know. But that seems to be out of the question at the moment. So we must hit on some other ruse to get you out into society."

"Well," Danila remarked sarcastically, "I can't say much for your ingenious idea. I do not want to be married! I haven't even had a chance to look for my Prince Charming."

53

"My love, you do have a rather unfortunate romantic prospensity. I'm afraid that an earthshaking love affair is not at all a common thing. You might end up a spinster if you mean to settle for no less. Besides," she added meaningfully, "I did not say married."

"You didn't?" Danila queried with an arrested look. "Eddy—just what *did* you say?"

"Betrothed, love, which is as far from married as you should wish it to be."

Danila stared at her friend with awed admiration and then said primly, "My dear Miss Eddington, you have the most wickedly Machiavellian mind of anyone I have ever known."

"Yes," the lady admitted sheepishly. "I suspect I am utterly depraved, actually, to be putting such ideas into your supposedly innocent little head. But the situation seems to call for drastic measures, and I have hopes of bringing this off. I am afraid that if we let Mr. Devereaux out of our clutches, we will find ourselves at *point non-plus*."

"How can you possibly think that you can bring him up to scratch? Mr. Devereaux obviously views me as a grubby little schoolgirl. And anyway, he may have an attachment, well-favoured as he is."

"I don't believe so. During our tête-à-tête he did not indicate any such thing, which he surely must have done when he told me of his circumstances. Only once did he mention another woman. She must be some sort of bluestocking because she works as his assistant and evidently has done so for some time. It hardly seems a proper forum for a romantic relationship."

"I wouldn't think so," Danila noted with distaste.

"Well? Are you willing to consider this plan?" Miss Eddington asked quizzically.

"Oh, I don't know," the girl wailed. "It seems so dishonest and uncertain and—are you sure it would not be a settled thing?"

"On the surface it would appear to be," her friend admitted. "But the actual commitment would only be as strong as you both wished to make it. At the moment, I would judge the wish to be completely nonexistent. I do not think you need ever worry that Mr. Devereaux would press his suit. If he agrees to this proposal, it will be because he sees it as the quickest way he can settle you and return to his work." She looked at the girl's woeful expression and said affectionately, "My love, I know this seems extreme, but you have been afflicted with one inauspicious turn after another, what with all your guardians dying off without planning for your future. It is apparent you are going to have to take your fate into your own hands. I did so once, and I have never regretted it," she confessed freely with a lovely smile.

Danila came to sit at her feet and asked softly, "Would you tell me about it, Eddy? I have always thought you had some wonderful secret because you would sometimes get this blissful, faraway look in your eye, and I knew you were remembering. Was it earthshaking, darling?"

The older woman smiled and put her hand on the girl's head. "Yes, Danila, it was."

"Oh, you perfectly wretched lady! And you have the audacity to want me to settle for less!" the girl accused indignantly.

"No, I don't want you to settle for less, my love, but I do want you to have a chance to find it."

"Tell me, Eddy," Danila coaxed, taking her hand.

"It was many years ago—twenty, actually. I was eighteen. I met a young soldier who was on leave and had escorted his mother to Bath. The town at that time, you know, was still a mecca for the fashionables and not the dull place it is now. We had a whirlwind courtship, but it was not long before he received orders to report to his regiment for assignment to India. Because there was little time, we badgered my parents into giving their consent. We were married by special license and had three glorious weeks together before he had to leave. He did not come back. A year later I received word that he had been killed."

"Oh, Eddy, how dreadful!" Danila mourned with tears running down her cheeks. "What was his name?"

"John. John Kendall."

"Then you are really Mrs. Kendall?"

"Yes, but I didn't want to share that part of my life with anyone, and I took the family name when I persuaded my grandfather to help me establish this school. I have received a great deal of satisfaction, you know, from my association with young people. I always regretted I was not fortunate enough to have conceived a child. Every once in a while—not often—I am sent a young girl whom I can imagine as my very own. But none so fully as you, Danila. You are my very self at your age."

The girl was sobbing uncontrollably now, and she buried her head in her friend's lap. Presently she announced jerkily with a little hiccup, "I have decided, Eddy. I do not want to be presented or betrothed. I want to stay with you."

Miss Eddington raised Danila's face gently but said in a crisp tone, "My dear girl, don't be absurd. It is all very well to indulge in a little maudlin sentimentality on occasion, but it must not be allowed to divert us from the main objective. It is just possible, you know, that, after you and Mr. Devereaux know each other better, you may form an attachment. And if you don't, you can maintain a status quo until you meet your prince or until you are twenty-one and can dictate your own life."

"Well, when you put it that way, it does seem perfectly harmless," Danila reasoned, taking a deep, quivering breath and rubbing her eyes with her fists. "There is no purpose to deceive Mr. Devereaux, after all, because he obviously couldn't care less."

"So I think, too, my dear. In fact, I shall put it to him in just such a practical manner so that he will not feel boxed in either."

"All right then, I'll do it if you can manage him. But, Eddy, we will still spend our summers together, won't we? You are my only family, you know," Danila said appealingly in sudden realization that she was about to break away from the only intimate relationship she had known these last five years.

"As you wish, darling. We will see."

"Do not speak to me in that odiously condescending manner," Danila bridled up, stamping her foot. "I hope you do not think me such a shabby creature that I would forget my true friends, like those other flightly females who have flown the nest."

"No, my love, I know you are not," Miss Eddington assured with a laugh, telling her to go wash her face with cold water and leave her to refine her plan of attack.

The next morning an unsuspecting young man walked blithely into the spider's web in rather good spirits because he imagined he had found the answer to his problem, and he could see no reason that it would not be acceptable. So he greeted his hostess cheerfully. "Good morning, Miss Eddington," he said. "I have given this matter serious thought, and I believe I have conceived an admirable solution."

"Have you, Mr. Devereaux? I must say that you have taken the wind out of my sails because I had a new proposal all wrapped up for you also."

"Well then, let us hope we find our minds running along the same channel," Jason said affably.

"Let us hope so," she agreed, "though I'm afraid I think that highly unlikely. But do proceed, Mr. Devereaux."

"Miss Eddington, I have noticed that you and Lady Danila are deeply attached to one another, and it is obvious that you are familiar with and have entry to high society, so it seems not at all unreasonable that you should remove to London for the Season and sponsor the girl yourself," he said with a triumphant expression.

The lady looked at the obviously hopeful young man, and she congratulated him, "Well, I do give you credit for trying, Mr. Devereaux. But you see, what you suggest is not at all plausible."

"Why not?" Jason asked, taken aback by this immediate negative reaction. "Surely you could arrange for the school to be run without you for two months."

"I can see you might think so, my dear sir, and of course, I am not indispensable. But we are speaking of one's responsibility. During the last fifteen years I have developed an unrivaled reputation based on performance and dependability, and the girls are enrolled particularly at Miss *Eddington's* Academy. This is my livelihood, and a very good one at that, and one I cannot afford to jeopardize with an abdication of my duties even for Danila, as she very well understands."

In the face of this adamant refusal Jason knew it was useless to pursue the idea, so he sighed deeply and said futilely, "There is nothing for it then but that she will have to be patient. I have no alternatives to offer."

"You have not heard my suggestion," Miss Eddington reminded him.

"Oh—of course. I'm sorry," Jason apologized. "Have you located another sponsor?"

"No, nothing so simple. Tell me, Mr. Devereaux, are you betrothed?"

The gentleman looked startled but replied, "No, I'm not."

"How is it you have not interested yourself in marriage?"

"I do not have time to think of such things, Miss Eddington. I am wholly dedicated to my work, and my time is fully occupied."

"I see," she said reflectively and then initiated her offensive. "Why do you suppose your uncle appointed you Lady Danila's guardian?"

"I don't know precisely," he said warily, having a faint impression of impending danger.

"I have been thinking about that," Miss Eddington advised, keeping to a straight line, "and it came to me that he left you two legacies, one connected to the other."

"What do you mean by that?"

"Merely that he left you your future home *and* your future wife."

"My God!" Jason ejaculated in utter astonishment. "You can't be serious."

"Oh, yes—yes, I am. It is perfectly logical and wholly suitable and certainly a proper answer to our dilemma."

"It is no proper answer to anything," Jason exploded, "and that is the most crackbrained notion I have ever heard in my life. I am positive my uncle had no such intention," he denied emphatically, having a vague recollection of some evidence that would confirm his opinion, though he could not raise it out of his subconscious.

"Well, of course, you did know him and would more likely be cognizant of his idiosyncrasies," Miss Eddington acknowledged in a conciliatory manner. "But it did strike me as excessively odd. Nevertheless, it would be an idea worthy of consideration, don't you agree?"

"No, I do not agree, as you are well aware," Jason said uncompromisingly. "I just informed you I had no time for marriage, and certainly no inclination to marry a scheming vixen, to say nothing of the fact that I have never had any sympathy with these so-called marriages of convenience."

"I am glad to hear you say so. I find the concept terribly gothic myself, and our agreement in this respect makes me much easier in my mind for what I am about to suggest. I do think you must accept the fact that you will have to shoulder your responsibility. And since there seems to be no other solution, you will have to take Danila to your home in Sussex, a totally unacceptable move under present circumstances. However, if you were betrothed, the situation would be considerably altered. There need be no question of an immediate marriage, and you would not be distracted from your work at Dismoreland, for I promise you Lady Danila would not expect you to dance attendance on her since she is an extremely enterprising girl and would not be at a loss for finding something to amuse herself. If in the future the idea should be mutually agreeable, then the ultimate step could be taken, although," she added quickly as she realized from his ironic expression that she had committed a faux pas and should qualify this last statement to allay his suspicions, "I am personally of the opinion that this eventuality is remote because I do not believe you are of suitably harmonious dispositions."

"Have you discussed this with Lady Danila?" Jason asked fatalistically.

"I have put it to her."

"Forcefully, Miss Eddington?"

"Reasonably, Mr. Devereaux."

"And she agreed?"

"Not without misgivings but yes, in the same context I have just made the proposal to you."

"She must be in desperate case to accept such a proposition," Jason said unbelievingly.

"Mr. Devereaux, Danila has had one unfortunate reverse after another to postpone her departure. And since circumstances show no sign of improving, we have decided to take the bull by the horns, so to speak."

Being backed into a corner, Jason felt the need for a breathing spell. He walked away to stare out the window as he turned the unpleasant, totally repellent idea over in his mind. Miss Eddington was audacious and determined, but he did not think she was of bad faith, so he accepted her dictum that this charade was not truly binding. It was true that he could install Danila at Devereaux House—not at first, naturally, because he would have to arrange for another female to live in, possibly Great-aunt Harriet. In the meantime perhaps he could ask Laurel and Lady Madeline to accommodate her. Laurel did say that she liked her already, and they might be good companions—when Laurel had free time, of course. Damn! What a hobble! He had been gone four days already, and if they didn't settle this now, he would have to go all through it again in a few months. This might be the best solution after all. He was anxious to get back to Sussex, and well, what would be the harm in it? He wondered how Laurel was progressing on the revised plans for the drawing room. If she were finished, they could begin work on that part immediately. It would be particularly satisfying to have at least one room completed so that they could see some tangible results after these many weeks of tedious preliminaries. Perhaps they would start on the kitchen area next, then on one of the bedchambers, and he would be able to actually move in. Yes, that would be the thing. . . .

"Mr. Devereaux—Mr. Devereaux—"

"Yes?" Jason asked abstractedly, still staring out the window."

Miss Eddington had a pressing desire to pull the rug from under this exasperating young man, for it was obvious that he had gone off in his own world, but she forced herself merely to chide him lightly, "Mr. Devereaux, I fear you have lost the point of our conversation."

He turned slowly and said with a vague look in his eye, "What? Oh—yes. Well, I suppose we can proceed as you have suggested since she is so determined to test her wings. Perhaps by the autumn we can arrange something else. In the meantime she will have to be satisfied with a quiet country life, which she will very likely find a good deal less amusing than the one she has been leading here. I trust you to point that out to her, for I do not entertain and do not intend to make any concessions on that point for her benefit. When would she wish to come to Sussex, do you suppose?"

"Why, immediately, I am sure. She could return with you."

Jason said sardonically, "I have the impression that you don't quite trust me, Miss Eddington."

"It's not that I don't trust you, Mr. Devereaux. It's just that I think you might get sidetracked," the lady answered with an apologetic smile.

"With good reason, I'm afraid," Jason admitted ruefully. "Well then, I will have to send word ahead, for I shall have to ask my friends the Ingrams to receive Lady Danila as their guest until I can make suitable arrangements in my home. Very soon I will be able to remove to Dismoreland, and there won't be any problem. I will send my coachman to Sussex immediately. I should like to leave as soon as Lady Danila can be ready."

"The day after tomorrow would be practicable, I think. I shall have to locate an abigail to travel with her, of course."

"Yes, I will appreciate it if you will handle all those details. I'm afraid I am quite out of my depth."

Miss Eddington privately thought that no truer words

had ever been spoken, but she merely said that she would make all arrangements and that she would inform Lady Danila of his decision. "Perhaps, Mr. Devereaux, you might come tomorrow afternoon to take her for a drive so that you may become better acquainted."

This prospect did not strike Jason as a particularly desirable objective, but he persuaded himself that he would have to make some effort, so he agreed and said he would call for her at three o'clock.

Having taken this fateful step, he returned to the White Hart to compose letters to Laurel and to his mother, a seemingly simple exercise that for some reason he found peculiarly laborious. After several false starts he finally scribbled off a few vaguely phrased lines. He instructed his coachman to hire a hack and ride as quickly as possible and to deliver the messages as soon as he reached his destination, "for I am going to bring an univited guest and I do not want just to pop in on them."

"Yes, sir," Jenkins replied with a look of surprise, thinking that the young master must have had a rough time of it if the bewildered look on his face told the story. "I'll get there tomorrow afternoon for sure."

"Don't break a horse's leg," Jason said, unimpressed. "You're not running a race. And I think, if you would ride back to meet me at Newbury the next evening, we could make the trip in two days, which might be a little arduous if I were driving alone."

"Yes, sir. I'll be there," the coachman responded, not exactly enchanted with the idea of spending three full days on horseback. He hurried off since it was past one o'clock already, and he would not get to Newbury until after dark.

"So, my love, it is settled," Miss Eddington told a somewhat apprehensive young lady. "It was very much as I suspected. Mr. Devereaux is so anxious to get back to his Dismoreland that he would agree to any plausible arrangement that would not distract him. However, he has warned me to inform you that you are going to have to adapt yourself to a quiet country life until such time as he can find some other solution. And I'm very much afraid he is not just shamming it. You may be in for a frightfully dull interlude. Do you wish to cry off?"

Danila thought for a moment and then decided, "I think I will chance it, Eddy. At least I will be able to discard this schoolgirl characterization, and besides, I have had the strangest feeling that my luck is going to change. Isn't that peculiar?"

"Perhaps you are just excited to be starting a new life. I must caution you not to be too optimistic because I should very much dislike to see you become distressed from a failure of expectation. And remember, Danila, you are not being cast adrift because you can always come back to me."

"Of course, dear Eddy. But you must not worry about me. You know I have a strong sense of self-preservation, and I will come about. I know I will!"

"I haven't a doubt of it myself, love," Miss Eddington said with a laugh as she hugged the girl affectionately. "But one feels a responsibility at least to pay token respect to hostile forces."

Danila giggled and returned the embrace, saying fervently, "I am going to miss you, Eddy. Will you write to me every week?"

"Yes, darling, I will. Now we had better begin preparing for your departure. Mr. Devereaux has decreed the day after tomorrow, so we shall have to bestir ourselves. And— oh, yes. He is coming to take you for a drive tomorrow afternoon at three to improve your acquaintance."

"At your suggestion, no doubt," Danila quizzed and was rewarded with what could only be described as a decidedly impish grin, totally out of the character one would have imagined for the proper headmistress of Miss Eddington's Academy.

The next afternoon Jason went to the stables and arranged to hire a curricle since the weather was particularly fine. He instructed the ostlers to harness his chestnuts to the vehicle and then drove out to the school.

He waited a very short time in the reception parlour, for the ladies had decided Mr. Devereaux very likely held punctuality high on his list of merits, until Danila, dressed in a smart yellow carriage dress and carrying a practical hooded green pelisse, presented herself with a proper deference and a friendly smile.

Jason said approvingly, "I am glad to see you are prepared for a day in the out-of-doors, Lady Danila, for I decided it would be more pleasant to drive in a curricle since there is little wind and the sun is shining brightly. It would be quite unsatisfactory to take a scenic drive in a closed carriage, especially as you are going to spend the next two days in one."

"I am delighted the idea occurred to you, Mr. Devereaux. I am particularly happy to be out of doors. It will please me very well to take one long last look at the lovely surroundings that have been so familiar to me these last few years."

And so, with a mutual mood of affability, they climbed into the curricle, and Jason proceeded leisurely to the Lansdown Road, heading towards Bath. They passed through rolling hills overlooking the town and presently turned right to drive by Lansdown Crescent and All Saints' Chapel and then back to the main road, which took them to the center of town, an area of a few blocks surrounding the Pump Room and Bath Abbey.

"Have you read any of Miss Jane Austen's books, Mr. Devereaux?"

"Yes, I have, and I see that you have been remembering them as I have."

"Sometimes I have come here with copies of *Northanger Abbey* and *Persuasion* and stood before the places mentioned in the books, imagining I would meet one of the characters," Danila confessed, giving credence to Miss Eddington's representation of her as an enterprising girl who could amuse herself. "Of course, it is dreadfully come down in the world now, and one can hardly believe it once was so grand."

"Only for a short period of its history, Lady Danila—

one great rebirth. And now it takes on its old character again, but with a much more charming face." They were driving slowly along the Bristol Road, and they looked up across the Crescent Fields to the striking full view of the architecturally stunning Royal Crescent. They turned right to proceed up the hill and then drove past the curved row of town houses to Brook Street, which led directly into the Circus, a three-part circle of similar design. Jason asked companionably with a new informality, "Is there anywhere else you would like to go, Danila?"

"Oh, I should like to go across Pulteney Bridge if you wouldn't mind," the girl said diffidently. "I have always admired it, and I am persuaded it must be of some interest to you, also."

"Yes," he agreed, "it is a most unusual structure, of the same concept as others I have seen, but on a smaller scale."

"What others?"

"The Ponte Vecchio in Florence and the Rialto in Venice."

"Have you been all over the Continent?" Danila asked enviously.

"No," he answered with a smile. "Just France, Italy, and Greece when I was studying ancient architecture."

"I should dearly love to travel," Danila said wistfully.

"Perhaps you will someday, Danila. Try to be patient."

She wrinkled her nose at him but did not get on her high-ropes and settled back to enjoy the very agreeable outing.

Jason drove around Sydney Gardens and then back across the river Avon to High Street and onto Broad Street, which led them back to the Lansdown Road.

Danila felt very much in charity with her guardian and was moved to assure him of her good faith. She ventured resolutely, "Mr. Devereaux, I should like to speak frankly with you for a moment because I feel that if we open our minds, we will be relieved of this liability of wariness. I think we are enough well disposed to each other that we might easily go along on a friendly basis, so," she continued hastily, forestalling any interruption, as she knew exactly what she wanted to say and did not mean to be diverted, "I wish to tell you that I am fully in agreement that our betrothal is merely a sham, contrived for appearances only. I mean—I know you cannot but be in high dudgeon with Eddy and myself for inveigling you into this compromising situation and must think us the most answerable of scheming females—and are entirely in the right of it for that matter. But I am very well aware that we are not compatible in—in that way, and so I hope you will not be too vexed with me, for I just had to do something," she finished in a rush.

Jason burst out laughing at the conclusion of this engagingly artless dissertation and declared unhesitatingly, "Danila, you are the most remarkable girl, and I am not the least worried you mean to set your cap for me if that is what is bothering you. And yes, I am sure we are going to be friends. In fact, it has just been revealed to me that you are going to be a delightful addition to our little family and that Laurel will like you very well, as she imagined she would."

"Who is Laurel?"

"My very good friend, neighbour, and assistant."

"Oh. But how do you know she will like me?"

"Because I needed advice, and I let her read your letter. It amused her extravagantly, much to my discomfiture, and she had you pegged in an instant with a favourable assessment," Jason said with a grin as they pulled up before the academy. He helped her down and escorted her to the door, telling her he would return for her the next morning at nine o'clock.

"I'll be ready," Danila replied. "Thank you for a lovely afternoon, Mr. Devereaux."

"You're welcome, Danila. It was my pleasure, and I think, under the circumstances, you might call me Jason," he suggested quizzically.

She curtsied and said, "Of course, Jason." Then, with a happy laugh, she ran up the steps.

Chapter
FOUR

It was just an hour later, about 125 miles away, that a thoroughly exhausted Jenkins rode up the treelined drive to the Ingram residence. He was admitted to the front hall, and a footman went upstairs to tell Laurel that Mr. Devereaux's man wished to see her. She came down immediately, exclaiming in concern, "Good heavens, Jenkins. You look worn to a thread. Have you been riding all day?"

"Yes, Miss Laurel. I have brought you a message from the master."

"Is he returning soon?" she asked eagerly.

"Yes, miss. In two days." He handed her the folded note and then hurriedly excused himself to ride to Devereaux House.

Laurel carried the letter to the drawing room, where her mother was sitting at her needlepoint frame working on a new cover for her favourite footstool.

"We have a note from Jason, Mother. It is rather strange when I think of it, however, because it was delivered by Jenkins, who said his master would not be back for two days. I wonder what is holding him up." She broke the seal and began to read:

My dear Laurel,

On arriving here, I discovered myself faced with a dilemma because my opponents and I were decidedly on opposite sides of the fence. After several proposals and refutations we adjourned to resume the negotiations the next morning but remained very much at odds. Miss Eddington, a formidable female, I must tell you, rose to the heights of the ridiculous when she suggested that Uncle George had intended that I should marry his ward, which I confidently rejected out of hand. However, after a series of forcible arguments and assurances, I somehow found myself outmaneuvered since it was apparent that I would have to remove Danila to Sussex, an obviously inadmissible scheme under existing circumstances. So I agreed to the betrothal, and I find myself having to ask you to play hostess until I can make proper arrangements at Devereaux House. I have been impatient to get back home, wondering how you have progressed on the plans, and I will see you two days after you receive this. Please make my apologies to Lady Madeline for my presumptuous imposition, but I will relieve you of your burden as soon as possible.

With affection,
Jason

When she finished reading this indifferently obscure, yet utterly afflictive, letter, Laurel felt oppressively faint. She leaned back in her chair, shaking uncontrollably. Lady Madeline looked up to question her about Jason's visit, and she was dismayed by the pained look on her daughter's face. "Laurel—Laurel, my dear, what is it?"

The girl tried to speak, but no words would come. She gestured feebly at the letter that had fallen to the floor.

Lady Madeline picked up the sheet and read hurriedly, feeling almost as great a shock as her daughter. "My God! How could this have happened so precipitately! I can't believe it." And then, being struck by the pallor of Laurel's face, she quickly moved to put her arms around her, lamenting, "Darling, I am so sorry. I am to blame for being so uncooperative. This would never have happened if I had agreed to your request. Laurel, my dear, do try to control yourself. You will become ill." She rang for the maid and directed her, when she came hurrying in at the urgent summons, "Carrie, Laurel has had a sudden indisposition. Please help me take her to her room." She put the offending paper into her pocket, and between them the two women got Laurel to her bed. They undressed her and settled her under the covers and then called for cloths and warm water to bathe her forehead because she felt cold as ice. All the while a worried mother was murmuring soothing phrases, but she received no response as the girl just lay back motionless without opening her eyes.

Half an hour passed, and finally Lady Madeline was relieved to hear a weak voice. "So much for my being able to handle it, Mama. I didn't know it would hurt so much."

"Hush, darling. I do not mean to say I told you so because I feel very much at fault. I shall never forgive myself. I don't know what possessed him, but it is outside of enough to ask us to take her in. I never realized until now that the boy is as shatterbrained as his mother!"

At this they heard a commotion in the lower hall, and a moment later the door flew open. A slightly disheveled lady, who looked as though she had just thrown herself together, burst into the room. She saw Laurel lying in bed, looking thoroughly done up, and she took her hands, sympathizing, "Oh, my dear, I was afraid the distressing news would affect you like this. I was completely overset myself and would have performed one of my famous withdrawal acts if I had not been so worried about you. I don't know how I could have such a nodcock for a son."

"How odd for you to think so, Theo," Lady Madeline marveled, ready to join issue. "I was just crediting him with being your true offspring."

"Maddy, I am not in the mood for battle, and I will not let you irritate me with your little darts," Theo Devereaux said with a frown.

"You seldom do," her friend said regretfully.

Even in her misery Laurel had to smile at these irresistible pricks, which were a trademark of the long friendship between the two women, and she took each by the hand. "Do not cut at each other on my account," she begged in a voice that still shook. "The thing is done, and I shall have to get myself under control because Jason and his—and Danila will be here the day after tomorrow. We will have to be ready to welcome her."

"Welcome her!" Theo Devereaux exclaimed incredulously. "Laurel, what a perfectly unrealistic assumption. I can only stare at such a notion! I hope you do not think I mean to accept her as my daughter. You have held that place in my heart for too long. It is absolutely unthinkable. I shall not receive her."

This impulsive declaration had the effect of bringing the tears that had refused to come, and Laurel pleaded, "Theo, I am overwhelmed by your love and loyalty, but we cannot be so heartless to a poor girl who has had so many misfortunes. If you love me truly, you will not make a scene or magnify a difficult situation. I don't know how I shall go on if everyone lets Jason know what a crushing blow he has dealt me. It would be unbearably humiliating. Don't you see? It is too late now for wishful thinking and second thoughts."

"I am to blame," Lady Madeline bemoaned again with tears running down her face, overwrought by her daughter's unhappiness. "If only I hadn't imagined I was so clever."

Theo demanded, "What is that supposed to mean, Madeline? And do stop behaving like a watering pot. We will have a flood between the two of you."

Her friend looked at her reproachfully but confessed with a guilty expression, "I refused to take Lady Danila to London unless Laurel would go with us."

"Well, as to that I'm afraid you are going to have to share the credit for this muddle because *I* refused to be involved at all," Jason's mother said magnanimously.

Laurel smiled again but had had enough of these backward looks and expressions of regret. She did not feel any the better for it and only wanted to be left alone. So she entreated with a quivering sigh, "My loves, I am not at all cheered by these lamentations, so I wish you will leave me in peace, for I feel frightfully knocked up and will try to sleep for a while."

"Of course, darling, we did not mean to be so dispiriting," Lady Madeline commiserated. "Do try to rest. I will look in on you later."

"All right, Mother, but—you will be discreet?" the girl asked dubiously.

"Yes, dear. Do not worry. We will not embarrass you."

"No, we will not," Mrs. Devereaux agreed. "But I do not mean to be entirely passive about this because betrothed is not married, and I am persuaded we should not bow to adversity without a fight. Besides, I just do not believe Jason would go through with it."

With this less than comforting assurance the two women left the room and went to Lady Madeline's boudoir. They proceeded to belabour the subject, until they had spent their indignation, and settled on a wait-and-see policy, after which Theodosia Devereaux returned to her retreat, where she composed one of the most expressive poems of her career, lamenting on a mother's agony kindled by filial iniquity.

Meanwhile Laurel found that being alone did not improve her spirits and in fact left her free to indulge her inclination to feel sorry for herself. She tried to muffle the heartrending sobs in her pillow, finally becoming so exhausted that she did fall asleep, which is how her mother found her a little later when she came to see if she could persuade her to eat something. She decided not to disturb her unhappy child, but she tenderly brushed the hair from the tearstained cheeks and felt the shockingly wet pillow, which brought tears to her own eyes again. She returned to her room and then came back once more to see that the girl still slept before she retired for the night.

In the morning Laurel woke feeling perfectly miserable after a fitful sleep, and she could hardly open her heavy, swollen lids. She tried to rise to bathe her face, but her body did not want to respond, and she could not believe how weak she felt. Nevertheless, she forced herself to get up. She held a wet cloth to her face but in a few moments went back to sit on the bed, leaning against the bedpost.

The door opened quietly, and Lady Madeline entered when she saw that Laurel was awake. "Good morning, love. How are you feeling?"

"Dreadful," came a pitiable reply. "I'm afraid I am showing myself to be a grievously poor-spirited female, for I seem to be all to pieces."

"My dear, it is nothing to wonder at after such a shock. Do go back to bed. You don't look at all the thing. Are you truly ill?" Lady Madeline asked with a worried expression.

"I do feel rather queasy," Laurel owned. "Besides, I have a beastly headache, and my legs don't want to support me, all of which can be attributed to an attack of the nerves. But I think I will follow your advice, Mother." She slipped back under the blankets, putting her hand on her aching head.

"I will bring a tray to you. You are probably weak from hunger for not having eaten anything since lunch yesterday."

"Oh," the girl groaned in protest, "don't mention food to me. I can't think of eating."

"Laurel, you must take something. You cannot let yourself fall into a decline. I will be back in a little while," her mother said resolutely.

When she returned, she could persuade her daughter only to drink some tea and to eat a small biscuit. The rest of the day she did not meet with much more success, and she was becoming truly upset that Laurel did not seem to be able to bring herself out of the depths, although she kept repeating anxiously that she was going to have to get hold of herself before Jason returned so that she could receive Lady Danila, each time immediately experiencing an aggravation of her headache.

Finally Lady Madeline determined the cause of these recurrences, and she informed her daughter, "Laurel, I am just come to realize that you are making yourself really ill, being afraid you will not recover sufficiently in time to face Jason. I see no reason for you to force yourself to do so until you have contrived some semblance of composure. When he arrives, we will tell him that you have been ill but are now on the road to recovery and will no doubt be in good case directly. That would explain your wretched appearance and give you a little time to take in the actuality of this unimaginable folly."

"Perhaps that would be the best thing, Mother," Laurel agreed with a relieved sigh. "I *have* been worried how I should explain my nervous state, so I will resign myself to playing the invalid for a few days. I will try to eat a little now."

Lady Madeline ordered a tray for her. Then, undertaking to forward their little deception, she sent a short note to Jason's mother, giving her a report on Laurel's condition, assuring her that the patient's indisposition had purged itself and that but for a lingering weakness Laurel was nearly herself again.

At precisely nine o'clock Jason and his valet, Smithson, had collected Lady Danila and her maid, a local farmer's daughter who occasionally helped out at the academy in a variety of jobs. Miss Eddington had approached the girl's mother and father to ask if they might release her to accompany Lady Danila to Sussex to act as her abigail. Since Danila was a favourite with most of the working-class families in the area, they consented readily, being pleased that their Katie would be possessed of such a fine position. The two girls rode inside the carriage. Smithson sat on the box with Jason, keeping a watchful eye as his master set a fast pace. Even allowing for changes of horses, they arrived at the inn in Newbury by four o'clock.

Both girls were weary but were so excited by their prospects that they made no complaints and showed themselves to be excellent travelers. Jason advised them to remain in their rooms, suggesting that they make an early night of it because they would have an even longer journey tomorrow. He was planning their departure for seven o'clock. He then rejoined Smithson in the public dining room, where they waited for the arrival of Jenkins. Within the hour they were rewarded for their patience when he entered, looking somewhat the worse for wear after his third consecutive day on horseback, having covered something like two hundred miles.

Jason had to laugh at his battered appearance, but he congratulated him on his feat and promised him a respite the next day. The three men dined together in an unusually casual fashion, as Jason had little sympathy for a strict separation of the classes, and then gratefully retired to their rooms.

The next morning it was almost eight o'clock before they started on their way, but it was as prompt as Jason had expected, so there were no expressions of reproval. Smithson rode behind the cab, and the other two men alternated driving until they reached the last checkpoint, where Jason recovered his horse, which he rode the rest of the way.

It was almost dark when they arrived at the Ingram house, and there were five thankful travelers that they had finally reached the end of their journey.

Jason dismounted and opened the carriage door to help Danila and Katie down the steps. He directed the others to see to unloading the baggage; then escorted the girls to the door.

Their arrival had been remarked by the household, and Lady Madeline was waiting in the hall to receive her uninvited guest with as much forbearance as she could muster under the trying circumstances.

Jason immediately went to embrace her affectionately and apologized, "My dear Maddy, I hope you will forgive me for this imposition, but I was driven to an extremity, and I counted on my good standing. May I introduce Lady Danila Wilmington and her abigail, Katie Thompson? Danila—Lady Madeline Ingram."

Lady Madeline started forward to extend a welcome but was forestalled by Jason's demanding, "Where is Laurel?"

"Jason, Laurel suffered some plaguesome disorder

74

shortly after you left and still is not fully recovered, but she is improving and will no doubt be back on her feet in a day or two."

"But Laurel is never ill," Jason demurred with immediate concern. "Are you sure it is not something serious? Did you call a doctor?"

"Jason, for heaven's sake, do not be in such a taking. These pesky things do attack everyone occasionally, you know."

He grinned sheepishly but insisted, "Nevertheless, to ease my mind, I shall look in on her." And before Lady Madeline could object, he had bounded up the steps.

In resignation an apprehensive lady turned to the two young girls to welcome them. She took Danila by the hand and apologized, "My dear, I hope you will excuse this ungracious reception. I'm afraid Jason is not always mindful and has a tendency to go off on his own."

Danila assured her with a light, unaffected laugh, "Oh, I am already well acquainted with *that* particular habit, Lady Ingram, but I am not one to be disturbed by such trifling omissions. I am so grateful to him for bringing me to Sussex that I cannot but feel well disposed toward him."

Lady Madeline did not know quite what to make of this artless confidence, but she reserved judgment and invited, "Do come with me to the parlour for a few minutes while your maid goes to arrange your things. Then I will take you to your room. Would you like some tea? We will plan dinner for an hour from now."

"Oh, yes, thank you. That would be very agreeable," the girl said appreciatively as she took off her cloak and her bonnet and handed them to Katie. She followed her hostess upstairs to the parlour, where she immediately went to stand before the inviting fire to warm her hands.

Lady Madeline studied her closely for a moment and was presently confronted with a pair of bright, questioning eyes. She brought herself to attention and said pleasantly, "You look very much like your mother, Danila. I knew her many years ago."

"Really, Lady Madeline?" the girl exclaimed eagerly. "I

still miss her dreadfully, you know, for we were great friends, being so similar, enjoying the same things and thinking the same way. But I was very fortunate, I am happy to say, to have been introduced to Miss Eddington. We took to each other on the instant, and she has substituted for my family. It was not entirely easy to leave her," Danila confided with a slightly forlorn expression, "but we were agreed that I just *had* to do *something*, you see, and we were reduced to snatching at straws. However, I hope you know that I do not mean to be a charge upon you and am very well used to finding employments for myself because, except for extra reading, I had long since escaped from the schoolroom and had stayed on with my friend because I had nowhere else to go."

Only a hardhearted, regular old brimstone could resist such an affecting *épanchement de coeur*, and since Lady Madeline could certainly not count herself in such reprehensible company, she unhesitatingly surrendered to the girl's ingenuous charm and embraced her sincerely, assuring her she had found a new home, then saw her to her room.

Jason knocked on Laurel's door and marched in when her maid came to answer. Laurel cowered in dismay and protested, "Jason! You can't come in. Oh, do go away. I am not at all up to receiving you."

"And since when is a sickroom off limits to one's friends?" he asked reasonably as he came to sit on the edge of her bed, taking one of her hands in his. "My love, whatever has beset you? You look a mere shadow. Haven't you been eating?"

"Not very much," she admitted. "But I am feeling a little better," a not exactly veracious statement because she found herself dangerously on the verge of a relapse as he sat there looking at her with a worried frown. "I am sorry, Jason, but I have not quite finished the work on the drawing room diagrams," she began, hoping to distract him from questioning her further.

He interrupted and said quizzically with a contrived

look of disapproval, "Oh, have you not? Well, I wonder if I should bring my whip when next I come."

This hollow threat made her laugh, and he admonished severely, "You are not to worry about such unimportant matters when you are feeling so low. We have no pressing schedule, and the first thing is to see you back in fine fettle. I do not mean to leave you again, I can tell you, if you are going to run this kind of rig the moment my back is turned."

She smiled at him wanly but could hardly hold back the tears as she forced herself to say, "Please tell Lady Danila that I apologize for not being able to receive her."

"Don't worry about Danila. She understands that she is going to have to devise her own entertainments," Jason said offhandedly. "Now I see you are tired, so I will leave you to rest." He stood up and then bent over to kiss her forehead with a look of concern. "Good night, love. I'll come back in the morning," he promised and barely had closed the door before a hard-pressed young lady dissolved into a fit of the vapours and cried her heart out.

Before going down to dine with her guest, Lady Madeline went to her daughter's room, anticipating the worst, and was not surprised at her lamentable condition. "He came before I could stop him, Laurel. I can see that you did not behave very well."

"I did when he was here," the girl said dully. "But—but he acted as if nothing had changed. It seems that he means to just go on as before, and I don't know how he can be so—so unfeeling."

"Well, you are not the only victim, I'm afraid. He treats Lady Danila as though he had to remind himself that she is there and in fact did not even bother to take leave of her."

"Oh, dear, the poor girl," Laurel deplored, feeling an immediate sympathy for a fellow sufferer. "Is she as we imagined?"

"Yes, I'm afraid so," Lady Madeline said ruefully. "I found my heart quite going out to her, and in spite of my resolve to remain aloof, I welcomed her into our home."

Laurel smiled at her parent's woebegone expression and

chided, "And why should you not, Mother? It was apparent from her letter that we would find her appealing."

Lady Madeline sighed. "I don't know how all this is going to be resolved, Laurel, but I have decided not to go to town for the Season. Things are too much in a muddle. It shall be my penance."

"Mama, do not be absurd. This is not truly your doing."

"Don't try to dissuade me from my decision, my love. My mind is quite made up. Now I shall join our guest for dinner, and I expect to have a report that you have eaten well."

"I will try," Laurel said unenthusiastically. "But I'm afraid I have had something of a setback."

Lady Madeline looked at the girl's drawn face and promised, "I shall try to keep him from oversetting you tomorrow, darling, though," she added dubiously, "I have no great hopes for it."

The next two days Laurel remained in her room, and while she was able to talk with a reasonable degree of equanimity to Jason, who, as was feared, would not be denied admittance, she still had not recovered her strength and felt unnaturally listless. By the third day, however, she was beginning to bounce back, and she ate her first full meal. On the fourth she resolutely decided to prepare herself for reentering society. So, after she had eaten, she asked Carrie to help her wash her hair. Then she took the plans she had been working on and sat before the fire.

All this time Danila had been suffering a tantalizing curiosity about the mysterious occupant of the sickroom. She had imagined Laurel to be of an indeterminate advanced age but was having to revise that image because she did not see any possibility that Lady Madeline could be more than forty, and even that would strain one's credulity. Finally, acting true to form, she decided to invade the hallowed chamber. When she judged that she would not be observed, for she suspected she would be deterred if caught, she went to knock lightly on the door.

Laurel, feeling considerably refreshed and eager to get back to work, called cheerfully, "Come in," thinking it was her mother with some writing materials she had requested. Looking up, she was surprised to see a small, piquant face, framed by dark curls, peering around the door as a questioning voice asked uncertainly, "Laurel?"

"Yes, Danila. Do come in. I had intended to come out of my infirmary today anyway. I am sorry I took so long to make you welcome, but I do, you know."

Danila was staring openmouthed as she walked slowly over to kneel beside a perfectly stunning vision, in a ample wrapper, sitting cross-legged on the floor, with long silvery hair streaming down her back. She burst out wonderingly, "I can't believe you're Laurel."

With a startled, amused expression Laurel asked, "Why not?"

"Well, you don't look any older than I am, and you're so unbelievably beautiful," the delighted intruder marveled.

"Danila, that is a lovely compliment, but I assure you I am several years your senior."

"How many?"

"Um—three and a half, I imagine."

"Why, that is hardly anything at all. Jason had said he thought we might become friends, but I supposed that he just meant we would be compatible. My very best friend, you know, is Miss Eddington, and she is thirty-eight," Danila attested somewhat irrelevantly. "I did not imagine we would be close in age. It quite sends me into transports because now I feel as though I have done the right thing in coming here. I had not been all that easy about it in my mind, you see, what with Jason telling me what a dull life I would have because he did not intend to go out of his way to entertain me."

"Danila, surely he would have said no such thing," Laurel protested with a little frown.

"Oh, yes. But he just meant to warn me not to expect any special consideration and did not intend to be unkind. I quite understand he is very much involved in his work, and I have promised not to be a bother," Danila chattered unaffectedly.

Laurel was considerably struck by these revelations, and

79

she began to think Jason the most disobliging and heartless suitor imaginable. In siding with the ill-used young girl, she found it easier to think of dealing normally with her persecutor. So she excused herself and went behind a screen to dress and then came back to twist her hair into a knot at the back of her neck.

Danila squealed in protest, "What are you doing to your hair?" even while privately deploring her new friend's unstylish, extremely modest gown.

"Getting it out of my way," came an unsatisfactory reply. "I have decided it is time I got back to work."

"Do you always wear it like that?"

"Yes. I'm afraid you are going to find me dreadfully sober and unfashionable," Laurel said apologetically.

"No, I am not, because I can tell that you have an agreeable sense of humour, and I am very good at amusing people," a dauntless girl advised confidently.

Laurel had to laugh and agreed, "I expect you are at that."

"Yes. And that is why I decided to come to see you today—because I thought to cheer you up," Danila announced and then added sheepishly when she observed Laurel's quizzical look, "Well, that *is* true even though I had another purpose to make your acquaintance."

Laurel impulsively gave the girl a hug and submitted, "Danila, you are a little imp, and I'm sure we are going to be much merrier now you are here." She knelt on the floor to gather up her papers and was just placing them on a table when Jason was announced.

Seeing that Laurel was not alone, he walked in and demanded unceremoniously, "Danila, what are you doing here?"

"I came to meet Laurel," the girl admitted boldly, undismayed by her guardian's abrupt, unfriendly greeting, "and we are famous friends already." Then she took the offensive, charging, "You did not tell me she was so lovely and not much older than I am."

"I don't believe I told you anything to make you think she was not," he objected defensively.

"What has that to say to anything? You told me she was your *assistant*!" Danila accused indignantly.

"And so she is," Jason acknowledged in amusement. "But I perceive you have a confined conception of female assistants. What are your prejudices?"

"For one thing I thought she would be—as old as you are," she told him defiantly.

"Quite ancient, in fact," he noted wryly as Laurel giggled in appreciation.

"Well, you did say you were friends since you were children," Danila explained in an attempt to soothe his wounded vanity. "And I did not imagine she would be so beautiful."

"And to think that I had such respect for your powers of imagination. Which reminds me. You did say you were especially adept at amusing yourself, did you not? Laurel and I have work to do," Jason noted significantly.

"I certainly hope you don't think I am going to go off and let you remain here alone in her bedroom!" a suddenly nice young lady declared primly.

"Considering that I have been here every day this week, you are a bit behindhand," Jason remarked caustically.

"No, Jason," Laurel said, laughing. "She is right. It's not as though I were in bed."

"Which, on the face of it, my love, would make it even more improper," he said mischievously.

"Jason!" Laurel exclaimed, blushing furiously. "That is a shocking thing to say!"

"I think it is the most interesting thing he has said yet," Danila offered conversationally. "There may be hope for him after all."

Laurel looked at them both quellingly and remarked dryly, "If you two improper jokesmiths will help me carry all these things downstairs, we can go over the drawings in the library."

When they had everything set up, Jason and Laurel sat at the table and began to examine the plans with Danila looking over their shoulders.

"Did you draw all that, Laurel?" she asked in admiration.

"Um-m-m—"

"How did you learn to do it?"

"Jason taught me."

"What is that funny little thing up in the corner?" she said interestedly, pointing her finger, and then suddenly realized she was on thin ice as Jason turned a baleful eye in her direction. Before he could make some unacceptable suggestion, she sped over to curl up in the big leather chair to continue reading the first volume of *Ivanhoe* by the "the author of Waverley" (who was generally understood to be Sir Walter Scott, despite his denials). She did not mean to be barred from the room.

Jason just shook his head but joined in Laurel's laughter. Then the two of them concentrated on finishing the sketches so that work on the drawing room could begin immediately.

Chapter
FIVE

After just a very few days it was agreed that there should
be no thought of removing Danila to Devereaux House
and that she was to remain with Laurel and Lady Madeline, an ironic circumstance if Jason had thought on it because there would have been no need to have to fabricate a
betrothal if he had known that he could have counted on
his friends taking the girl off his hands. But the fictitious
commitment was so far in the back of his mind that it did
not occur to him to set the record straight. The little group
settled into a comfortable relationship, and even Jason's
mother could not hold to her threat to bear malice toward
such an engaging child. She contented herself with verbal
barbs directed at her provoking son, which escaped his notice entirely because he often listened to her with half an
ear since they seldom spoke on the same level. And so,
failing to elicit a satisfactory response, she disappeared
with a righteous indignation into her sanctum sanctorum
and was not seen for over a week.

Danila thought she was a marvelous card and described
her tellingly in her running letter to her friend. All of her
new acquaintances were similarly introduced, and Miss
Eddington found the representations extremely entertaining:

> . . . When I arrived here, Eddy, I perceived at
> once that things are not as they seemed, for Lady
> Madeline does not look old enough to have a spinster
> daughter, but I have not yet met Laurel because she is
> recovering from some indisposition. . . .

> . . . Today Jason took me to meet his mother, and
> I have to tell you that Lady Madeline is much more
> pleasant. But I am persuaded it may just be Mrs. Dev-
> ereaux's way, being a poetess, you know. . . .

And then, with an obvious resentment:

> . . . I am come to think Jason has inherited a mild
> version of his mother's detachment from the world.
> He is very hard to talk to because he always seems to
> be preoccupied. But after all, he did not offer us Span-
> ish coin, so I cannot be too critical. . . .

> . . . Today I met Laurel. Eddy, you will not be-
> lieve! She is only twenty-two and extremely agreeable,
> and she is the most beautiful girl I have ever seen in
> my life. That is, she would be if she did not dress so
> unfashionably and wear her hair in a knot. It is the
> most unusual colour—a silvery blond. And she has
> the loveliest blue eyes with darker brows and lashes
> and such a perfection of features that it makes me feel
> absolutely the antidote. And to cap it all, I don't be-
> lieve she even knows, or at least doesn't wish to know,
> what a diamond she is. But I can tell you, I have
> some ideas on that. . . .

In Bath Miss Eddington read these vignettes almost with
pity for the unsuspecting puppets in Danila's sphere. Obviously the minx had a lot of material to work on, and she
was afraid that Mr. Devereaux might find the girl's enterprising nature a little more than he bargained for. With a
feeling of relief, she replied:

My dear Danila,

I am delighted that you seem so happy in your new surroundings, but I beg you to be judicious in your manipulations. . . .

Danila's advent upon the scene generated a number of minor changes in a normally limited social schedule that were only mildly disruptive and that Lady Madeline privately regarded as all to the good. She was especially gratified by the natural affinity that had developed so quickly between Laurel and Danila, which, considering the circumstances, presented a bewildering incongruity. Even though Laurel continued to spend most of her time with Jason at the mansion, she did occasionally allow herself to be persuaded to accompany her mother and Danila to visit a few of their closest neighbours, although she usually declined to join them on their short trips to Horsham, other nearby villages, and local points of interest.

Sometimes Danila would ride to Dismoreland with Jason and Laurel to roam through the house and around the grounds while they worked. She usually did not stay long because there was just so much architectural palaver she could countenance. Their evenings were unfailingly uneventful except for family amusements, and they were unhappily constrained to refuse invitations to little suppers or informal dance parties held by one of their neighbours because Jason refused to be coerced into acting as escort, an untractable position which clearly demonstrated to Danila that ostensibly being betrothed to such an unaccommodating man constituted an unpropitious handicap, and she meant to break that yoke in the very near future. In fact, she would have done so immediately if there had not been some vague reservation in the back of her mind that she should not rush her fences but should let things stand as they were for the moment.

Lady Madeline took her young charge under her wing to improve her wardrobe, and they spent many afternoons browsing through the fashion magazines, eagerly awaiting the new edition of the *Belle Assemblée*. After making a list of their fancies and requirements, they were ready for the next step. So one fine day they set out early in the morning with Jenkins and two of their own grooms for an excursion to Brighton to choose a quantity of fabrics that they would present to Lady Madeline's dressmaker for fashioning into elegant gowns of their own special designs. They were not in the least conservative and bought anything and everything that caught their eyes—orange blossom sarsnet, fine French cambric, Mechlin lace, Indian muslin, shimmering silks, and the silvery gauze Lady Madeline had imagined for Laurel. She was encouraged in her cherished ambition by her young confederate because Danila was determined that sooner or later Laurel was going to be drawn out of her cocoon, and she persuaded Lady Madeline to buy several other materials that would compliment Laurel's colouring. In addition, they selected hats, shoes, gloves, and all the other presumably necessary feminine fripperies that would complete the costumes they had visualized.

Since they had allowed themselves to indulge in a veritable shopping orgy with little thought of time, they had to forgo exploring the famous resort and could take only a slow drive through the town, merely stopping briefly to admire the famous Steine boardwalk and Marine Parade before riding around the enclosure of the Royal Pavilion.

"Oh, good heavens!" Danila exclaimed in astonishment, a not unusual reaction to this fanciful creation of John Nash. "That is the most peculiar-looking building I have ever seen. I don't know if I admire it or not. I don't think I do. What do Laurel and Jason think?"

"They both think it is appalling," her companion replied in a manner which proclaimed her agreement.

"Have you ever been inside?"

"Yes, several times," Lady Madeline affirmed.

"What is it like?" Danila asked curiously as she strained her neck to look back once more.

"Overdone, like the king himself," Lady Madeline judged expressively. "There are some beautiful pieces in the pavilion—practically all of them, in fact, if viewed individually. But everything is so exotic that it offends the eye. It is certainly an anomaly, considering the king's discriminating taste in other areas, particularly in art. Perhaps you will see it one day."

"Oh, I should like to," Danila exclaimed with only a mild enthusiasm because she could think of a lot of other places she would rather go. Brighton had lost some of its glamour since George IV had become more reclusive in recent years, being painfully self-conscious about his weight.

On the return journey both ladies were thankful to rest and spoke very little, contenting themselves with visions of their finery, and took short naps to restore themselves after what they had suddenly come to realize had been an exhausting, if thoroughly delightful, day.

Laurel came to meet them at the door and was dismayed by the mounds of boxes that were accumulating on the hall floor as the carriage was being unloaded. Many of the packages had been strapped on top, and considering that there did not seem to be an inch to spare, she guessed that this was not all and that more was yet to come, a suspicion that was confirmed by two genuinely bewildered, but shameless, ladies. They professed themselves frightfully hungry, having taken very little time out for eating, so Laurel sent word to the kitchen that dinner should be served in half an hour. She amiably suffered a detailed recount of all their discoveries and purchases, although no mention was made of the things they had chosen for her. Danila and Lady Madeline seemed to have come to a tacit understanding that it would be best to postpone any importunities on that point.

With detached amusement Laurel watched the two animated faces as they described one fabulous find after another, and she was pleased that her mother had met with a kindred spirit to minister to her preoccupation in the world of fashion.

As these days followed pleasantly one on the other, the compatible little group seemed to have forgotten the troubling betrothal because no mention was made of it, and there was no evidence of intimacy between Jason and Danila to remind them of the inauspicious circumstances. Occasionally Laurel was made intensely aware of the unnatural situation, usually when Jason demonstrated his affection for her, which lamentably occurred with greater frequency. He often planted a light kiss on her forehead or cheek, either in greeting or parting or when he was particularly pleased with one of their designs. And when they sat together at the table, he would sometimes absently take her hand in his, which she always drew away as soon as she could without making an issue of it. After almost a month of this perplexing behaviour Laurel's nerves were becoming frayed, and she told Lady Madeline, "Mother, I am so confused. Jason seems to be totally ignorant of the fact that he is an engaged man, and I don't seem to be able to bring myself to the point of remarking on his unseemly conduct."

"I know, my dear. It has become apparent that neither of them is the least attracted to the other in a romantic way, and they are perfectly content to go on like this indefinitely. I would not worry about it, if I were you, for Danila is not hen-witted, and she will see the absurdity of the situation."

"Yes, but—well—while the betrothal stands, I cannot but judge myself a Jezebel," Laurel said with a droll, rueful expression that brought a sympathetic smile to her mother's face.

Lady Madeline's surmise that Danila would soon catch on proved to be a little behindhand because that sharp-eyed young lady had *Gotten to the Bottom of Things* as soon as she had met Laurel. It was no wonder Jason had been so concerned about her health and had demanded to see her every day. The man was a perfect gudgeon not to have the slightest notion of the true state of his feelings. Whenever she was in their company, Danila amused herself being an interested observer, and it soon became apparent to her that while Jason lived in a daze, Laurel did not. The poor girl obviously adored the muddleheaded gentleman and could not hide her sentiments from one as discerning as

Danila. It was evident that Jason had not fully explained their situation, which naturally accounted for Laurel's unhappy embarrassment. Even so, an enterprising young lady postponed a full confession until she could determine a promising course of action, and she gradually began to devise a way to use this mock betrothal to advantage. One evening she sat with Jason and Laurel in the library and was feeling definitely out of charity with her guardian because of the deplorable lack of sensibility in his treatment of such an exceptional girl as Laurel, and she indulged herself with imagining all sorts of plaguesome inflictions to his person.

Jason absently reached out to place his hand on Laurel's as they discussed one of their conceptions, and she, as usual, felt extremely uncomfortable, especially with Danila in the room. She looked up guiltily and was dismayed to find the girl's speculative eyes drawing an understandable conclusion. Laurel gave her a miserable look of apology and then instantly stood up to stretch, remarking in an unusually abrupt manner, "I am too tired this evening, Jason. I don't seem to be able to concentrate."

Her unnatural manner surprised him, but looking at her sharply, he was struck by the strained expression on her face, and he suddenly realized that they had been working single-mindedly for several days. With a keen feeling of guilt he apologized, "I'm sorry, Laurel. I have been too demanding. Let us take a few days off. It is not as though we have a deadline." He gathered up the drawings and smiled. "I will take these with me now, so you won't be tempted to work on them, and I will come tomorrow afternoon to place myself at your disposal for whatever the two of you might wish to arrange." He stood to put his hand under Laurel's chin and said gently, "Get some rest, love. I do not mean for you to fall ill again." Then he patted Danila affectionately on the head and left the two girls alone.

Danila went to take Laurel by the hands and drew her over to sit on the couch, announcing purposefully, "My dear Laurel, I think it is time we had a little talk."

"Oh, Danila, I know," Laurel agreed miserably. "But I

am at a loss as to how to handle the awkward situation. Jason is certainly behaving improperly, but he doesn't mean anything by it. It is the way it has always been. If our positions were reversed and I were the guest, I would go away. But that solution just isn't practicable."

"It's not even desirable," Danila interrupted unceremoniously, "and do stop being such a ninny. Laurel, I don't know how you can be so moonstruck over such an abominable man, especially when he has been the vilest wretch alive not to have fully explained our situation. I can only imagine how he put it, but it is obvious that he left considerable room for misunderstanding. We are not truly betrothed, darling. We just made a pretense of it so that he could bring me to Sussex."

Laurel just sat staring for a moment, then leaned back and let the tears of relief run down her face. She took a deep breath and said shakily, "Well, that does explain a few things. I have been so confused, Danila, that I began to fear for my sanity. I didn't see how I could go on like this indefinitely."

"I did not mean to cause you such distress, Laurel, but I couldn't decide exactly what to do about it. I mean, I have serious reservations about letting Jason off the hook entirely, and I don't mean because I intend to have him," she advised hastily as she observed Laurel's hurt expression, "but because it isn't safe to let that man loose on his own! Really, love, he is the most vulnerable greenhead when pitted against designing women and would be an easy mark for some determined lady who is up to snuff."

"Danila, he is not all *that* naïve," Laurel protested in defense. "He has not reached the age of twenty-eight still unmarried by being an easy mark."

"I am inclined to view that circumstance as pure luck," Danila advised, totally unconvinced. "Fortunately he has been pretty much isolated from the clutches of the more desperate schemers, having been too involved in his work to make any impression on society. But that is not to say that someday he might not find himself in a less secure environment, and I wouldn't give a penny for his chances to escape the snares of wily young girls and their mamas, particularly if they are aware of his wealth and his family connections."

"Danila, you are not painting a recognizable picture at all," Laurel demurred reprovingly. "I have known Jason forever, and he has never shown himself to be as tractable as you imagine."

"Well, maybe not so far, my poor innocent, but I can tell you he was putty in our hands, Eddy's and mine," the girl declared, undeterred.

"Danila!" Laurel exclaimed with a look of dismay. "I cannot believe you to be so unprincipled as to practice deliberate deceit."

Danila was moved to hang her head in shame as she admitted with an appealing honesty, "Well, I was, Laurel. But I did not think it would cause any harm because from Jason's manner when he spoke of you, I could not have imagined that you and he had a long-standing attachment. I mean, how was I to know that he was such an out-and-out numskull that he did not even realize he loved you deeply and, moreover, that you returned his sentiments, especially when both cases are so apparent to everyone else," she concluded defiantly.

Laurel smiled blissfully as she asked softly, wishing to have the lovely sentiments repeated, "Do you truly think he loves me that way, Danila?"

"Really, Laurel, I think it was Fate that sent me here to take a hand in things," Danila said disgustedly. "Why, the man can't keep his hands off you, and well you know it"—an indelicate statement that caused Laurel to blush uncomfortably. "I think," Danila said reflectively, "that loving you is so much a part of him that he doesn't see it for what it is. And now I realize that the real attraction for him here was not Dismoreland, but his lovely lady. He really can't bear to be away from you."

All of these auspicious professions were music to Laurel's ears, and she could have lost herself in such pleasurable thoughts forever. But she could not quite accept them for the absolute truth because he had, after all, let himself be talked into this betrothal. She asked diffidently, "Danila, how did you and Miss Eddington maneuver Jason into this compromising position?"

"We had only to determine his vulnerability, my love. It soon became obvious that he would accept any reasonable solution that would allow him to return to Sussex post-haste. We naturally assured him that we had no fixed intention that the betrothal would stand, so he felt perfectly safe and did not let the implications disturb him. I can't believe he allowed you and the others to believe it was a legitimate agreement. Whatever did he tell you?"

"The letter *was* vague," Laurel admitted, "but he did say specifically that he had agreed to a betrothal."

"And *that* was *it?*" Danila queried unbelieving. "I don't know why I should be surprised, however," she attested disparagingly. "It sounds just like him. Well, my dear girl, I think it is time that we opened his eyes. I shall speak with him tomorrow."

"No!" Laurel objected forcefully. "I forbid you to do any such thing. It would put him in an extremely compromising position, and I should never be sure he did not feel obligated to offer for me."

"Laurel, you are being ridiculous. He adores you!"

"If you are right, then I would rather he discovered that fact for himself," Laurel said incontrovertibly. "If you go against my wishes in this, Danila, I shall never forgive you."

"I begin to see how this lamentable situation came to pass," Danila observed trenchantly. "You, my dear, are a coward."

Laurel did not take offense but said ruefully, "You are beginning to sound like my mother."

"You should have listened to her long ago," Danila advised.

"But you don't understand . . ." Laurel began.

"What I understand, my addlepated friend, is that you are being extremely scrupulous and could end up losing him. You are just lucky that I am an honourable girl, for I could press this commitment and he would find himself at

92

the altar. So! I have no intention of making a public renouncement until you have him safely baited. And if you will not agree to a straightforward approach, then we will have to begin an underhanded campaign to open his eyes. Now, I have been thinking—"

"Not tonight, Danila, please," Laurel protested, putting up her hand. "I have had all the momentous revelations I can handle, and I feel completely exhausted. Let us retire for the night, and I promise you I will listen to your proposals tomorrow. Perhaps I will be more receptive when I have had some time to consider what you have already told me."

"All right, love. We will set things to rights, do not doubt it. So have lovely dreams, and I will have a marvelous plan all ready for putting into action."

Laurel laughed at the purely Machiavellian look on her friend's face, and she embraced her affectionately. "Danila, you are absolutely the most abominable girl, and I pity the man you finally do set your sights on. He won't stand a chance."

"It's just possible, you know, that I might please him very well, and he would have no cause to be pitied," Danila advised huffily.

"Actually, my love, your gentleman, whoever he might be, will be extremely lucky to have you, and I humbly retract my unworthy observation," Laurel assured her sincerely. And then they went arm in arm upstairs to their rooms.

The next morning all three ladies slept late, Lady Madeline because it was her habit; Laurel because, after finally calming her nerves, she fell into the first deep, untroubled sleep she had had since she received Jason's letter; and Danila because she had lain awake for hours, inventing all sorts of opportunities to shock Jason into awareness. She did not concern herself if any of her schemes should cause him distress, seeing no reason to go easy on him, for she would not forgive him for hurting her dearest friend.

At breakfast the two girls informed Lady Madeline of the true state of affairs. After giving fervent thanks to the powers that be, she readily joined in Danila's assessment that it was time that Jason was brought up to scratch. "Danila is right, Laurel," her mother affirmed readily. "If this could happen once, it could happen again, and you know very well that you would not be able to handle it as well as you thought. You have not been yourself since this all began. I hope you realize now you must put forth some effort to make him understand."

"Yes, I've thought about it, Mama, and I shouldn't want to have to go through this again," the girl agreed with a shudder. "I have been utterly miserable."

Danila reached out to put her hand on Laurel's and apologized abjectly, "I am so sorry I didn't tell you sooner, darling. I was trying so hard to think of what to do after I told you that I lost sight of the main point. But," she added with a determined expression, "now that we have cleared the air and are all agreed that we must take action, I confess I have been bursting to tell you of the perfectly fabulous idea I thought of last night. I could hardly sleep for the excitement of it, and I have been on tenterhooks for fear you will disappoint me!"

"Danila," Lady Madeline said, forestalling an immediate exposition of this divine inspiration, "let us take our coffee where we can be private. Our household maintains very close ties with Jason's, and I would not depend on our chances to maintain any measure of secrecy."

"Well, then, we must be very discreet," Danila affirmed promptly and rose from the table, not meaning to be deterred in her purpose to apprise the others of her plan. Laurel and her mother looked at each other and laughed but stood up, and Lady Madeline directed the butler to bring them fresh coffee, leading the way to the cozy library.

When they settled themselves, Danila immediately began to set the stage for her proposition, announcing. "First of all, Laurel, you are going to have to allow yourself to be the stunning girl you can be. This pose of yours is absolutely ridiculous. Anyone who has so much good taste and an appreciation of beautiful things as you do just cannot be so unaware of her own beauty. So it follows that you have been disguising yourself deliberately, and I am hard put to it to comprehend your reasoning."

She raised her brows questioningly, and Lady Madeline answered, "She has some sort of misguided notion that Jason would not feel as comfortable with her if she made a pretense to be fashionable."

"Well, as to *that*," Danila remarked acerbically, "she is perfectly right. But comfortable is hardly a desirable state in matters of this kind."

Laurel put her hand to her pink cheeks and looked at her mother helplessly. "Mother, I feel dreadfully unworldly compared to this shockingly shameless vixen we have taken to our bosoms. I am persuaded we should not let ourselves be inveigled into any of her schemes. I am sure I could not carry them off."

"Personally I have been thinking my prayers have been answered," Lady Madeline differed enigmatically with a twinkle in her eye.

"What do you mean by that?" both girls asked simultaneously.

"Well, some weeks ago I called on the Fates to send me an ally, and I couldn't have been better served," she said, a whimsical confession that made the three of them lapse into easy laughter.

Danila went to hug her accomplice affectionately and then returned to her chair, declaring, "I am glad you feel that way, Lady Madeline. It makes it easier for me to tell you what I propose. I had hoped you might reconsider and go to London for the Season after all."

Lady Madeline grinned appreciatively and advised, "You don't have to convince me, my dear. Our problem is to make Laurel see the advantages of it."

They both turned their eyes on the third party and were met with a stony look that told them they had a battle on their hands.

Danila pleaded, "Laurel, do be reasonable. It would be the perfect thing. When you appear on the London scene, the effect will be devastating. The gentlemen will swarm about you, and Jason will have to stand in line." She rose and walked over to stand a little away and simpered, batting her eyelashes, "My eyes are like deep pools? My lord, I am persuaded you say that to all the ladies. I am sure I should not—"

Her silly performance was interrupted by a knock, and the butler entered to announce, "My lady, Viscount Oxborough has called."

Immediately Jason's cousin burst into the room. He took Laurel by the hands. "My love, I came as soon as I could after I heard. How the devil did Jason let himself be caught by some scheming schoolroom chit? I have known him for a nodcock, but I did not imagine him a complete fool. Do not worry. I shall never allow him to treat you so abominably. I will put it to him in no uncertain terms, and he will have to send the bold baggage packing."

"Oh, dear," Lady Madeline gasped in dismay as she observed the belligerent look on Danila's face.

Laurel smiled broadly, pressing Philip's hands gratefully as she said, "My dear Philip, it is extremely gratifying to find myself with such a fierce champion, and now that I have two, I cannot doubt that everything must be happily resolved. Philip, I should like very much to introduce you to my very good friend Lady Danila Wilmington."

He looked at her in astonishment but turned as she directed and was met by the most scathing look it had ever been his misfortune to receive from any young female, being usually well regarded by all such generally susceptible persons.

"Your good friend! But, Laurel, isn't this—"

"The bold baggage," Danila finished for him, smiling sweetly but with a dangerous glint in her eye. She turned from him lazily and asked, "And who is this—uh—gentleman, Laurel?"

"Oh, Danila, I'm sorry. May I introduce you to Jason's cousin Lord Philip Ashburn, Viscount Oxborough."

The girl curtsied and said cordially, in the manner of one who intends to comport herself properly, even under the most trying circumstances, a deliberate courtesy to point up Lord Philip's uncivil conduct, "I am pleased to make your acquaintance, my lord." And then she sat on the couch next to Lady Madeline, regarding the newcomer with an interested eye.

Philip had to give the girl credit, for in a trice she had turned the tables on him. From her obvious good standing in the household, it was clear that things were not as he imagined. He looked at Laurel's amused face and backed off ruefully. "I have an ominous feeling that I am going to pay dearly for that regrettably ill-advised bobble."

"Well, you might have been a little precipitant," Laurel allowed with laughing eyes, "but considering the circumstances, it was understandable, and Danila is not one to hold a grudge. Are you, my love?"

"Well, no, considering the circumstances," the girl relented, smiling impishly. "But I must say, my lord, that your arrival is exceedingly untimely because just before you came on the scene to make your vile accusations and hateful aspersions, I was elaborating on my plan to make Jason come up to scratch."

"Then I am not misinformed, after all," Philip surmised in a definitely unfriendly manner.

Danila looked at him in disgust and scoffed, "Is everyone in your family lacking in comprehension? Not for *me*, my lord. For Laurel!"

"Oh," Philip said with a chagrined expression, feeling very much the fool. "Uh—perhaps you will explain how I came to be so off the mark," he suggested humbly.

Danila decided reluctantly that this constituted a reasonable request, but first she asked, "How did you find out about it?"

"Jason's mother wrote to my father and insisted that he do something," Philip confessed apologetically.

Lady Madeline noted caustically, "One of her more effective moves, considering he was touring on the Continent."

"Oh, so you're *that* cousin," Danila spoke out, suddenly comprehending.

"What cousin?" Philip asked dubiously, with a wary expression.

Danila smiled at him reassuringly and replied, "When Jason was telling me who could not sponsor my debut, he mentioned his aunt, who was away from England at the time. That was the problem, you see," she continued indignantly. "No one was available so . . ." And then she explained how the betrothal came about. "But," she added, feeling for some unaccountable reason a pressing need at least partially to excuse her behaviour, "of course I had no idea that he was committed to Laurel, even though he doesn't seem to realize it. However, now that I am here, we have decided it was Fate that arranged it because Laurel has come to perceive how gullible Jason can be, and we are going to bring pressure to bear in some dramatic fashion!"

"Couldn't we just tell him?" Philip suggested equivocally, diverted by the girl's animated manner.

Danila smiled at him approvingly and concurred, "So I think, too, my lord. But Laurel has vetoed that idea absolutely, and actually I can appreciate her sentiments, for it would be much more romantic if Jason should suddenly be enlightened and throw himself at her feet."

"Danila, do stop fantasizing," Laurel begged with a horrified expression. "There is no way that Jason would throw himself at anyone's feet."

"That was just a figure of speech," Danila advised scornfully. "What I mean is that he should be floored by your appearance—"

"Sounds much the same thing to me," Lord Philip interposed mischievously, as he was beginning to relish baiting the malapert little schemer.

"—which," Danila continued with a withering glance at the gentleman, "means that we cannot allow him to see the new you piecemeal but must hit him full force. Oh, I can imagine his astonishment now as he sees you with your hair dressed elegantly, coming down the winding stairs in a beautiful blue gown—"

"*What* winding stairs?" Laurel asked dampeningly, suddenly having serious reservations about putting herself in this girl's hands and experiencing a renewed determination to resist her impositions.

"Well," Danila conceded, "I don't precisely know if they are winding or not." Turning to Lady Madeline, she asked interestedly, "Where are we going to stay in London?"

Lady Madeline was wholly caught up in Danila's enthusiasm, and she exclaimed, "Oh, my! I don't know. I usually rent a house on Brook Street, but I'm sure it is no longer available. I shall have to write my solicitor, directing him to find something acceptable."

"Mother!" Laurel exploded, totally exasperated. "I had hoped you would suppress this wretched girl's presumptions, but instead, you have allowed yourself to be seduced. I wish you will both listen to me. I am *not* going to London or lend myself to any of your other schemes, so you may stop taxing your brains."

"Laurel!" Danila began but desisted when she received a warning look from Lady Madeline, and she had to be satisfied with just having brought the matter into the open.

Philip had been thoroughly enjoying the spirited exchange and was disappointed to have it end. But he was sure that this was not the last of it, so he quickly decided he would remain in Sussex to watch the drama unfold. He stood to excuse himself, telling the ladies he meant to stay with Jason for a time and would be seeing a lot of them, a prospect Danila viewed with considerable interest.

Chapter
SIX

Philip had gone directly to the family seat in Kent after he crossed the Channel but had stayed only two days before speeding to the rescue. He had ridden on ahead and had ordered his coachman and his valet to follow with his carriage and trunks, so he was prepared for an extended stay. When he arrived at Devereaux House, he was informed that the master had gone to Dismoreland but was expected back shortly for lunch.

"Is my aunt in or out?" Philip asked facetiously with a crooked grin.

"I believe, my lord," the butler answered blandly, "one would have to say that Mrs. Devereaux is—uh—in."

"All right, Foxworth, thank you. I understand, and I won't disturb her. I'll wait for my cousin in the library."

"Yes, my lord. I shall inform him you are here."

Within the hour Jason had returned and went immediately to welcome his unexpected visitor. "Phil, when did you get back?" he greeted him affably, clasping his hand strongly.

"Just a couple of days ago," the younger man answered without elaboration.

"Were your mother and father ready to come home? I had thought they intended to stay awhile longer."

"Well, actually, they are. I returned alone," Philip stated indifferently.

"It's a little early in the year to go to London, isn't it?" Jason asked quizzically.

"Didn't come back for that reason. Confound it, Jason! I might as well tell you. The truth of it is that Aunt Theo wrote to my father telling him that you had lost your reason and had gotten yourself engaged to a brazen hussy just out of the schoolroom. She said she had washed her hands of you and demanded that he take some action to bring you to your senses. And so, being properly suspicious of his sister's propensity to exaggerate, he prudently sent me to investigate and report."

"Damnation!" Jason exploded, kicking at the fire irons. "Now I suppose the news is all over town."

"Depends on whom else she told," Philip commented unencouragingly.

"You seem mighty cool about it if you believe the story," Jason remarked caustically.

"A couple of hours ago you would have thought differently, but I have been to see Laurel and have met the 'brazen hussy'," his cousin admitted with a wry grin.

"Do you mean to tell me that you actually considered I might have been such a gudgeon?"

"Don't rip up at *me*, old man. Even allowing for your mother's excesses, one can hardly be expected to think that she had fabricated the whole thing," Philip retorted testily. "We presumed she had some cause."

"My God! If she misunderstood, I wonder if Laurel and Lady Madeline did also," Jason speculated with a look of panic.

"I would imagine so. You do have a tendency to be a bit vague now and then," Philip noted unpromisingly.

"Let's ride over now," Jason said anxiously, moving toward the door. "I have to explain."

"I don't think that's a matter for urgency at this moment," his cousin advised calmly. "Your ward has already set the record straight."

"How do you know?"

"Because I put my foot in my mouth, making unwarranted accusations, and received the most magnificent setdown of my life. That girl is alarmingly spirited," he said with a daunted expression. "I expect some sort of imbroglio was inevitable once she entered the scene."

Jason laughed and agreed as he came back to sit down, "Yes, she is a minx, but charming for all that. Let's have lunch, and then we'll go back, so you can mend your fences."

"Oh, I've already done that," Philip advised with a roguish grin. "But I have no objection to consolidating my provisional status."

Jason raised a quizzical brow and warned, "If you are developing an interest there, you had better resign yourself to being led a merry dance."

"Don't worry. I mean to tread warily, but I admit to a certain curiosity," Philip replied cautiously.

As they restored themselves with a hearty lunch, they touched cursorily on a variety of subjects, remarking only the main points, for Jason was obviously impatient to see Laurel. They both changed to more proper attire for an afternoon call and decided to take the barouche in case the ladies could be persuaded to go for a drive since the weather had turned warmer now that the sun was shining brightly after the morning's light shower.

They were expected because Jason had said that he would come, and naturally it was presumed that he would bring his cousin. Danila and Laurel were immediately receptive to a drive around the countryside and hurried to get their bonnets and light pelisses. Jason asked Philip if he would take the reins first because he wanted to talk with Laurel and suggested that Danila might like to ride on the box with him, a proposal that met with that young lady's unequivocal approval. "Oh, I should like that very much. I have always wanted to learn to drive."

"Who said anything about your learning to drive?" Jason asked quellingly as he helped her up.

"Jason, I wish you would stop talking to me as if I were a child!" Danila declared with asperity. "Of course, I should not expect to take the reins today, but I do

102

not think it is asking too much to be instructed in the art of controlling the horses and other pertinent matters."

"Well, you may try to convince Philip," her guardian relented with an unrepentant grin. "He is generally considered a very amiable fellow."

She cast him a blighting look, then bestowed a lovely friendly smile on the other gentleman, who realized he had been thoroughly flimflammed. He resigned himself to his fate, which, as it turned out, was not all that objectionable since he discovered Danila to be an altogether deft and engaging pupil who obviously scorned a maidenly pose of diffidence and behaved in a perfectly natural fashion as if she had known her companion for years.

They drove towards the Sussex Downs along the banks of the river Arun and admired all the subtle evidences of the coming spring. After a while Jason turned purposefully to Laurel and broached the matter that had been preying on his mind. "My dear, I'm afraid I have unwittingly created a misapprehension, and I should like to apologize because I am come to think it might have caused you some distress. Laurel, did you actually think that I was betrothed to Danila?" he asked incredulously with an air of reproval.

The girl looked at him in surprise but smiled as she said, "Really, Jason, how could I think anything else when you specifically wrote that you were?"

"But surely I gave you to understand that it was merely a sham," he protested.

"No, I didn't divine that," she denied truthfully. "Nor did Mother or Theo for that matter."

"Good Lord, I must have made a sad mull of it! What the devil *did* I say?"

"I believe your exact words were that you had 'agreed to a betrothal'," Laurel told him dryly.

"Well, so I did. But if that was the sum of it, I can see how it could lead to misinterpretation," he admitted sheepishly. He took her hand and pleaded, "Please forgive me, Laurel. Is that what caused your illness?" he asked hesitantly.

"I expect so," the girl replied candidly, deciding to treat

the question lightly. "It just came so suddenly, and I couldn't imagine how things would work out. I mean—the young lady might take exception to your spending so much time with another female, and I had gotten so involved in the work at Dismoreland that it quite cut up my serenity to consider that our close association was in jeopardy. But of course, after I met Danila, I was not so nervy."

"I am relieved that she had the good sense to tell you the whole of it. I should not like to think that you had been worried all this time."

"I found out only yesterday, Jason," Laurel told him softly.

"Yesterday!" he exclaimed in astonishment. "But you and Danila have become good friends!"

Laurel could barely hide her amusement at this unconscious acknowledgment of the incongruous circumstances, but she just said mildly, "Of course, Jason. I am very fond of Danila, and I learned to live with my apprehensions."

This casual revelation caused Jason to experience an undefined letdown, and he suddenly realized that there had been a subtle change in his relationship with Laurel these last few weeks that would bear some serious examination. But the time was not propitious, and for the moment he merely spoke a deflated "Oh," then devoted himself to playing the attentive escort.

When they turned to head back, Jason offered to change places with his cousin, but Danila protested immediately, "Oh, no! For Lord Philip just said he would let me hold the reins for a short time when we are in the open."

"All the more reason for him to relinquish them to me," Jason declared promptly. "I am not so imprudent."

"Lady Danila," Philip asked whimsically, "how did you come to be plagued with such a stodgy guardian?"

"Oh, I don't know!" the girl responded passionately. "I have had such dreadful luck!"

At this fervent declaration Philip had to pull the horses to a halt because he was laughing so hard, and Danila, who had been perfectly serious, found his amusement infectious and joined in immoderately. Since this delightful sort of contagion is easily spread, Jason and Laurel were soon almost in as sad case as their companions.

Finally they all regained their composure, and Philip said breathlessly, "Danila, if you will promise to curb your comic predilections, I will give you your first lesson."

"Well," the compulsively honest girl said doubtfully, "I would very much like to promise you, but I should not want to be accused of telling a Banbury tale because, you see, sometimes I say perfectly serious things that other people think are very funny."

Philip had to laugh again and acknowledged, "Yes, I see what you mean. Well then, I will not place you in such a compromising position. We will just take our chances that our horses will not take advantage of us if they suspect us of being less than mindful."

She favoured him with another of her brilliant smiles of approval, and the young man realized at that moment that his visit to Sussex was certainly fortunate. He handed her the reins and said lightly, "Here you are, my girl. Now let us see if you can get us moving again."

She took them eagerly but sat for a moment and considered the matter carefully before tugging on the ribbons as he had demonstrated. The horses responded satisfactorily with only the slightest jouncing of the passengers, and they were soon tooling along the straightaway at a steady, if sedate, pace.

"Give them their heads a little," Philip directed. The girl looked at him apprehensively but slightly loosened her hold and was so pleased by the horses' admirable performance that she was minded to carry the experiment a bit further. Philip looked at her intent expression with amusement and, after a moment, told her to slow down the pace. She did so reluctantly but had no intention of showing herself to be an unruly pupil and behaved with the utmost discretion. They were approaching a more demanding stretch, so he reached to take the reins. "That's enough for today, Danila. Your hands will soon be rubbed raw. You will have to have a strong pair of driving gloves before our next excursion."

"Oh," she cried delightedly, "do you really mean to teach me?"

"Yes," he promised. "I'm sure I should enjoy it immensely. We shall certainly have to contrive our own amusements since our friends have rather one-track minds."

Danila found this proposal wholly agreeable, and she exclaimed happily, "I am *so* glad you came, Lord Philip. Everything is working out just beautifully, and you may be sure that I shall give Eddy—Miss Eddington, you know—a very good report of you."

"I am pleased to hear you say so," a hard-pressed young man said thankfully, struggling to keep a straight face. "I am sure it would not be at all comfortable were I to start off in her black books."

Danila looked at him suspiciously and said darkly, "You are laughing at me again. I only meant that—well . . ."

Jason finished helpfully, "What she means, my dear cousin, is that there are those of us who have not fared so well. I must congratulate you on your discretion because, I assure you, Miss Eddington is an extremely redoubtable female."

Danila felt moved to offer a mitigating explanation, and she ventured, "It's not that I made you out an ogre or anything like that, Jason. I just said . . ."

"Never mind," her guardian interrupted. "I think I would just as soon not know, and I, too, am glad Philip has come. I have been fearing that your unusually good behaviour might take a turn for the worse for lack of enterprising opportunities."

Philip turned his head with a quizzical expression and said suggestively, "Well, Laurel?"

"Make it unanimous, Philip. I am beginning to share my mother's peculiar communion with Fate," she told him.

Having reached this happy accord, they continued their agreeable banter and very soon found themselves at the gates of the Ingram property. The gentlemen were pressed to remain for dinner and did not have to be coaxed. A lively foursome went in search of Lady Madeline to announce their return and soon discovered her in the upstairs drawing room, entertaining a surprise guest.

Theo Devereaux pounced immediately. "Well, Philip, I must say it is beyond anything that I should have heard from the servants that you had come but did not have the courtesy to attend me before you took off on one of your jaunts and that I should have to come look for you."

Philip laughed and went to give her a strong hug and a kiss on the cheek as he admonished teasingly, "Aunt Theo, you know very well that if I had bearded you in your den, you would have given me a monumental setdown for my presumptions. You are looking in fine fettle and as puckish as ever. The earl and my mother send their love."

She looked at him skeptically and noted caustically, "I suppose the lofty Earl of Schofield elected to procrastinate and send you as deputy."

"Yes, love, he did. But I must take exception to your unkind derogation because I assure you I am altogether competent, and I have every intention of resolving this matter to everyone's satisfaction."

Word was sent to the kitchen that there would be three guests for dinner. The young people went to refresh themselves, returning shortly to join the ladies for tea and to be regaled by Philip's stories of his latest Grand Tour. They continued their lively conversations all through a leisurely dinner and then retired to the library to play cards and to be entertained by Danila's performance on the piano, which all agreed had to be one of her superior female accomplishments.

The next several days the two couples generally went their separate ways, joining forces only at meals and occasionally in the evening, although even then Jason and Laurel often worked on the plans for Dismoreland. They were in the midst of a major alteration, having decided to modernize the exterior of the house, adding false fronts to the lower façades to eliminate the rustic appearance of the ground floor. The interior would be remodeled to accommodate a comfortable family living area in a U shape around a conservatory that would open directly to the outside at the back of the house and so unite with the vista that extended to the lake. One of the wings would be completed to contain a new kitchen and the servants' quarters. Jason had been rather stymied by the inutility of the spacious domed hall but finally decided to employ it as a gallery. He had accumulated a number of excellent artworks—sculptures, paintings, and tapestries—purchases he had made when he was on the Continent and those acquired by his father on his travels. He and Laurel were altogether pleased with this conception because it was one of the few rooms that would not require any extensive renovation since it had been beautifully decorated with marble columns and floor and exquisite wood carvings on the stairs and balcony and around the clerestory windows. It has been designed with classic simplicity and would lend itself to displaying the treasures without detracting from the artworks themselves. To accommodate several of the more magnificent pieces, Laurel set to work designing special moldings, pedestals, and an elevated platform in the center of the room under the dome to display a spectacular collection of armoury that the admiral had confiscated from some of the prize ships he had boarded, including some jeweled scabbards and daggers from the Barbary pirates and gold-handled, decorated dueling pistols received as a gift from one of the electors of Saxony for some personal service.

With Laurel and Jason being so preoccupied, Danila and Philip spent a good part of each day together and usually rode in the morning, often accompanied by Lady Madeline and occasionally by Jason and Laurel for a short time before they excused themselves to ride on to Dismoreland. In the afternoons, weather permitting, Philip continued to instruct Danila on driving. She progressed rapidly, having only a slight tendency to set a fast pace, although her tutor had to admit that she had excellent reflexes, and he always kept a sharp eye.

One fine day they all planned a special picnic excursion to Lord Egremont's estate, Petworth, which was of particular interest to Jason and Laurel because of the famous landscape gardens, which had been designed by Capability Brown.

Most evenings they spent in the Ingram library, but once Lady Madeline and Danila were delighted when Philip agreed to escort them to a supper dance party at the home of the squire, who enjoyed a respected position as the local justice of the peace. Danila was elated to be able to wear one of her new dresses and bowed to Lady Madeline's choice after being informed that the high-fashion creation she had her heart set on was not at all suitable for an informal country party. Nevertheless, she pronounced herself slap up to the mark in her jonquil yellow round dress embroidered with green scrollwork and was even more set up with herself when Philip complimented her on her appearance, remarking that she looked like a breath of spring, ingratiating himself still further by kissing her hand, even though the practice was considered dreadfully old-fashioned. Lady Madeline also received her due, being adjudged almost scandalously youthful-looking for the natural presumption that she must have been a child bride to have a twenty-two-year-old daughter. And so it was a rather puffed-up threesome that set forth after having been extravagantly admired by the two who had elected to remain behind.

They were among the first arrivals, gratifying the host and hostess inordinately, for there were few titled families in the immediate vicinity, although a number of the larger landowners or their wives had connections to younger sons of the aristocracy. Their appearance was a feather in the cap for the squire and his wife, particularly when they showed themselves to be so amiable.

In the carriage Danila had cautioned her two companions not to reveal the truth of the betrothal because she still had some sort of vague feeling that Jason should remain in the ranks of the ineligibles.

"But, Danila," Lady Madeline had argued, "it will seem excessively odd that he is not acting as your escort."

"No, we will just tell anyone who is inquisitive that he is too deeply involved in his work at present but thoughtfully

109

appointed his cousin as his deputy," the girl invented easily.

Philip laughed and assured, "That will serve, Lady Madeline. It would not be questioned."

"Not unless the two of you have been observed these last few days that you have been together constantly. I do feel responsible for Danila's reputation, you know, and I should not like to have her labeled as fast."

"We will be very discreet," Philip promised. He then turned to Danila with a mischievous grin. "Do not fly into a miff if I ask you for only two dances, my girl, and try not to be too friendly."

"Oh, you insufferable man!" she spouted indignantly. "I hope you don't think that I mean to hang on you when I am going to my first party since Eddy and I visited her cousin at Christmas!"

"Of course not!" he agreed unconcernedly. "I have it on good authority from Jenkins that all beaux and belles of the neighbourhood will be on hand, so I expect neither of us will be lacking for partners."

"Oh," a small voice said unenthusiastically, and its owner fell into a thoughtful silence, which was duly noted and appreciated by her two companions.

In the course of the evening both Danila and Philip appraised the other guests interestedly and confidently decided they had nothing to worry about. They proceeded to comport themselves admirably, making themselves agreeable to the other young people and winning the approval of most of the dowagers, there always being in any group at least one malcontent who makes a career of finding fault. After partaking liberally of the sumptuous supper that easily surpassed the usual repasts served at many of the *ton* parties, which were often provided by the same caterers and became almost predictable, the guests began to depart. Some of them with longer distances to travel arranged to drive in the same direction by three or fours, which would discourage any attack by would-be highwaymen, a decreasing, but still potential, danger.

Philip rode outside on the box with Jenkins on the return journey of some seven miles and within an hour saw the ladies safely home.

Danila slept very late the next morning, waking in unusually high feather even for a girl who was generally cheerful. Her subconscious had obviously been playing tricks on her since the first thought that came to her mind concerned a certain Lady Ashburn, Vicountess Oxborough—Lady Danila Ashburn, to be precise. She smiled to herself and stretched lazily, luxuriating in this delightful fantasy. Her mind began to work furiously because she realized a renewed ambition for settling Laurel's affairs now that she had lit upon some pressing ones of her own. She decided that she would talk the matter over with Lady Madeline and with Philip, who, she had a pleasant sensation, would see the advantages of an early resolution himself. She was determined, whatever her own aspirations might be, that her darling Laurel, for whom she had developed an immoderate partiality, would realize her happiness.

She called for Katie and asked her to discover if Lady Madeline had risen yet. The girl came back shortly to report that Lady Ingram was having a light breakfast in her sitting room and invited Danila to join her if she wished. The girl rose immediately, put on a warm wrapper, and allowed her maid to brush her hair.

She greeted Lady Madeline and accepted a bowl of fruit with cream and a cup of coffee. Then she promptly launched into an animated discourse, propounding a number of precepts with which Lady Madeline could find no fault at all.

"We simply *must* persuade Laurel to go to London," Danila declared fervently. "We cannot allow her to put us off any longer. In just a couple of days it will be Easter and the Season will be getting under way."

"I am totally in agreement with you, my dear Danila, but as I have been importuning her for the last three years without the least success, I am afraid I do not have much hope for her cooperation."

"Yes, well, it is apparent that there is no way that she will go while Jason remains in Sussex, working on his fusty

111

old mansion, so the only solution is that he shall go with us."

"I admire your logic, Danila, but I will consider you a magician if you can pull that off. Jason has never gone to London for the Season in his life. He has a definite antipathy towards that particular rite of spring."

"I will think of something," the girl promised optimistically. "I shall enlist Philip's aid, and I am persuaded we shall find some compelling argument. I thought perhaps you would wish to have Mrs. Higgins begin work on some of Laurel's gowns since most of ours are finished. She could do the cutting and some of the preliminary work so that when Laurel does fall in with our plans, the dresses will be ready for fitting."

"Danila," Lady Madeline said with an indulgent laugh, "you do have the most enterprising nature I have ever encountered, and I suddenly have every confidence that you will manage somehow. So I will send for the dressmaker today and have her begin immediately."

With a satisfied smile the girl sat back, anticipating her meeting with Philip. Lady Madeline watched her with fascination as the changing expressions on her face gave evidence of the nimbleness of her mind. She wondered what schemes were being hatched, hoping they did not progress to the outlandish, although given Danila's vivid imagination, she would not bet against such a possibility.

The day was not particularly pleasant, and Danila felt deliciously lazy besides, so she decided it would be much more comfortable to plan their strategy in the cozy library before a warm fire. She took special pains with her appearance that afternoon, choosing a magenta-coloured velvet gown with matching slippers and a light paisley shawl of subdued blues and reds to drape over her shoulders. She then went to the drawing room to play the piano until Philip arrived. She heard his carriage but managed to control the impulse to run madly to greet him and remained at the piano until he entered the room. She started to rise, but he motioned her to continue as he settled himself in a chair, stretching his long legs before him, leaning back with his eyes resting pleasurably on this enchanting girl who had won his heart almost from the first moment he saw her.

When she finished the sonata by Schubert, they looked at each other and smiled in perfect communion. He went to sit by her and took her hands. "Danila, my love, that was beautiful. I am so pleased that you enjoy music, and I look forward to many lovely, peaceful evenings at home."

This allusion to a conjugal future for them roused butterflies in her stomach, and she smiled at him sweetly. As always, feeling obligated to set the record straight, she said, "Well, you know, my teacher was not all that happy with me. He would compliment me on my technical facility and my expression, but I do not always play in the correct tempo. I am really not that proficient, and I do not attempt any demanding compositions."

Philip laughed at her seriousness and vowed, "Danila, you are the most enchanting little imp I have ever met, and I love you madly." Taking her chin in his hand, he kissed her lightly. She felt so happy she wished to melt and cling to him. But as he began to gather her into his arms, she remembered her resolve, and she pushed firmly against his chest, protesting, "No, darling, please don't."

An affronted young man looked at her incredulously and demanded testily, "Why not? I thought you would like it."

"Oh, Philip, you know I do. I like it excessively, but I have promised myself to put an end to the impasse between Jason and Laurel before I will let myself be distracted. And you know," she added provokingly, "it is exceedingly improper to be cuddling with you when I am engaged to another man."

"That won't fadge, you ramshackle girl," a nettled suitor pronounced sternly. "You are *not* betrothed to another man, and I don't wish to hear you joke about it. I have been finding even this pretense hard to swallow. And while I am expressing my displeasure, I must tell you that I hold it hard to believe that you never had any speculation about becoming Mrs. Devereaux at some time because Miss Eddington obviously did, and I don't doubt she whispered in your ear."

Danila had the grace to hang her head as she admitted reluctantly, "Well, perhaps at first, before I came to Sussex, I did consider such an eventuality. Jason, after all, is a very handsome, estimable gentleman, when he isn't playing at being a guardian, and would seem a nonpareil to any impressionable young girl."

"Impressionable you are not," Philip denied dampeningly. "Scheming, without a doubt, but definitely not impressionable."

"I allow you are right," she granted, not taking exception to his trenchant observation. "But I have since analyzed my susceptibility to such a prospect, and I have decided it was positively inevitable. In many ways you are much alike, you know, which explains any attraction I may have imagined, for," she continued artfully, "how could I have possibly known that Jason was just a forerunner?"

"My God!" Philip exclaimed, looking at her in fascination. "You are the most outrageous, designing female and will probably make a shambles of my life, but I might as well face up to it. I haven't a prayer for resisting you, and I admit that I am fairly caught. However, I warn you, you are definitely on borrowed time. Now," he asked with a rueful sigh, "just what trials are you going to set me before you will concentrate on our situation?"

"Darling Philip," Danila purred happily, placing her hand on his cheek, "I do admire your lovely sentiments and am finding all your professions extremely exciting, but I must finish this business, and I'm afraid we are going to have a bit of a problem."

"I beg you will just come out with it, Danila. I am in no mood for riddles," he said ill-humouredly.

"Well, first of all, we have to persuade Laurel to go to London," Danila began.

"I had rather hoped that was no longer one of your priorities," Philip remarked in obvious disappointment.

"Actually, I am not nearly so enamoured of the idea as I

114

once was," she admitted placatingly. "But I do think it would be fun to experience the excitement of it just once," she said wistfully.

Philip reached to take her hand and apologized, "I'm sorry, darling. I am a selfish wretch to want to keep you all to myself, but from my own experience I know how popular you are going to be with all the gentlemen. I shall probably have to call out some overly ambitious fellow before a week is out."

Danila laughed at the rueful expression on his face but assured him, "You won't have to worry about that, my love, because naturally everyone will think I am betrothed to Jason."

"The devil they will!" Philip exploded. "You can abandon that part of your scheme right now. If you go to London already bespoken, it will be to me."

"Philip," Danila cajoled shamelessly, "everyone will have heard of the betrothal anyway, so how could a few weeks make any difference?"

"Because I have no intention of cooling my heels in the wings while you go gallivanting around with my cousin."

"But it wouldn't be like that, you know. We would always be with you and Laurel," she explained patiently.

"My dear girl, you do have a remarkably ingenuous view of an extremely knotty situation. For one thing you are presuming that Jason is going to be in London, which is the most fanciful aspect of your whole concept, except for your even more addlepated presumption that he would allow the misunderstanding about your betrothal to persist. Even further, I doubt very much that you can persuade Laurel to fall in with your plans."

"Well," Danila proclaimed indignantly, "I didn't say it would be easy. That's why I need your help. We are going to have to force the issue right away because by the time we could be ready, the Season will probably be half over. I mean to collar Laurel the next chance I get, so I will appreciate it if you will keep Jason occupied tomorrow morning."

"Just how do you propose to resolve all these complexities?" Philip asked quizzically.

"I don't know precisely," she acknowledged frankly with sparkling eyes, "but I am persuaded that everything connected with this business is destined to turn out swimmingly, given the exceedingly auspicious results that have been realized thus far."

"Danila, if you go around making these extremely leading and forward remarks to other gentlemen as you have to me, you are going to find yourself in the suds," he admonished severely.

"Darling Philip, I hope you do not think I am so free in my conduct with just anybody. I know that you and Jason are very honourable gentlemen and would not mistake my meaning."

"And just how is it that you are so confident of your ability to judge correctly about such matters?" he asked deprecatingly.

"Just because I have spent my last five years with Miss Eddington does not mean I have not had the opportunity to observe the lecherous propensities of certain members of the opposite sex, I'll have you know," she declared with asperity. "During the holidays I was invited occasionally to spend two or three weeks at the homes of some of the other girls, and besides, when my mother was alive, she entertained often. She was a very beautiful, vivacious lady and always had gentlemen vying for her company. Several times I could see that she was almost ready to accept some dreadfully unsuitable aspirant, so naturally I was compelled to throw a spoke in his wheel," she confessed with a scowling expression as she remembered some of those unsavoury characters.

"Naturally," he agreed as he burst out laughing. "I suspect, my love, you are very much your mother's daughter."

"Well, we did look and think a lot alike," she told him, "but my mother was beautiful, and I am merely—"

"Beautiful, Danila, extremely beautiful," he assured her as he put his hand on her head lovingly. "Now tell me," he

116

coaxed, "why does it have to appear that you are engaged to Jason? I would like it so much if you would let me give you a ring and introduce you as my very own."

"Philip, please don't look at me like that. It makes me feel all shivery. It's just that I have this dreadful feeling that if I release Jason publicly before he commits himself to Laurel, somebody else is likely to compromise him."

"I believe, my dear girl, that you have this maggoty vision of yourself as your guardian's guardian," the gentleman remarked quizzically.

"Oh, Philip," she said, clasping her hands delightedly, "that's it precisely. I knew you would understand."

"Danila, do not try to twist my words. I do not understand. The whole thing could be happily concluded if I would just take Jason into a corner."

"Oh, no! Promise me you will not, Philip. Laurel would be so crushed. She has her own little odd humour, you know, in that she doesn't wish him to have to be told. You won't do her a backhanded turn, will you, darling?" she begged.

"All right, Danila. I suppose I have no choice but to sit back and let you direct this charade. What would you have me do?"

"I'm not sure yet. We will have to take one step at a time. I first have to talk to Laurel."

"I suppose Lady Madeline is also your confederate?"

"Oh, yes! She is already into her part and is closeted upstairs with the dressmakers working on Laurel's new gowns, which, of course, she knows nothing about, so do not let the cat out of the bag," she reminded.

"I take it this is part of your plan to hit Jason full force," he said teasingly.

She grinned and then changed the subject purposefully. "Now that we have made all the progress that we can on the matter today, I should like for you to tell me about your family. We have never talked very much about them, and I didn't want to make bold to ask for fear of its being too leading a question."

117

"Baggage!" Philip accused appreciatively and motioned for her to come to sit by him. She placed a footstool at his feet and looked up at him attentively, leaning against his knee, tempting him to reach out to place his hand on her hair and finger it caressingly. "My father is deeply involved in government affairs and is a leading figure in the Lords, so he prefers to live in London, where he can stay on top of things. My mother delights in her role as a political hostess. She has always encouraged his ambition, so I have been very fortunate to have met most of the prominent leaders in the country and have found the experience extremely fascinating, but not to the extent that I would wish to follow in my father's footsteps. I'm afraid I have the soul of a country gentleman, and I mean to spend a lot of time at Schofield Hall in Kent. The steward we have had for the last few years has not been particularly competent, and the estate has deteriorated noticeably. The earl really does not have the time or inclination to oversee and correct the problem, so he wants me to take over its management as soon as I marry. How would it suit you to be a country lady?" he asked tentatively.

"I'm sure I should find it wholly delightful," she assured him enthusiastically. "Is it a large property?"

"Yes, and it needs a lot of attention."

"Oh, dear. I'm afraid we are going to be very much occupied, my love. I have some extensive holdings myself, including a castle in Derbyshire. Fortunately, however, Mr. Halliburton has installed an excellent manager, so perhaps it will not be too burdensome."

"My God! I forgot you were an heiress! Between the two of us we will be rich as Croesus. That is, we will be if we can keep the estates profitable so they don't drain our resources."

"Well, actually, Philip, it would take some monumental catastrophe to drain my resources," she told him apologetically. "However, we can make good use of the money to modernize the estates. I know we will be able to install all sorts of improvements to make them model properties. I will not lack for ideas because I have the reputation of being a very enterprising girl."

"Yes, darling, I know you have," he said tenderly, leaning over to kiss her nose.

They heard Jason and Laurel below in the hall, and Danila went to sit in a chair just as they entered the room. "You two look cozy," Jason remarked. "Did you forgo your driving lesson today?"

"Yes," Danila replied. "I was too lazy, and the weather was unpleasant so we have just spent a quiet afternoon here by the fire."

"Consolidating your provisional status?" Jason asked whimsically, looking significantly at his cousin.

"Wrong tense, wrong adjective," Philip answered complacently, and before Jason could pursue the matter, he asked, "How is it you're back so early?"

"The house is particularly drafty today with the strong winds," Laurel said as she warmed her hands, "so we decided to come back here to work for a while."

Then, as usual, she and Jason spread their work out on the library table and were soon engrossed in a technical problem involving lights and mirrors. Philip and Danila came to look over their shoulders. Philip asked, "What are you working on now?"

"When we redesigned the ground floor," Jason explained, "we found ourselves with a windowless area in the center of the house under the domed hall. We will open it into the conservatory, but it will still be dark, so we are hanging several mirrors, with candelabra on either side, facing each other, and dropping a gaslighted chandelier in the center so that all the light will be reflected *ad infinitum*. The concept is very effective. I'm sure you've noticed the same arrangement in other houses."

"Yes, now that you mention it, I have, though I won't precisely say that I realized that it was deliberately contrived," Philip said admiringly.

"How much longer are you going to have to bury yourselves in those drawings?" Danila asked impatiently.

119

"Only another month or so," Jason said confidently. "We have done the hardest part, and already we have the men working on the remodeling."

"A month!" Danila wailed unhappily. "And then you will have to supervise the work, I suppose. Really, Jason, it is beyond anything that you monopolize Laurel in this perfectly outrageous fashion. I never am permitted to enjoy her exclusive company anymore."

"And when would you have time to do so?" Jason asked teasingly.

"In the morning," Danila answered promptly. "So I wish you will excuse her tomorrow, for I have some things I particularly wanted to talk to her about." She looked significantly at Philip, who, dutifully remembering his assignment, seconded the suggestion, reminding Jason that he had agreed to accompany him to Epsom one day and that he could just make up his mind to take time off.

Jason grinned and agreed sheepishly, "All right, Phil. We'll take our coachmen with us, for they would be in high dudgeon if we tried to go to the races without them."

Danila smiled approvingly at her love, and he just shook his head dubiously at the smug look on her face. The gentlemen declined to remain for dinner, deciding to make an early night of it, but warned the ladies they had only one day's grace and must be prepared to receive them again the following morning.

Chapter
SEVEN

Since they were left to their own devices for the evening, Danila decided to initiate her campaign after dinner. When they were all pleasantly settled for a comfortable coze, she ventured resolutely, "Laurel, these last several days I have been distracted from my purpose, but time is getting short, so we are all going to have to concentrate on your situation."

"I had hoped you had given up on that tiresome, maggoty notion, Danila, and had found another, more particular interest," Laurel remarked regretfully.

"That's just it," Danila told her impatiently. "I can't attend to my own affairs while yours are so muddled, so I have even more reason to set things in motion."

"I don't hold to that line of reasoning, my dear girl. You are not obligated to concern yourself in my behalf."

"You have forgotten about Fate, love," Danila said with a winsome smile. "Now—the way I see it—your main objection is that you will not leave Jason here to work on Dismoreland alone. So if we could persuade him to go with us, would you then consider the proposition?"

"Danila, there is no possibility of that. The question is entirely irrelevant."

"Laurel, will you please just answer yes or no?"

"What nefarious trick have you got up your sleeve now?" Laurel asked suspiciously, narrowing her eyes.

"Would you?" Danila pursued doggedly.

"Well, yes, but—"

"No buts, darling. The answer is yes. So tomorrow you can stand for some of your fittings," a precocious young lady declared triumphantly.

"Danila, I will not believe that you have wheedled Jason into acquiescence with your schemes, and just what fittings are you talking about?"

"I haven't asked him yet, Laurel," a confident strategist admitted candidly. "I am proceeding one step at a time. Now that I have jumped the first fence, I will put it to him next time he calls."

Laurel shook her head incredulously as she looked at her mother. "I suppose you are a willing accomplice, Mama, for I imagine you have something to do with these fittings which have so casually entered the conversation."

Lady Madeline, in the manner of one who has been caught stealing candy, stammered uncertainly, "We just thought—well—we wanted to—ah—surprise you, darling. We could not resist buying some lovely things for you when we were in Brighton, and, Laurel, you do need new clothes."

"Not the kind you have in mind, I suspect," her daughter observed accusingly.

"Laurel," Danila said patiently, "I think you have lost track of the main point. We wish Jason to notice you as a desirable, lovely girl. You have fallen back into your old routine and have already forgotten how devastated you were when you thought he was going to marry someone else. If you don't stop procrastinating, you will likely find yourself in the basket again. However, I do mean to stay engaged to Jason, at least in the eyes of society, until he is safely tied to your apron strings. But you know I have my own concerns, and I wish you will make some effort to help yourself."

"Please, Laurel," Lady Madeline echoed, "try to suppress your anxieties. It would make me so happy if you would come to London. You know how much I have wished for it."

"And Laurel," Danila continued, keeping up the attack, "you will no longer have to play the dowd. I should think it would be a relief to you, for I cannot believe you actually like those extremely virginal, unfashionable gowns you wear. And as for the maggoty notion that Jason would not feel the same toward you if he knew you for a ravishing beauty, you are perfectly right, though why you are afraid of it I cannot comprehend. The change could only be for the better. This whole thing could be resolved in a matter of minutes if you would let Philip have a man-to-man talk with him—"

"No!"

"—but since you won't, then you will have to seduce him."

"Danila! You have the most shocking conversations for a young girl, and your extremely indelicate utterances have the distressing effect of putting me to the blush. I'm sure I could not behave as you envisage."

"Laurel," Danila admonished, thoroughly exasperated, "if you refuse to take part in this little drama, which is being enacted strictly for your benefit, then I will not honour your wishes and shall open Jason's eyes in a perfectly straightforward manner. You have your choice."

Laurel looked balefully at the bulldogged expression on her self-professed champion's face but knew she was beaten, for the girl had obviously managed to convince herself that she was destined to perform a mission and was not going to rest until she had seen it through.

She turned to her mother and questioned seriously, "Do you really think the situation is as consequential as this hysterical child imagines, Mama?"

"I have always been apprehensive about your relationship with Jason—you know that," Lady Madeline affirmed. "I'm afraid you are so wrapped in cotton wool that you cannot see the pitfalls."

"I think you are both grievously wide of the mark," Laurel told her two tormentors critically. "You, Mama, have let your misgivings build up over the years and are extremely susceptible to this outrageous girl's impositions. She has shown herself to be the most unabashed meddler imaginable and should certainly be dealt a sharp rebuke for her presumptions, which, I am persuaded, you would have delivered long before now had you not been so receptive to her particular enthusiasms. I know Jason better than either of you, and he is not the nodcock you are trying to paint him. There is no way, Danila, that you could have inveigled him into actually marrying you, artful and charming mischief that you are."

Danila prickled uncomfortably at these accusations, but she still had enough spirit to retort defensively. "You weren't so sure of that a few weeks ago."

"No, but I am now. I don't think it is at all necessary to become unstrung about this because I have come to feel very confident that he will declare himself without all these machinations."

"But when, Laurel? A couple of years from now when Dismoreland is finished? And no matter what you say, I am not convinced that he isn't vulnerable. It was too easy to manipulate him," Danila persisted, having recovered from her momentary mortification. Still, she did not wish to be ousted from Laurel's good graces, so she apologized, "I'm sorry, love, if I have been too immoderate, but I have this fierce ambition to see you happy. I have never had any friend who has been so dear to me."

Laurel looked at the shamelessly designing girl and advised with a faint reproval, "Danila, one could become exceedingly wearied and suspect of this uninhibited propensity of yours to reveal your partiality, except that," she added with a soft smile, "it is impossible to doubt your sincerity. And so, naturally, one must inevitably fall victim to your blandishments."

Danila impulsively threw her arms around Laurel and then stood back to ask impishly, "Does that mean you will go to London?"

Lady Madeline burst out laughing, and Laurel sighed in

surrender, shaking her head dubiously. "All right, you abominable girl. But only if you can convince Jason without compromising me."

"Well, of course, I would not do that, Laurel, for you have told me you would not like it. I will think of something, so do not sit there with that odiously smug look on your face. You had best resign yourself to being a belle."

"I only said I would go to London—not that I would join the fashionables," Laurel reminded coolly.

"But one goes with the other," Lady Madeline protested. "And we already have several things for you to try on. Mrs. Higgins and her assistants have been working feverishly all day."

"Now, Laurel," Danila said hastily, forestalling an impending outburst, "let us fight that out tomorrow, for I have something exciting to tell you." With an ecstatic smile she confided, "Philip has declared himself and wishes to give me a betrothal ring. Of course, that is not possible right now, so I have persuaded him to wait for a few weeks."

"But why, Danila? You certainly mean to accept him," Laurel said with a puzzled expression.

"Well, of course. I already have. But I cannot be engaged to him when I am supposedly betrothed to Jason."

"Do you mean to tell me that you intend to continue that farce when we go to town?"

"*Especially* then," Danila attested firmly with a wide-eyed expression. "That is the whole point. We cannot have anyone thinking he's eligible!"

"Of course not," Laurel said, rolling her eyes upwards. "I am minded to forget this insistent delusion that besets you. Uh—what about Philip's ostensible eligibility?"

"Well, you shall help me fend off the vultures," Danila replied promptly. "And besides, I know he loves me and wishes to marry me because," she added unkindly, to make a point, "he has said so."

"And how do you propose to convince Jason to play his part?" Laurel queried skeptically, refusing to be piqued.

"I shall discuss it with Philip, but I will think of something," the undaunted girl remarked, using one of her standard arguments.

Laurel had to laugh at her tenacious, one-track mind, and she teased lightly, "I am sure I have nothing to worry about. Long before the time of departure you will be in a state of exhaustion from having had to think so hard."

"Oh, no, you need not hope for that, Laurel," Danila denied with an innocently serious face. "I thrive on any sort of challenge to my ingenuity, you know. I am really very good at resolving dilemmas and have never been checkmated yet."

"Well, my dear girl, you have your work cut out for you this time," Laurel told her doubtingly.

Danila just smiled complacently and suggested, "Why don't we retire early tonight so that we can have a full day tomorrow to work on your clothes? I am so glad that Philip and Jason will be occupied and will not distract us, for we will be able to apply ourselves wholly to designing your wardrobe. Oh, I am so excited, Laurel. Wait until you see some of the lovely things. I just know you won't be able to resist, and we will try new ways to dress your hair. We have even bought some bonnets and shoes and—"

"No wonder the boxes were piling up," Laurel noted ruefully. "I did think it was a rather extravagant display for just two people."

Lady Madeline smiled guiltily and decided, "I think I will retire now. I am quite inspired by Danila's encouraging professions, and I am anticipating an extremely welcome diversion which I had begun to imagine would never come to pass."

Laurel looked at the happy expression on her mother's face and experienced a surge of affection for her, belatedly coming to recognize how deeply disappointed she had been all these years that her only child refused to indulge her in her ambition to present a beloved daughter to the *ton*. Laurel embraced her and declared penitently, "Mama, I am sorry I have been such a stubborn, freakish girl, and while I stand firm in my conviction that Jason could not be hoodwinked, I will not tempt Fate because the one shock was almost too much for me. So since I have a new confidence that I am now firmly enough established in his affection to be more independent, I will do as you have wished and place myself in your hands for a complete transformation."

With this extremely propitious statement of total surrender the two conspirators expressed their heartfelt approval and privately congratulated themselves on the success of their campaign. All three went upstairs, agreeing to join each other for an early breakfast before throwing themselves into the pleasant project at hand.

Danila woke a little before seven and immediately went to Laurel's room to waken her, for she did not mean to waste any precious minutes and intended that they should all be ready to get to work as soon as the seamstresses arrived. Laurel was not asleep and had been about to get up, being a habitually early riser. But when she heard the door open, she turned over and closed her eyes to see if that wretched girl had actually come to drag her out of her bed. She soon discovered the extent of Danila's effrontery, finding herself being shaken rudely and exhorted, "Laurel, Laurel, wake up. We have a frightfully busy day ahead of us, so you cannot be a slugabed."

"My dear girl, I must take exception to your excesses. I defy anyone to define a person as a slugabed when it is not yet seven o'clock," Laurel protested uncivilly, sitting up and throwing off her blankets.

"Oh. You're awake," came a fatuous observation.

"Lucky for you," Laurel murmured darkly.

Danila grinned and asked, "How soon do you think Lady Madeline will join us?"

"I expect it won't be too long, but she takes only a light breakfast in her room, so we can go down to fortify ourselves for what promises to be a very trying day," Laurel replied with an injured air of forbearance.

They went to the morning room, surprising the cook with their early appearance. She soon had some appetizing dishes to set before them, and they ate hungrily until Dan-

127

ila decided that they had had a sufficiency and coaxed Laurel to have some coffee sent to the sewing room because she could not wait to show her the lovely things that were waiting her approval. Having resigned herself to her fate, Laurel allowed herself to be persuaded, and she followed the bubbling girl up the winding stairs to the spacious attic room with several large dormers that served as a storage and sewing room.

Laurel was dismayed at the total disarray that greeted them, for there were boxes everywhere and several partially completed gowns in beautiful pastel shades draped over chairs and tables all about the room. "My word!" she exclaimed in consternation. "Surely these are not all for me."

"Most of them, darling. Lady Madeline's and mine are mostly finished," Danila told her enthusiastically, then asked eagerly with a hopeful expression, "Do you think you will like the colours, Laurel? I know it is always more satisfying to choose for yourself, but you were so disobliging that we had to just buy what we thought would suit you best."

"You showed excellent taste, love," Laurel assured her. "You are right that pastels are best for my colouring. I have worn these darker gowns because they are more serviceable when I am working." She went to finger the exquisite fabrics, delighting in the feel of the silks, velvets, soft muslins, and tulles and looked quizzically at Danila when she noticed the azure blue silk. "Is this the one that I am to wear when I come down the fictitious winding stairs?"

Danila giggled happily, overjoyed that Laurel seemed to have reconciled herself to her lot. She affirmed, "Yes, isn't it beautiful? And look at this embroidered white muslin and the pale apricot tulle and—"

She was interrupted in her enthusiastic ramblings when Lady Madeline entered, followed by the seamstresses, who were anticipating this assignment with pleasure. They had never been happy making the things Laurel usually commissioned and practically attacked her in their eagerness to see her in some of their high-fashion creations.

The two assistants set to work doing preliminary work on additional outfits while Mrs. Higgins slipped on one elegant costume after another, making necessary adjustments and passing them on to the other admiring ladies. Danila and Lady Madeline participated in the admirably efficient operation by tediously going through the boxes to locate the trimmings or accessories that would complement each gown. After three hours of this almost frenzied activity they allowed their puppet to take a recess so that the dressmakers could put together other garments. Laurel was glad for the respite, but her relief was short-lived because Danila meant to make the most of her friend's compliant mood and decreed that while they were waiting for the next round of fittings, they would ask the maids to dress Laurel's hair in a variety of styles so they could see which ones would be most flattering.

Laurel groaned and looked pleadingly at her mother, who unfortunately proved herself to be a Judas, evincing not a vestige of sympathy as she suggested unfeelingly that they remove to her boudoir.

Both abigails were summoned. By virtue of seniority Carrie was allowed to test her creativity first. There was no thought of cutting Laurel's hair, and so the coiffeuse was somewhat inhibited by the heavy mass of fine, silky strands. The girl had only worn it simply, merely brushing it vigorously back away from her face, letting it part naturally and then pulling it tightly into a heavy knot just above the neckline of her gowns.

Carrie drew it up on top of her head and secured it loosely so that it fell in soft waves about her face. Then she rolled the long tresses into large curls on the crown of her head. The effect was totally charming and made Laurel look years younger, causing Lady Madeline to comment gratefully, "Thank goodness! Now I won't have to put it about that I was married very young."

"Mama!" Laurel exclaimed in astonishment. "Has my plain image really distressed you for that reason?"

"Well, I am ashamed to admit it, but I'm afraid I do have a lamentably excessive vanity. I mean, I am not so toplofty that I do not wish to own up to having a twenty-two-year-old daughter, but I did find it rather galling to be supposed older than I am," a shamefaced, lovely, youthful-looking matron confessed ruefully.

"Mama, I have been a perfect dunderhead!" Laurel declared contritely. "I have not once considered that aspect. I must say you have been extremely tolerant, and it is time I made a push to please you. So," she said resolutely, "I will show you how I think I should dress my hair for formal occasions." And taking the brush, she pulled it tightly to the top of her head, asking Katie to tie it securely in place and to fashion a cluster of curls at the back of her head with one long curl hanging forward over her shoulder.

When the young maid finished, Laurel turned to her audience for approval and was surprised to see tears in her mother's eyes.

"Mama, you silly goose, surely it isn't that bad," she teased.

Lady Madeline smiled happily and said, "Oh, darling, you are so beautiful. It quite sends me into raptures. I'm afraid, when I appear on the scene with two such lovely young ladies as you and Danila, I am going to find myself in the black books of several ambitious mamas."

Danila had been sitting lost in admiration, imagining all sorts of dramatic opportunities for enlightening Jason. On hearing Lady Madeline's last flattering remark, she brought herself back to the moment and concluded, "Well, since it is obvious that Laurel has given up the fight and seems to be the best judge of the styles that suit her, I do not think we need to spend any more time on this experiment."

"No," Lady Madeline agreed. "So let us have a light lunch and then return to the sewing room to put our noses to the grindstone. We can have most of the things fitted today, and they can be finished later without taking much of Laurel's time. If all goes well, we should be able to leave for London in two weeks."

"Two weeks!" Danila squealed in dismay. "Oh, dear! I

had better turn my mind to the prime factor in this scheme. Tomorrow I will ask Philip's advice."

The rest of the afternoon there was a flurry of activity, with all the ladies helping in some way, and one by one the gowns began to take on a finished look. Occasionally changes were made to satisfy the aesthetic eye of one or the other of them, and they were generally in agreement except in the matter of what Laurel considered a too revealing décolletage on several evening gowns, which, in compromise, was not satisfactorily resolved for any party.

By evening they all felt totally done up and after dinner remained only a short time in the drawing room before going upstairs to their beds.

When Laurel wakened the next morning, she ached in every bone in her body from having stood on her feet for so long through all the fittings, and she got up to do a few stretching exercises before dressing. She didn't know when Jason would come today, so she went to wait in the library, occupying herself with studying some of her architectural books until Danila came in to join her about nine o'clock. An hour later they heard a carriage approaching, and in a moment two cheerful gentlemen presented themselves. In his usual informal manner Jason replaced the drawings on the library table and was unfolding them even as he asked if the two girls had enjoyed their free day.

"Well, in a manner of speaking, we did, Jason, but Mama decided it was a good opportunity to order some new dresses for me, and I can't say I found the ordeal exactly entertaining," Laurel told him ruefully. "How did your day go?"

"Passably. Much better for Philip than for me, I'm afraid. I don't seem to have a knack for choosing the right horse. I have it figured out now, however, and the next time I shall merely bet on the same ones he does. I'm sure he has some secret percipience. His success cannot be all luck."

"Oh, Philip, how exciting," Danila admired with shining

eyes, hinting wistfully, "I should like very much to go to the races sometime."

"You can just forget *that* bit of conceit right now," the viscount said unequivocally. "Young ladies do not go to the races."

"I think that is monstrously unfair!" the girl complained indignantly. "And I think you are trying to flummer me because I have heard perfectly respectable ladies speaking of having attended them."

"Perhaps on some special occasion."

"Well, when is the next special occasion?"

Jason and Laurel laughed at the harrassed look on Philip's face, and Jason said facetiously, "It seems you have another battle on your hands."

"You're her guardian," Philip charged testily. "Can't you teach her to show some respect for her elders?"

"It appears not. Actually, I wasn't doing too badly until you came because I am not as amiable as you are. She showed a little more circumspection in her dealings with me."

"Well," Danila remarked acerbically, "if you imagine it to be to your credit to seem so bearish, then you may live with your delusions. Personally I like your cousin much better."

"Thank God!" Jason retorted expressively, making them all laugh.

In good humour Philip relented to the point of promising, "Since we are so close by, we *could* go to Goodwood one day. Richmond has one of the best stables in the country and often holds trials. Perhaps Charles is in residence and will give us a tour. I haven't seen him since he succeeded to the title last year."

Jason seconded the suggestion. ". . . because I have been a bit remiss there, though I did write to offer my condolences when his father suffered that agonizing death in Canada—he was bitten by a rabid fox," he explained to the girls. "It would be a pleasant excursion because the house is extremely interesting. The third duke commissioned Chambers and Wyatt to add to the old Jacobean house, and its domed corner turrets make it rather unusual. Besides, it houses a spectacular collection of paintings—some Canalettos, Stubbses, and Van Dycks, among others."

Philip shook his head and accused, "Jason, you have the most remarkably one-track mind. If this is what comes of having a profession, then I am thankful I have no such inclination. However, since you are so agreeable, we will take advantage of your obsession and arrange to go early the next fine day. Now," he ordered a perfectly delighted Danila, "come on, you shameless little baggage. Get your bonnet and a wrap, and I'll take you for a drive."

"Oh, famous! I was hoping you meant to ask me!"

"And if I hadn't?"

"I would have asked you, of course," she replied impishly, making a face at him, and hurried from the room to dress for their outing.

When they had driven for a mile or so, she launched into an account of their auspiciously fruitful day. ". . . and, Philip, you are going to be so astounded when you see the new Laurel. I am glad you have declared yourself, or I should have reservations about exposing you to such a spectacularly beautiful girl. When her hair is pulled up off her face, the classic perfection of her features is truly extraordinary, and she has such a marvelous figure that I could just die from mortification in comparison."

"That is extravagant praise indeed," Philip observed in amusement, having to laugh at her pouting expression. "When are we to be introduced to this vision of loveliness?"

"That's what I wanted to talk to you about. Of course, we shall have to find some winding stairs," she said impishly, "and we have to persuade Jason to go to London with us because that is the only way Laurel will go."

"That last will take a little doing," Philip commented dubiously, "but I can help you out on the first part."

"You can?" Danila asked in surprise. "How?"

"Actually it is ridiculously simple, my love, so I can take no credit for being enterprising. You see, my father has a quite large town house on Portland Place. There is plenty

133

of room for all of us, to say nothing of the fact that there is a lovely curved stairs in the center entrance hall," he added whimsically.

"Oh, Philip!" Danila exclaimed excitedly, throwing her arms around his neck, causing a temporary unruly demonstration by the horses. "That is a famous idea. May I tell Lady Madeline? Oh," she said dubiously as a sudden afterthought dampened her enthusiasm, "perhaps it is too much of an imposition, and your mother and father might think us the most rackety group to make ourselves free with their house. Besides, they might return and wish us all to Jericho."

"I'm sure they will return, darling, because I mean to give them a full report on all the happy developments of these past few days. When my mother learns that I mean to present her future daughter-in-law to her, you can be sure we will find her waiting for us."

"So soon? Lady Madeline says we should be able to leave in two weeks."

"Then I shall write this very day and post it immediately, for Mother is only in Paris and could possibly precede us. In fact, I am not at all sure she isn't on her way back now because I rather suspected my father was becoming a little resty when I left, what with all the political shenanigans going on now that the old king finally stuck his spoon in the wall. So, to make sure they do not miss my letter, I will send a duplicate to the London house. As for their not being receptive to our invasion, you need not worry about that, for Laurel is a favourite with them, and Lady Madeline is one of my mother's dearest friends. Jason and I have always felt welcome in each other's homes, and when I think on it," Philip noted with a wry grin, "I wouldn't be surprised to find Aunt Theo trailing along."

Danila giggled and voiced a nagging thought that was causing her some anxiety, "Philip, do you think the countess will like me?"

"She will adore you, my love, I promise you," her prejudiced swain replied confidently.

"But she might think me uncommonly forward for going to Sussex and then involving myself in Laurel's affairs."

"She and the earl will both be intrigued by your enterprising nature, just as I am, darling. I assure you they are not at all impressed by simpering girls who haven't an original thought in their heads. They are going to be entirely in charity with me for showing such perception to claim you before you make your appearance on the Marriage Mart."

"Oh, Philip," Danila vowed softly, being deeply affected to the point of finding herself with tears in her eyes, "that was a lovely thing to say. I do love you so dreadfully, you know, and I shall be so happy when we can announce our betrothal. Do you think the countess will understand about my immediate purpose?"

"I shall explain, love, and while I'm not promising she will understand, she will not cry rope on us because she will trust my judgment in the matter. I do not think we shall have to pretend very long anyway. Jason is well aware of how things stand and will come up to scratch very soon."

"Do you think we will persuade him to go to London?"

"We can try. Do you have any ideas on our strategy? I shouldn't wish to go beyond the line."

"Are you just trying to humour me?" she asked suspiciously.

"Yes, my sweet, I am," Philip replied frankly. "You know perfectly well my views on the subject do not coincide with yours, and while I have committed myself to forwarding your designs, I do not mean to pretend that I find them entirely reasonable."

"Oh," she said diffidently, being momentarily crushed, an attitude that her strong personality could not sustain for any noticeable length of time, a fact which accounted for her immediate reversion to positive action as she speculated, "I have promised Laurel not to compromise her, which means that I cannot make an obvious reference to her attachment. However, I do not think that we are prohibited from contriving some sort of argument that will

135

cause Jason to have scruples about how he has monopolized her time and deprived Lady Madeline of the pleasure of introducing her to society. Yes, I think that might serve very well," she mused as she began to have a feel for this particular strategy. "We shall call him to book for being an unmindful woolgatherer who has proved himself the veriest coxcomb for blindly accepting that everything should be ordered for his benefit."

"That's coming it a little strong, Danila," Philip reproved gently, making allowances for her *idée fixe.* "Jason has a great deal more sensibility than you give him credit for."

"Well, Philip," she explained in tacit agreement, "we cannot be *too* nice in our complaints because we have to convince him that he should make amends for his past omissions."

"And even if we do, how does it follow that he will go to London?"

"Naturally we should put it to him that Laurel will not consider going if he does not. So he is obligated to be cooperative."

"Of course. I wonder I did not make that simple deduction myself," Philip said humbly.

Danila looked at him timidly and asked with an unnatural hesitancy. "Will you talk to him?"

"Yes, love, I will," he promised, reaching to take her hand. "Perhaps not following your line precisely, but I will use my considerable influence, and before you warn me, I will tell you, yes, I do understand that we are in a bit of a hurry. Now take the reins and show me if you remember the little trick I taught you the last time we drove out."

True to his promise Philip approached his cousin that evening after dinner, when they remained at Devereaux House because of the heavy rainstorm that had developed late in the day. "Jason, I have a particular assignment that will no doubt set your back up, but I am not going to apologize for my complicity since you must assume chief responsibility in this imbroglio for injudiciously having

136

pitched yourself into the briars when you aligned yourself with that disgracefully scheming girl."

"What has she inveigled you into now?" Jason asked warily.

"She is determined to go to London," Philip informed him, "and she has decided that we must go *in toto* since she and Lady Madeline have every hope of persuading Laurel to accompany them. And because it is certain that Laurel will not desert you when you are so involved in Dismoreland, Danila naturally concluded that you would just have to go, too."

"My God, Phil! Can't you control that girl? I wouldn't give a penny for your future peace of mind if you are going to let her run riot and drag you into her little games."

Showing a lack of concern, Philip just looked at his cousin and advised humourously, "I find myself exceedingly entertained by her antics, though if I should decide that she shows signs of going beyond the permissible or if I disapprove of her machinations, you may be sure I will draw bridle."

"I suppose that little speech is a none too subtle hint that you are in agreement with her in this particular flight of fancy," Jason noted sardonically.

"Yes, I am, as a matter of fact. Lady Madeline has always had an ambition to show Laurel off to her friends in town. I can understand that, for she is very much a part of the fashionable world. You have rather scotched that hope, you know, with your joint projects that give Laurel an excuse to refuse, and don't imagine you can persuade her to go without you because any such attempt would likely just hurt her feelings."

"I don't think Laurel has any desire to be subjected to that extremely tedious, barbaric ritual," Jason attested confidently.

"No, she is not the least interested," Philip admitted. "But I am telling you in confidence that she has agreed to go to please her mother if you could be persuaded. Naturally she is counting on your refusal to get her out of it, so

137

I said I would acquaint you with the crux of the matter and let you put it to your conscience."

"My God! If that isn't the most flagrant abuse of friendship I ever saw in my life!" Jason protested vehemently. "You seem to have to adapted yourself very well to that vixen's unscrupulous methods."

"Well, the way I look at it, it is never too late to learn new tricks, especially when they are so effective," Philip said, laughing at his cousin's baleful expression. "Come on, Jase, look at it from Lady Madeline's side of it. Laurel is her only child. They are very close to each other, and she has a natural mother's pride to want to show off her beautiful daughter. Surely you can manage things to go along without you for a while. It will take months for the craftsmen to catch up with your instructions. Besides, you can shop in London. You must have to buy some furniture, and the auction houses are always bringing in new things. Just change your schedule a little."

Jason looked at his cousin with admiration and asked, "Did you ever have an ambition to be a lawyer, Phil? I am persuaded you would have been a tremendous success."

"No. It's an intriguing thought, however. But one can't do everything, and I have a mind to be a country gentleman, which I am sure you can appreciate, for I have it on good authority that we are much alike in many ways, though of course, I rate higher, not being obliged to play the guardian."

Jason laughed, shaking his head, and then said tentatively, "I suppose I could take a recess and in fact could occupy my time very well as you suggested. It might come as a welcome diversion, for Laurel has been making a study of furnishings. She could be very well pleased to have this opportunity to browse around. Unless," he interrupted himself as an unhappy thought came to his mind, "you think Maddy would object to our working in town."

"Not if you don't carry it to excess," Philip assured him.

"All right then, I'll go," Jason decided with a sigh of resignation. "Where are they going to stay?"

"At Schofield House. There is plenty of room for all

of us. I hope you are going to be able to organize things in a hurry because they want to leave in two weeks."

"That's pushing it a bit, but I'll manage. Thank God we are close enough that I can come down once in a while for a day or two to keep an eye on things."

"Just don't make too much of a habit of it, or we will both lose our credibility," Philip warned.

"Yes, my lord," Jason said in mock reverence, "we certainly could not have that." And then he added quizzically, "Just what, may I ask, is the reason for that incredibly foolish look on your face?"

"I was just anticipating the extravagant expression of approval I am going to receive tomorrow for the success of my efforts," Philip replied, a roguish admission that predictably, being consistent with the male's physically attuned sense of humour, sent them into immoderate laughter.

Chapter
EIGHT

The next morning the two households attended Easter services, this second day of April, and then returned to Devereaux House for a sumptuous breakfast. The poetess seemed a bit abstracted, and the others, recognizing the signs of an impending withdrawal, looked at each other in amusement, being not the least surprised when she vaguely excused herself and left the company. Soon afterwards the other ladies returned to their own home, inviting Jason and Philip to join them later.

When the two young couples congregated in the Ingram library in the afternoon, Philip asked the butler to inquire if Lady Madeline could join them. This unusual specific request caused the girls to sit up and take notice, and they both looked searchingly at the two men. Jason smiled softly at Laurel with an almost apologetic look in his eyes, and Philip winked significantly at Danila, leaving neither young lady with any doubt as to the efficacy of Philip's powers of persuasion. In disbelief Laurel turned to Danila, who quickly lowered her eyes so she would not be caught gloating.

Laurel had a strange sensation in her stomach with this realization that things were going to change. She knew that she really had not prepared herself for that eventuality, and she was forced to admit to herself that she was bedeviled with more than a little cowardice, for as she drew nearer to the moment of truth, she found herself becoming more and more apprehensive.

Jason remarked her curious reaction and was bewildered by the look of dismay that revealed her disquiet. It was true that she had always declared adamantly that she did not want to go to London to be presented, and he believed her, thinking that she merely scorned such frivolous pursuits, just as he did. But it appeared that there was more to it than that, for she seemed almost frightened. It had never occurred to him that she might be reluctant to be uprooted from the somewhat sheltered, uncomplicated existence she had become accustomed to. He began to perceive that Lady Madeline's purpose was not merely self-motivated because Laurel could not remain isolated from the sophisticated world indefinitely since she by birth was naturally a part of it. Having thus erased some of the cobwebs from his mind, he resolutely committed himself to easing her delayed entry into society while blaming himself for his insensibility in having unwittingly pandered to her irresolution, sentiments for which he would have received high marks from Danila had she known he had reached such commendable conclusions.

Lady Madeline entered to find a strangely pensive group. One look at Laurel's anxious expression told the story, which was instantly confirmed by Danila's barely contained excitement. She turned to Philip, and he grinned roguishly as he advised, "My dear Maddy, I hope you know you have a challenge in store for you. Launching these two lovelies into the *ton* is going to be a full-time project."

She glanced guiltily at Jason but was met with an affirmative nod and such a look of affectionate understanding that she had an almost irresistible impulse to embrace him. She went to put her arm around her daughter instead and said soothingly, "Don't worry, love. It will be all right."

Laurel had recovered from her shock sufficiently to turn

accusing eyes on Jason. She demanded, "Did you really allow yourself to be wheedled into agreement with this scheme?"

He smiled sheepishly, admitting defensively, "I prefer to look at it as bowing to reason."

"Jason! We are too busy! How can you think of leaving Dismoreland now? Unless," she added suspiciously, "you do not mean to stay long in town."

These plaintive objections only augmented his sense of guilt, and he went over to sit next to her, taking both her hands in his. "My love, let me tell you the plan, and I'm sure you will see its merit. First of all, we have both shown a selfish lack of consideration for your mother's wishes, and we will go to town to please her. But I am hoping she will allow us to spend some time at our particular enthusiasm because we do need to choose furnishings, wallpaper, and other things for interior decoration. Sooner or later we would have had to scour the London shops and auction houses, so we can take this opportunity to begin our search. And do not suppose I mean to desert you once you are established, for I promise you I will not. But two months *is* a long time, and occasionally I will take a day or two to see how things are going, though I will hurry back to give you a report."

She looked at him stubbornly for a moment but concluded he was serious and committed, so she said with a resigned sigh, "Jason, I am persuaded that you are not all that happy to be distracted at this moment. However, if you are determined to be the gentleman, it appears I am without support, and I shall just have to follow the crowd. But," she added spiritedly, glancing significantly at her mother, "as to whether or not I will be allowed to follow my own pursuits, I beg you to remember that I am *not* a cat's-paw."

This reluctant admission of surrender followed by a contradictory posture of defiance prompted the others to laugh disrespectfully. Jason experienced one of his frequently recurring desires to crush Laurel in his arms, an impulse that was no longer easy to suppress, and but for his resolution

142

to honour Lady Madeline's wishes, he would have become more particular in his attentions, now having a new confidence in their mutual attachment. However, he would have to wait until after the Season so that Maddy might have her day, but he was gratified to hear her assuring, "Laurel, my love, I will not badger you unduly. I'm sure we can come to some accommodation. You know I merely want to introduce you and have no purpose to subject you to the indignities of the Marriage Mart, so you will not have to rush madly from engagement to engagement as most girls do to assure themselves of the greatest exposure."

"And what of this proposal that I should companion Danila? I cannot believe that she means to practice any significant exclusion when she has been so mad for establishing herself in the *ton*," Laurel noted caustically.

"Laurel!" Danila protested with a hurt expression. "You *know* that my ambitions have been considerably altered these last few weeks. When I was in Bath, I naturally had fanciful visions of creating a stir in London, but that particular foolishness is entirely passé. Still, I should like to see the sights and meet people and wear fashionable clothes and go to glittering affairs just one Season. But I promise you I do not mean to try to burn the candle at both ends."

"Actually any attempt on your part to do so would be severely hampered if you mean to hold to your original plan," Laurel reminded inauspiciously.

Danila looked puzzled, then said as the light dawned, "Oh, yes, I see what you mean."

"Why don't you disclose that proposition now while we are all assembled? I don't doubt it might be extremely diverting," Laurel pursued quizzically, having an unworthy desire for revenge.

Danila was caught a little behindhand because she had not had time to "think of something," having just learned that the second fence had been cleared. She searched frantically for some way to approach her guardian on the matter of the mock betrothal. If she could have read Jason's mind, she could have saved herself all the bother, but since a lack of openness, combined with the pitfalls of a vivid imagination and a monomania, inevitably sets the stage for misunderstandings and confusion, she unwittingly delayed a resolution of the main point and pitched them all into a comedy of errors.

As Jason was the only one unaware of her "original plan," he naturally inquired ominously, "Danila, just what May-game are you contemplating now?"

"Jason, you have a lamentable tendency to suspect me of chicanery," she objected, sparring for wind.

"With good reason, as you well know. Now, if I am going to be ready to leave here in two weeks, I do not have time to stand here to listen to your discursions. You will please cut line and get to the point."

"Well," she said, being forced into a precipitant revelation, "I—I want our betrothal to stand when we go to town."

He stared at her incredulously and then added, "Have you gone mad? There *is* no betrothal."

"Society thinks there is because the news has gotten around," she told him slyly. "It has even been reported to Eddy by some of the girls."

"Well, society can easily be enlightened," he replied bluntly.

Beginning to develop her strategy, she mustered an injured manner and objected pleadingly, "I can't go to town and admit it was all a hum. I would be so *humiliated!*"

"I don't doubt Philip could think of something to sweeten the bitter pill," Jason said leadingly, "unless you have already grassed yourself in that quarter."

"You know I have not!" she spouted angrily, tricked into a somewhat incriminating declaration.

Jason raised his eyebrows skeptically, and Danila recognized her mistake, privately giving her opponent his due. She turned desperately to Philip, who had been listening to these arguments with a special interest, but he contrived to ignore her plea for help since this was one part of her scheme with which he was definitely not in sympathy and had no intention of advancing.

With the realization that she was on her own, Danila's

natural sense of initiative came to her aid, and she asserted, "Well! I can see you have no concern for my reputation and show yourself a regrettably indifferent guardian. If it were supposed that I was bespoken to one man and should show up in town betrothed to another, I would be unhappily remarked as a fickle, flighty female with no scruples!"

"Since the changeover is the eventual outcome anyway, I fail to see how you are going to avoid that particular charge," Jason told her, unimpressed.

Reaching deep once again, she argued, "It's a matter of timing! It is too soon. But once we get to London and it is apparent that you and I are not the least compatible and that Philip and I have a natural affinity, it will be more reasonable. Especially when it is seen that you are deliberately throwing us into each other's company." And so saying, she sat back with a triumphant look, feeling monstrously pleased with herself.

Philip burst out laughing and slapped his thigh. "I don't believe it! Danila, you are absolutely awesome, and I am persuaded you and the earl will get along famously. You may even teach him a few things about politicking."

Jason looked at his cousin and remonstrated incredulously, "Phil, you surely do not mean to encourage this wretched girl's delusions."

"I find her dexterous powers of persuasion irresistible, my friend, and if you will but try to subdue your prejudices, you might see the reasonableness of her final argument."

Lady Madeline decided it was time to lend her support, and she concurred, "Really, Jason, I do think it makes for an admirable solution. Everything could be straightened out after we get to town. It would certainly eliminate the necessity of having to make embarrassing explanations."

"You all are forgetting one extremely salient fact," Jason informed the company laconically. "*I* have a marked antipathy about lending any credence to this supposed betrothal. And don't tell me I should not have allowed myself to be compromised in the first place. I am well aware of

145

that degrading circumstance, and I have no intention of continuing the charade. It wouldn't be believed anyway since without a ring it would not appear to be official. And," he added ungraciously, looking malevolently at his plaguesome ward, "don't suppose you have any chance of getting one."

"Well!" Danila sputtered in high dudgeon. "I hope you don't think I would wear just *anybody's* ring!"

Being hoist on his own petard, Jason looked as if he could strangle the girl until he was forced to admit the rare humour of it, and he joined the others in their unsympathetic laughter.

Finally Danila bemoaned ruefully, "Oh, dear, I did it again, didn't I? I *am* sorry, Jason. I did not mean to be so insulting, and I do see your point. However, we could just put it about that we have an understanding, letting people think what they will."

Faced with this new cryptic representation, he looked questioningly at Laurel, but she refused to venture any opinion and merely spread her hands and shrugged her shoulders to show her disinclination to be involved in the deliberations. Reminding himself of Lady Madeline's approval, Jason decided that as now programmed, it would not cause any further misconception, so he agreed uncivilly, "All right, Danila. I don't pretend to understand the vagaries of the feminine intellect, but if you really cannot comport yourself in a forthright manner"—a calculated dig that almost provoked a ruffled young lady into upsetting the applecart, though she controlled herself with gritted teeth—"I shall allow you your little deception. But as of now I wash my hands of you, and you may apply to Philip for any future advice or services. Is that clear?"

"Well, of course! It is only proper, after all," she told him with asperity, "since we are bespoken."

Jason just shook his head unbelievingly at her remarkably vacillating positions and then gave it up, saying impatiently, getting his papers together, "If you will excuse me, I have to check on the work at Dismoreland."

146

"I'll come with you," Laurel announced promptly, determined to show her independence. She was not deterred as Danila and Lady Madeline had no wish to turn the knife, being content with having progressed to the point of no return, and they indulgently allowed her time to accustom herself to the fact.

The next few days the seamstresses worked feverishly on all the gowns and sent to Brighton for additional help. In spite of her protests, Laurel was often trapped into standing for fittings and was pressed to choose from a formidable selection of hats, gloves, and shoes that had been sent for approval. Little by little she became familiar with the new image in the mirror, although when she escaped from her confinement, she immediately put on one of her old gowns and redid her hair before meeting Jason. Danila was not in the least disturbed by this show of rebellion because, as she told Lady Madeline, "You know I have this romantic notion that Jason should be dumbstruck when he sees her in her new finery the first time." And she imagined all sorts of scenes to provide Laurel with a dramatic entrance.

One pleasant afternoon, when she and Philip were out for a drive, Danila said musingly, "I have been thinking, Philip—"

"You have?" he asked wonderingly with a twinkle in his eye.

She wrinkled her nose at him but continued, "It probably would be best if we went to London to settle in before Jason came so that—"

"No—wait. Don't tell me. Let me see if I can read your mind," he said teasingly and then exclaimed facetiously, "I have it! You want to set the stage, and I suspect there is a vision of winding stairs in the setting."

She smiled sheepishly and requested his appraisal. "Well, what do you think?"

"It would probably suit Jason very well because he has been stewing about not having enough time to get things properly organized," Philip told her.

"Let us give him an extra week, and we will then be ready for him," she suggested even as she realized she would likely have a battle with Laurel. "We can bring it up casually tonight when we are at dinner." With this further strategy easily agreed upon, they turned their minds to their personal concerns and spent a happy afternoon making plans for their future.

Theo Devereaux, having come out of isolation and learning that the entire company was making plans to go to town, invited the Ingram household to dinner to celebrate Danila's birthday with the hope of uncovering the interesting circumstances that led to this unusual decision. That Jason and Laurel should be going along testified that some out-of-the-ordinary forces had come into play, and she tried to discover how her recalcitrant son had been maneuvered into a situation he had successfully avoided for years.

Not having a great deal of faith in her discretion, the conspirators held to the public explanation, which only partially satisfied her. Suspecting there was a great deal more to it and for once regretting having missed the action, she was brought to the perverse conclusion that she did not mean to be left out again. She promptly announced that she would accompany them, causing Danila to look mischievously at Philip, who favoured her with a knowing wink.

Jason regarded his mother with amusement and suggested, "Why don't the two of us stay at Dismore House? I received word from Larry yesterday that Helen and the new baby are doing well and that they plan to remain in the country for several months. He has given me carte blanche to use the town house whenever I am in London."

"Of course," his mother agreed readily, "that would cut down on the congestion on Portland Place and work out very nicely since we would be separated by only a few blocks. Besides, we would have more room to spread out to work, which I am sure has entered your calculations. When are we leaving?"

"In just a few days," Lady Madeline replied. "We are

already nearly packed, and if we start out directly, we will arrive in town before the Season is in full swing."

"A few days! I *do* think I might have been informed of these arrangements before the eleventh hour. I can't possibly leave that quickly," a nettled lady protested indignantly.

Philip turned to his cousin and suggested casually, "Why don't you and Aunt Theo come a week later? It will take us awhile to settle in anyway," a leading proposal which exalted his already high standing in the heart of a thoroughly enamoured, admiring young lady.

"That would be a better schedule for me," Jason admitted. "Some tiles for the kitchen haven't arrived, and I had hoped to look them over before they were installed."

"Well then, why don't you wait to bring your mother, Jason?" Danila seconded. "And perhaps we can plan our first theatre party the day you arrive," she proposed, having quickly perceived the opportunity presented by this arrangement.

Jason looked at Laurel, who had remained quiet, knowing full well that the ordering of events was out of her hands. She decided to make it easy for him, having accepted that he had been duped again, and she assured him, "Of course, you must wait for Theo, Jason. I am delighted she has decided to come." She turned to the older lady and apologized with a look of affection, "Please forgive us, love. We have been so caught up in settling our differences that we have been abominably remiss about informing you of our plans."

"Well," Lady Madeline noted artfully, "we have even more cause to set the *ton* on its ears now that we will have a resident celebrity," a calculated provocation that brought admirable results.

"Do not think to parade me like a monkey," the poetess warned acerbically," for I will not play the buffoon. I am not a posturing fool like that languishing overrated Lord Byron, though I have to admit that his latest offerings show more substance. I have been minded to consider him more palatable since he became an expatriate, a sentiment no doubt evoked by the fact that we are no longer obligated to suffer his affectations."

"I hope you do not mean to barricade yourself in town. You could just as well stay here," her friend remarked succinctly.

"Of course I will not. I am well aware that there is something smoky about this sudden pilgrimage, and I mean to uncover the mystery," she told them resentfully.

Philip laughed and promised, "And when you do, Aunt Theo, you will find yourself provided with all sorts of ideas to versify."

"So there *is* something behind all this," she exulted immediately.

"Naturally, love. You know nothing has been the same since Jason brought his ward to Sussex," her nephew replied whimsically and suddenly found himself being pummeled.

On the following day Philip did not drive over to see Danila until the afternoon, for it had been established that mornings must needs be devoted to preparing for their imminent departure. When she came to join him, he informed her propitiously, "My love, I have received a letter from my mother, and as I predicted, she is in town waiting for us and is planning all sorts of entertainments, including a ball in your honour to introduce you to society. She promises to keep mum, as I asked, but she finds the dissimulation a little confusing and hopes to have it explained to her more believably. She has written a special message to you." He handed her a scented folded sheet, which she opened eagerly and read:

My dear Danila,
    It is my great pleasure to tell you how much I am looking forward to meeting you. Philip assures me that I shall be pleased with him and that I will love you as he does. I have no qualms on that score, for he rarely disappoints me. (I hope you will excuse a mother's pride in her son.) I am so happy that he has found someone to share his life. The earl sends his

felicitations, and we are both waiting impatiently for your arrival.

> *With kindest regards,*
> *L. Clarinda A.*

Danila looked up with a happy smile and acclaimed, "What a lovely gesture, Philip. I am sure we will get along famously, for we are in agreement already."

"You are? What about?" he inquired with an innocent face.

"You know perfectly well, you shameless man. But since you have proved such an admirable confederate, I shall feed your vanity and admit that we both think you are wonderful," an altogether gratifying statement that earned her a fervently amorous demonstration.

Danila had been recording a running history of the last few days to keep Miss Eddington apprised of all the latest developments, but the note from Philip's mother put her in such high feather that she decided to send off a letter immediately.

> *. . . I had thought to wait until we arrived in London to post this and so surprise you, but I could not wait to tell you about receiving a lovely note from the countess. Everything is working out so beautifully, Eddy, and I hope you will come to town as soon as the school term is over because I am anxious for you to meet my love and all my new friends, and I particularly want them to meet you.*

The young people managed to squeeze in their planned excursion to Goodwood, which afforded them a great deal of pleasure from having held something of interest to each of them. Danila, in one of her enterprising moods, decided that she might be very well pleased if they would set up a stable on one of her several properties, a prospect Philip was disposed to view with considerable favour.

While the others made all the necessary arrangements for departure and supervised the packing, Laurel and Jason worked steadily to finish some of their diagrams and sketches that would be needed in the next few weeks and soon had enough work programmed for the rest of the summer. Fortunately the master builder was well known to Jason, and he had every confidence that Master Corcoran would contract only the most able craftsmen for the various categories of skilled labor. So it was with a relatively easy mind that he began to contemplate his removal to town. His main problem was to guarantee that his mother kept to the planned schedule, though it seemed that she intended to discipline herself, having an aroused curiosity about what had been going on under her very nose, and was keeping the household in a bustle, ordering the placement of covers and directing the housekeeper on a number of dreary domestic matters with which she rarely concerned herself.

And so it was that the Ingram ladies and Danila, accompanied by their two abigails and escorted by Philip riding postillion, left Sussex with two carriages, both piled high with boxes of finery, on the tenth of April to join the exodus from the country estates to the confinement of the London town houses for the annual ritual to greet old friends, make new ones, enjoy the diversions of a vibrant city, and compete for attention in their circumscribed beau monde. It was a prospect viewed with little enthusiasm by one member of the trio, but the other two blithely refused to let her gloomy spirits dampen their own.

Chapter
NINE

The trip to London was easily within a day's travel, and even though they did not leave until nine o'clock and stopped for a leisurely lunch at Dorking, they arrived at the Thames about half past four. The city skyline was not an unfamiliar sight to any of them, except for Katie, because both Danila and Laurel had spent some time there with their parents in earlier years and Laurel had often accompanied her mother in the off-Season for short visits. Still, the bustling atmosphere of the sprawling giant, which now boasted about one and one-quarter million inhabitants, created an air of excitement and anticipation. Even Laurel could not deny a sharpening of the senses and interestedly remarked all the diverse images of the teeming metropolis as they crossed Westminster Bridge and drove up Regent Street, which was in a continuing state of construction under the direction of John Nash, to the Earl of Schofield's house on Portland Place.

The horses were reined in before a large Adams-designed town house. Philip dismounted to help the ladies out of the carriage and escorted them to the door, which swung open auspiciously. They stepped inside to a small hall that led to a richly appointed and decorated reception salon with a central curving stairway, which Danila noted immediately with an approving eye.

153

Philip handed his hat and coat to the butler, asking, "Are my mother and father at home, Digby?"

"Yes, Lord Philip. Lady Schofield suggested the ladies be allowed to refresh themselves before joining her and the earl in the red drawing room for tea."

"That is very thoughtful of Clarinda," Lady Madeline approved. "I, for one, feel totally disheveled, and I shall be glad for the opportunity to repair the damage." The other two travel-worn ladies agreed and gratefully followed the housekeeper who showed them to their rooms.

Laurel and Danila merely washed and tidied themselves, but when they went to collect Lady Madeline, they found her undergoing a complete change of toilette. She looked at them guiltily and apologized. "I felt so draggletailed, my dears. I just had to remove that heavy traveling dress, but I won't be long," a promise kept with some effort. In a quarter of an hour the three went to present themselves to their host and hostess.

Lady Madeline entered first, followed by Laurel, with Danila trailing a little behind.

Lady Clarinda jumped up immediately and embraced her good friend. "Maddy, it is so good to see you. We have much to talk about, and I am glad you changed your mind and came for the Season after all. And, Laurel, my dear," she said affectionately as she embraced her also, "you are as beautiful as ever. I am so very pleased that you have finally agreed to come to us for the Season."

She then turned to Danila, who had been joined by Philip, and he spoke proudly, "Danila, my love, it is my pleasure to introduce you to my mother and my father—the Earl and Countess of Schofield."

Danila curtsied prettily and acknowledged. "I am very happy to meet you, my lady, my lord," and then smiled brightly, revealing her natural animation.

Lady Clarinda clasped her to her and professed, "Danila, my dear, we welcome you with all our hearts and hope you will learn to accept us as your family."

"Yes, Lady Danila," the earl concurred as he came to

stand by his wife. "We are immensely gratified that Philip has decided to set up his own household, and we wish you every happiness."

"I thank you both for your gracious reception," Danila responded becomingly and then irrepressibly launched into one of her confidences, as she usually did, never being able to sustain a subdued demeanour. "I will be so happy to be part of a family again. For several years, before I went to Sussex, my only close friend was Miss Elizabeth Eddington, you know, and suddenly I have a lovely new family. I am *so* lucky and am terribly ashamed to have complained about how *unlucky* I had been. Now that everything is working out so beautifully, I am come to believe that all my setbacks have been part of a Grand Plan, and I am *convinced* that I have been protected by a guardian angel!"

"I'm sure Jason would be astounded to hear himself so represented," Philip teased with a devilish grin.

Danila giggled and scolded, "You *know* I didn't mean *him*. That was just—"

"I know, love. A figure of speech," Philip said, laughing, as he drew her over to sit by him on the couch.

The earl and the countess looked at each other and smiled, for they both readily understood how their son had lost his heart. The girl was utterly charming and had such a cheerful and unaffected manner that it was impossible not to like her. They were both delighted with the prospect of having such an amiable daughter-in-law.

Lady Clarinda sat by the tea table and served her guests. Then they spoke briefly about what social events would merit their priority, and the countess assured Danila that she was looking forward to presenting her to society in just two weeks so that she could realize the full benefit of the Season and that already she had requested vouchers to Almack's for her and Laurel from her good friend the Countess Lieven.

Danila's eyes sparkled with excitement. She smiled hopefully at Laurel, who could not resist the girl's winsome face. And since she had promised her mother in that regrettably weak moment at least partially to enter into the spirit of the occasion, she returned her friend's smile, remarking ruefully, "Danila, sometimes I think you must have made a study of Herr Mesmer's experiments."

"Who is *he?*" Danila asked warily, wondering if she were being gulled.

The earl replied with a laugh, "A German physician, my dear, a charlatan, some say, who reportedly had a facility for making people do what he commanded them."

"Oh," Danila acknowledged with a sheepish grin, perceiving the joke.

After the laughter had subsided, Lady Clarinda remarked cheerfully, "I am sure we could continue this very agreeable conversation for hours, but we have planned dinner for seven. The earl wishes to put in an appearance at the House this evening, so perhaps we had better go to dress," a suggestion that was quickly acted upon, and the guests excused themselves to go to their rooms.

Philip remained with his mother and father and waited confidently for their appraisal, being wholly gratified when his mother declared immediately, "My love, she is an absolute darling, and I have fallen captive to her charm already. She looks very much like her mother and has the same vivacity, though I am thinking she likely has a great deal more sense. Caroline was a shocking featherhead, and I admit I had some reservations when you told me whom you had chosen to be your wife. But I do apologize for that unworthy sentiment because I should have known you were extremely discriminating. I can see why you have not been interested in any of the other girls who have been thrown at you these last few years. I began to be afraid you had a *tendre* for Laurel and were destined to remain a bachelor since she has been committed to Jason forever. Is that *ever* going to be resolved?"

"Very shortly, I have no doubt. Danila has taken the matter into her hands, and having watched her move unfalteringly from step to step, I am confident of her success," her son told her readily.

"Yes, well," the earl requested abruptly, "I wish you will

explain just why it is that we must pretend she is engaged to Jason. It sounds like a deuced pack of stuff and nonsense to me."

"Yes, dear," the countess agreed. "I would so much like to introduce her as your betrothed."

"So would I," the young man admitted ruefully.

"Well, can't you bring her to heel, my boy?" the earl asked bluntly.

"Yes, I'm sure I could," Philip acknowledged, "but I don't have the heart to demand that she give up her little game. She is determined, you see, to precipitate the denouement of the match between Laurel and Jason. She has been scheming furiously, and successfully, I must add, to make them come to London so they do not have their work to preoccupy them. She has even convinced Laurel to drop this plain image she has been affecting. I suspect we are going to be introduced to a new Beauty at dinner."

"She has my vote for that particular objective, and Maddy's, too, I am sure. But I fail to see just how it follows that she should appear to be engaged to Jason," the countess said with a bewildered expression.

"She has a positive obsession that Jason should not be permitted to enter the London scene as an unattached male."

The earl and his wife stared at their son, and when they realized that, in spite of his wry grin, he was serious, they burst out laughing.

"Philip!" the Countess exclaimed. "However did she come by that odd humour?"

"She says it was too easy for her and Miss Eddington to maneuver him into acceptance of this mock betrothal, and so, having come to the conclusion that he is something of a gudgeon when pitted against designing females, she is determined to keep him out of circulation until he sees the light and offers for Laurel."

"Oh, dear," Lady Clarinda demurred, laughing again. "Wouldn't it be a great deal easier just to whisper in his ear? I'm sure it has been a settled thing in his mind these ages."

"Yes, it would be easier, and of course, you are right. But Laurel has overruled any such direct enlightenment because she has a sensitivity about Jason's coming to feel an obligation to offer for her."

"Foolish girl. Sometimes I think he has held back because he felt she wasn't ready, and I'm afraid I have to say that I cannot agree with Danila's estimation of Jason's vulnerability. There is no possibility that he would marry anyone but Laurel."

"I know," her son agreed again, "but you will admit that the matter has been at a standstill for years, and I think Danila is just the *agent provocateur* who can provide the impetus. She means for Jason to feel a little anxiety when Laurel becomes the new rage."

"Really, Philip, you are letting that girl get carried away by her romantic fancies. I don't understand why you are indulging her like this," Lady Clarinda reproved.

"I can't see the harm in it, Mother. I am amused by her dedication and singleness of purpose and have rather a fascination to see how she will manage it."

"I do hope, my boy," the earl commented dubiously, "that she will not develop into one of those damnably managing females who always meddle in other people's affairs."

"Don't worry," his heir assured with a roguish grin. "She thinks rather well of me, and I wield a great deal of influence. She has not had much opportunity to concentrate her energies on her own affairs, having been somewhat cut off these last few years. She was used to concerning herself with keeping her mother in line and playing the marplot to rout undesirable suitors and then, at Miss Eddington's Academy, involving herself in other people's problems. But she won't have time for that sort of diversion once we are married, so I am of a mind to humour her in this."

Lady Clarinda smiled and remarked whimsically, "Well, that explains why Caroline never remarried. All right, Philip. I can't say I approve, but I will let you work it out for yourself. Now we had better go to dress, or we will not be ready for dinner."

Before going to their own rooms, Lady Madeline and Danila stopped to help Laurel choose one of her new gowns. She looked at them resentfully and objected, "I do wish you will stop treating me like a puppet. I am perfectly capable of dressing myself, and I am not going to suffer your interference another day. I am here, I have a wardrobe full of elegant clothes, all of which meet your approval, and I have said I would become a fashionable. But I *will* not submit myself to review every time I have to make a public appearance." And with this adamant declaration she sat down defiantly, refusing to budge until her persecutors had left the room.

They both had to laugh, and Lady Madeline apologized, "Laurel, I am sorry. I just thought you might be a little hesitant yet and would need some encouragement."

"Well, I don't. I am committed to this comedy, and even though unwilling, I can assure you I will be able to act it out. I will meet you downstairs before dinner."

Having successfully routed her ardent advocates with this bellicose posture, Laurel looked ruefully in the mirror, admitting she had unequivocally compromised herself, and in order to avoid any other such lowering demonstrations, she would have to prove her adequacy. So when Carrie came to her, the abigail found a subdued young lady dressed in the puffed-sleeve apricot tulle that revealed her lovely neck and shoulders, and she met with no objection when she dressed the girl's hair in the striking fashion that Laurel had favoured.

Much to her discomfiture it was in the way of a Grand Entrance when the transformed Laurel entered the drawing room to find the household waiting for her.

Philip was the first to find his tongue, and he exclaimed, "My God! No wonder you have taken pains to disguise yourself." He began to laugh, saying cryptically, "Poor Jason."

Laurel looked at him menacingly and then found herself being embraced by Lady Clarinda, who professed fervently, "Laurel, my dear, you are absolutely stunning. It is going to be such fun to present you and Danila to our

159

friends. I am very excited about it, and Maddy and I will certainly put the other sponsors' noses out of joint with our two beautiful charges."

The earl came to kiss the new Beauty's hand and teased with a twinkle in his eye, "Laurel, you remind me of one of Botticelli's madonnas. At the risk of incurring your displeasure I find I am inclined to agree with Philip's sympathy for 'poor Jason'."

The girl blushed and gave an embarrassed laugh. She said apologetically that she hoped, now that they had expressed their approval, they would not feel obligated to shower her with compliments at her every appearance, "for I find it exceedingly unnerving and I shall never be able to develop a casual attitude if I am forever singled out for notice."

"Of course, my love," Lady Clarinda affirmed. "It is extremely ill mannered of us to cause you to feel ill at ease, but it was such a delightful revelation we could not hide our enthusiasm. Come now, we will go in to dinner and speak of other things."

Philip winked at his love, who looked like a cat that had swallowed a mouse, and offered his arm to his mother. The earl followed with Lady Madeline, and the two girls brought up the rear, giving Danila the opportunity to whisper reassuringly, "You see, it wasn't so bad!" beguiling her friend into a more relaxed manner.

With so many things to discuss the conversation jumped from one subject to another, ranging from Dismoreland to the Grand Tour to Danila's arrival to the exciting Season in store for them, and Philip asked his father interestedly, "What is your position on the queen's divorce?"

"Damn! That is the most sordid affair I have ever witnessed in all my years in politics. If only Queen Caroline were as tractable as the Empress Josephine showed herself and would accept her dismissal with dignity, we would be saved the ignominy of a royal set-to. But she has expressed her intention of returning to England to be recognized as queen, which is sending the king into a frenzy. If he cannot be talked out of instituting divorce proceedings, we are going to be faced with a scandal of monumental proportions when her indiscreet immorality is aired in public. I, for one, am against making an issue of it because the royal house has lost enough prestige these past several years without this new tempest in the teapot."

When the footman cleared the covers to serve the dessert course, the earl excused himself to go to Westminster to join his colleagues. The others soon retired to the drawing room, where they made their plans for the next few days and continued their discussions of the several topics that had been raised at dinner.

Chapter
TEN

During that first week the ladies spent many hours visiting among themselves and helping with the plans for Danila's debut. Occasionally they received morning visitors and made excursions to some of the shops. Usually Danila and Laurel rode with Philip in the mornings, when they were introduced to several of his friends, who began to call in the afternoons, hoping to further their acquaintance with the two new beauties. But Danila had no interest in these inferior specimens and was content to mark time until Jason should come and they could appear as a foursome.

The day before the Devereauxes were due to arrive a message from Jason was received on Portland Place, saying that they would be leaving on schedule and that he would present himself the next evening to accompany them to the theatre, as he had been directed.

Laurel by now had become accustomed to her new image and was beginning to feel comfortable with it, but she dreaded that first meeting with Jason. She hoped he would not think she had suddenly changed into a frivolous coquette. She still had misgivings about trying to bewitch him.

"Laurel, you have the most absurd scruples!" Danila accused when they were relaxing in her sitting room to rest for the evening out.

"I know, love, but I can't help wishing it weren't necessary to practice seduction to make Jason want to marry me."

"I wish you will get your head straight on your shoulders!" an exasperated mentor admonished. "It is not as though he doesn't love you, for you know he does and for every reason you want him to, so there is no way you should feel guilty about bringing him to the point of wanting to make love to you. It is the only thing missing—but it won't be after tonight."

"Danila! Why I ever put myself in your hands I will never comprehend. You make the most discomposing remarks, and I don't think I could face Jason if I imagined he knew what we were about. Do you suppose he will divine our motive?" Laurel asked with a look of panic.

"No, you silly goose. He will just think that Lady Madeline and I have drawn you into our schemes, which is only true, after all, so you need not scruple to lay the blame at our door. Do *not* be such a faintheart, and *do* try to get yourself in a proper frame of mind."

"All right, Danila. I suppose I shall have to go through with it," Laurel submitted and went to her own room to lie down for an hour or so.

Lady Madeline came in while Laurel was dressing, though she was careful not to antagonize her daughter with any suggestions and only once allowed herself to tell her how beautiful she looked. The azure blue gown had a silvery sheen and was fitted to show off her lovely figure. It fell only to her ankles, revealing matching slippers and glimpses of silk stockings. Carrie had dressed her hair to perfection, bringing one long blond curl forward over her right shoulder. Laurel reached for her jewel case to choose something, but Lady Madeline opened a velvet box she was holding and said, "No, darling. I have brought you one of my pieces." And she slipped a single-strand diamond necklace with a pendant around her neck, exclaiming, "This is perfect, my love. I knew it would be just the thing."

"Mama," Laurel protested in embarrassment, "I can't wear that," as she noticed the position of the pendant.

"Of course you can, darling."

"Really, Mama, I cannot believe you would wish your daughter to be so brazen. It is so—so *leading*. And this gown is cut much too low."

"My love, you think so only because you have been in the habit of covering yourself up to your chin. I assure you it will not be thought the least remarkable."

Danila came to announce that Jason had arrived and that he and Philip were waiting downstairs. Then she hurried away to make sure that the stage was properly set. She was so intent on anticipating the moment of Laurel's appearance that she did not realize what a charming picture she made herself in her light rose gown with a pink petticoat as she came down the stairs. Jason complimented her, "Danila, you look very lovely, and that colour is especially flattering."

"Thank you, Jason," she said, pleasantly surprised.

She looked expectantly at Philip, who placed a hand under her chin and kissed her lightly. "My cousin has excellent taste."

She grinned impishly and informed them, "Laurel will be down in a minute and—oh, here she comes now."

Jason followed her gaze and experienced a violent shock. He stared unbelievingly at the ravishing creature who was slowly gliding down the steps, and he seemed rooted to the spot. She came to stand before him, saying softly, "Hello, Jason."

He murmured wonderingly, "Laurel," and then exploded, "My God, Laurel! What have you done to yourself?" an inauspicious outburst that shattered her fragile composure. She looked in dismay at Danila, who frowned at her warningly, a completely worthless encouragement when Jason proffered the coup de grâce with the angry remonstrance "Surely you do not mean to show yourself in public in that shockingly immodest gown. Go find a shawl to cover yourself!"

This uncivil confirmation of his disapproval so unnerved

Laurel that she burst into tears and ran upstairs to her room, to be met by her mother, who unsympathetically insisted she stop indulging herself with a fit of the vapours or she would ruin her toilette.

"It doesn't make any difference. I'm not going anywhere," the girl wailed. "Jason was disgusted and does not wish to be seen with me."

Lady Madeline knew that was not precisely the crux of the matter, though he had certainly behaved badly, and she meant to have a little talk with him. At present, however, she concentrated on calming Laurel because she did not doubt that Danila would take appropriate action on the other front.

After the staggering contretemps Philip pulled his cousing unceremoniously into the small salon. Danila followed and closed the door with fire in her eye.

Philip looked at Jason incredulously and said to Danila, "You are right, my love. He *is* a gudgeon."

Jason was perfectly well aware of the preposterously infamous faux pas he had committed and did not have to search for a reason for it. In frustration he vented some of the anger he felt at himself on his two companions. He demanded bitterly, "What did you expect? To spring it on me without warning was the height of folly."

"Well!" Danila came back militantly. "How did we know you were going to behave so abominably? Now you have ruined everything! It took Lady Madeline and me weeks to persuade Laurel to stop playing the dowd. Now you have embarrassed her unforgivably. And," she demanded angrily, "what right do you have to speak to Laurel in that shockingly highhanded manner?"

"Danila," Jason said with a pained expression, "you don't have to rake me over the coals. I know I made a cake of myself. If you will go ask Laurel if she will talk to me, perhaps I can put things to rights."

His ward looked at him with a mulish expression, as if she did not credit him with a modicum of sensibility, until Philip told her, "Go on, love, or we will be late for the theatre. Why don't you wait in the drawing room, Jason?

You won't be disturbed, for my mother and father are out to dinner."

Danila went to Laurel's room and found that Lady Madeline had succeeded in pacifying her daughter somewhat. She announced, "Laurel, Jason asks if you will see him, and he is waiting in the drawing room."

"No! I can't see him—not like this. He—he didn't like it at all."

"My love, you are a peagoose. The truth is he liked it too well and didn't want anyone else to see you looking so beautiful," Danila informed her wisely. She went to Laurel's bureau and selected a light diaphanous shawl to place around her shoulders, saying caustically, "Maybe *that* will satisfy his prudery. Don't let him ruin our evening, Laurel. He may as well accustom himself to your new look, for it is too late for you to backtrack. Now show some mettle and go face him down."

Lady Madeline smiled encouragingly, so the girl let out a long, quivering sigh and stood up slowly, feeling like a lamb being led to slaughter.

When she entered the drawing room, she saw Jason standing forbiddingly with his hands behind his back, and she wanted to turn and run again. But he came forward quickly and took her hands, apologizing abjectly, "Laurel, please forgive me. I don't know what possessed me to fly off like that."

She lowered her eyes and remained silent, not knowing what to say, waiting for him to make it easier for her.

"I think I was so stunned to see such an unfamiliar image in place of my Laurel that I felt I had lost you, and I couldn't bear it." He paused and then observed huskily, "You do look incredibly beautiful."

She found this unwitting evidence of his susceptibility passably hopeful, though she ventured timidly, "But you do not like me like this."

"That is not precisely true, my love. It *is* disconcerting, but I'm sure I can become accustomed," Jason reassured lightly with a teasing grin.

She gave him a tremulous little smile and admitted, "I

thoroughly agree with you about this gown, you know, though even Mama assured me it was all the crack."

"It is the fashion, Laurel; however, I would prefer that you would wear your shawl—at least while we are out."

She primly ignored his *mot* and agreed, "Oh, yes, I feel much more comfortable with it."

"Am I forgiven?" he asked hopefully.

"Of course, Jason. I should not have allowed myself to be so misguided," she replied magnanimously.

He took her hand, feeling pleasingly lighthearted, and pronounced firmly, "Then let us join the others and enjoy a lovely evening."

When they appeared together in apparent harmony, Danila breathed a sigh of relief and, without comment, allowed Philip to slip her short cloak over her shoulders, preceding him to the waiting carriage.

Their appearance at the theatre created a mild sensation. Even in the midst of dozens of bejeweled, glittering ladies the dark-haired and silvery blond beauties stood out, especially as they were in the company of two elegant gentlemen, one of whom could not be immediately placed by the dowagers of the *ton* until one young man told his party, "Oh, that is Jason Devereaux, Viscount Oxborough's cousin. I believe the dark-haired girl is his ward, Lady Danila Wilmington, but I'd give a monkey to know who the other is. She is a regular dasher," a superlative compliment not well received by the two young women in his party. He was eventually enlightened when, after several confidences were whispered from box to box, the Beauty was identified as Lady Ingram's daughter, who was accompanying her mother for the first time. Obviously this unusual circumstance required some investigation, and during the intermissions Philip's box was swamped with visitors who hoped to discover the standing of the two ladies with their escorts. The inquisitives came away thoroughly confused. Although it appeared that both girls were bespoken in some fashion, it was not precisely confirmed, leaving a lot of room for speculation. But the Season was just beginning, and the chase was on.

Jason realized he was not going to have much free time because he obviously was going to have to circumvent the gallants. But since that meant that he would be often with Laurel, he did not find the prospect unwelcome. He decided he would postpone their tour of the auction houses for a while—at least until after Danila's debut and the first round of social obligations had been honoured. And so, much to their surprise, Danila and Laurel and Philip found him entirely receptive to any proposal, and he dutifully presented himself punctually for their engagements. They became an inseparable foursome, still causing some perplexity in the *ton*, and while they were invariably amiable in company, they did not accept single invitations.

The day of Danila's come-out arrived all too soon. Last-minute preparations were being checked frantically, there always being an apprehension that something would not arrive in time, so that Schofield House was in a turmoil until an hour before the first guests were to arrive, when suddenly everything came under control.

Jason and his mother arrived for dinner, bringing with them a surprise visitor, much to Danila's delight. Without her knowledge Philip had arranged for Elizabeth Eddington to come from Bath.

Danila threw her arms around her friend and introduced her enthusiastically to the others. "Oh, I am *so* happy you came, Eddy. How long are you staying?"

"Just two nights, Danila. You know this is not a good time for me to leave, but I could not resist Lady Schofield's gracious invitation," Miss Eddington replied affectionately.

"Well, tomorrow we will have a long visit. Will you promise?"

"If you have time," her friend temporized.

"Eddy!" Danila said menacingly, persuading Miss Eddington to agree without any further patronizing objections.

During dinner Miss Eddington was drawn readily into the family group, and it was soon discovered that she and the three older ladies had several acquaintances in common. She expressed her admiration of Theo Devereaux's

168

poetry, and that lady, usually taking no notice of other people's opinions of her work, affecting a rather insular posture, found the headmistress extremely *en rapport*, and she promised to send her an autographed copy of her next volume, which was even then being printed.

As usual, this animated and compatible company became deeply involved in their conversations until Lady Clarinda realized that they had delayed too long and would have to hurry to refresh themselves before they were caught napping by early arrivals.

Danila dragged Elizabeth Eddington with her. In her excitement she kept up a flow of chatter, prompting her friend to warn her that if she did not put a damper on, she would find herself croaking like a frog, if not losing her voice altogether, a convincing argument that was duly noted.

In a short while Lady Clarinda came to collect Danila and Laurel to tell them it was time to form the reception line. In spite of Laurel's protests that it was not seemly for her to be so honoured because she was not a major attraction at this grand affair, she was not allowed to remain in the shade and found herself standing next to Danila at the bottom of the stairs waiting for the three hundred guests who had been invited.

Danila was dressed in a white full-skirted ball gown, embroidered with roses, and Laurel wore the silvery gauze her mother had chosen specially for this occasion. Jason and Philip stood across the room, both wholly enchanted with their ladies. Jason found it extremely difficult to maintain a cool expression as he watched all the bucks turning back to look at Laurel with speculative eyes. He swore inwardly, regretting that he had agreed to this excursion, fervently wishing he had suppressed his gentlemanly instincts and had offered for Laurel while they were still in Sussex, as he had wanted to. This venture promised to be one maddening ordeal, and it definitely went against the grain that he had agreed to pretend that he and Danila had an understanding besides.

"Looks as though we are going to have a problem on

our hands," Philip said with a wry face. "I hope you are up to keeping the wolves away from Danila's door since you are doubly responsible as her guardian and her 'betrothed'."

"At least the pretense serves as something of a barrier, but Laurel is not so protected. I don't like the looks she has been getting from the rakehell element of the crowd. I'm afraid she is going to be pursued unmercifully," Jason deplored with a dark expression.

"I'll handle that," Philip told him and then suggested they claim their ladies. The stream of guests had dwindled to an occasional late arrival, and it was time to enter the ballroom to begin the dancing.

He smiled mischievously at both girls but offered his arm to Laurel, and Jason, resigning himself to his role, escorted Danila. They were immediately surrounded by several smaller groups, and when it became apparent that Laurel was having difficulty, Philip made every effort to give the impression that he was first oars with her. In instant perception of his motive she cooperated willingly, dampening the hopes of a number of aspiring gentlemen who felt extremely ill used that these two lovely creatures were all but snapped up before they even came to town. Jason and Philip were chided resentfully for their extremely nefarious methods of flummoxing the competition.

With a hands-off policy established Laurel and Danila were able to fend off undesirable attentions and to refuse unwelcome invitations. They were instant successes, nonetheless, because it was never unpleasant to be in the company of beautiful and charming girls who had no tiresome affected mannerisms and who, besides, were agreeably conversable and showed themselves to be interested listeners.

With so many new faces swimming before them, Laurel and Danila found themselves overwhelmed and finally gave up trying to remember everyone, leaving recognition to future meetings. Some of Danila's former schoolmates rushed to her side, suddenly delighted to see their "good friend," and so insinuated themselves into the company which held an excess of gentlemen. Danila, in benevolent humour, received them all with geniality, willing to forgive, if not forget, their obvious fair-weather overtures.

The competition for dances and favoured positions continued relentlessly and interminably, and Laurel was soon disaffected. By one o'clock she had begun to have a glazed look in her eye as if she were walking in her sleep. Jason took pity on her and led her to a vacant couch in a corner, urging, "Come sit down, love. You look fagged to death."

"I am so tired, Jason. Is it true that these people do this almost every night?" She groaned expressively.

"Some do. But then they sleep all morning," Jason told her with a tender smile.

Danila, too, was finding the ordeal a little less than felicitous but partly for another reason. She had been simmering for hours, observing the bold as brass young women who obviously had it in mind to set their caps for Philip, and she was incensed by the forwardness of these females, some of whom Philip seemed to know rather well. But she made a resolution *not* to tease him because it was her own fault that he was thought to be eligible, and she meant to do something about *that* in the very near future.

Finally the musicians stopped playing, and the girls deserted the straggling guests to go to their rooms to fall exhausted on their beds.

Laurel did not waken until almost noon the next day and took her time about getting up because her eyes still felt heavy. She was just bathing her face with rose water when there was a light rap on the door. She called, "Come in," and Danila entered, still in her wrapper also. She flounced ungracefully on the bed and drew her knees up, announcing, "Well, Laurel, we made it through, but I have to say that the ritual is monstrously overrated. I am glad it is over."

"Danila, I very much agree with you, though I had no Great Expectations in the first place. I do hope you will not express yourself in that excessively frank manner to anyone else because Mama and Lady Clarinda are all set up with themselves about their spectacular success."

"Oh, I know, Laurel, and I will not disappoint them, I

promise you. I suppose, if I had had an ambition to find my Prince Charming, it would have been more pleasurable. But when one has already found him, it is no great thing to have to suffer the attentions of those tedious, smooth-tongued Bond Street fribbles. Some of them are pleasant, but most have a regrettable tendency to preen themselves like peacocks."

Laurel giggled in appreciation but felt obliged to admonish, "My love, sometimes you do have an inelegant way of expressing yourself."

Danila made a little face and said sincerely, "Laurel, you *did* look so beautiful that everyone was quite spellbound, and Jason couldn't keep his eyes off you. It was positively shocking, in fact. If he doesn't behave more discreetly, no one will believe we are betrothed."

"I know," Laurel said with an almost smug expression. "Considering the lamentably inauspicious beginning, it is turning out rather well."

Danila grinned but refrained from crowing and said, "I came to ask if you would accompany me to see Eddy this afternoon. I know it is the custom to receive visitors the day after a come-out, but I so want to visit with her before she leaves town. I am very much attached to her, you see."

"Why don't you explain to Lady Clarinda? I'm sure she will understand, and I will surely go with you because I am not of a mind to be obligated to hold court by myself."

"I'll get dressed and go ask her," Danila said, hopping off the bed, leaving Laurel to finish her toilette.

Lady Clarinda did not exactly approve of the girls' truancy, but she was pleased that Danila showed so much sensibility and loyalty. She suppressed her reservations and agreed that while it would be thought curious, it would not lower their standing since they had so admirably established themselves at the ball.

Danila impulsively kissed the lady's cheek and vowed, "Lady Clarinda, you are a regular trump, and I am so glad you are not—uh—"

"Stuffy is the word, my dear," the countess finished for

her with a twinkle in her eye that clearly proclaimed where Philip had come by his delightful sense of humour.

"Yes—well—I thought perhaps I ought not be so saucy," Danila said with her impish grin.

"I beg you will not feel hesitant with me, Danila. I'm sure we will all be much more comfortable if we behave naturally with one another."

"So I think, too, my lady, and I am so relieved to have you say so because I have a natural disinclination to dissemble, though perhaps I should not behave quite so freely with the earl," she added dubiously.

"You might show a little more reserve in his company, my love, for he does have a lingering sympathy for the old order, though I can assure you he is not stuffy either."

Danila smiled happily and hurried to tell Laurel of their release. They both put on one of their new walking dresses and commissioned Philip to escort them to the Clarendon Hotel, where he deposited them and then went on to White's, promising to return for them in two hours.

Elizabeth Eddington more than half expected them because she had great faith in Danila's credibility, and she received them affably. She exchanged amused glances with Laurel, whom she found to be a lovely, intelligent, agreeable young lady and readily understood the younger girl's exuberant attachment, as they listened to Danila's verbose expositions. The girl, having been so used to entrusting her friend as a confidante, felt moved to acquaint her with all the particulars of these eventful three months.

Miss Eddington suffered this compulsive loquacity with admirable tolerance, but when it appeared that Danila was about to take breath, she suggested that they repair to the dining room, where she would treat them to a refreshing tea when she hoped that Danila would permit her to become better acquainted with Laurel, a subtle reprimand that was taken in good part.

Since the girls had not eaten anything yet that day, having had a surfeit of delicacies the evening before, they found this suggestion eminently agreeable. And so it was that Philip returned to find three ladies indulging themselves immoderately.

He sat down to join them, saying, "I welcome this opportunity to further my acquaintance with Miss Eddington. I have a powerful feeling that it would be much to my credit if I were able to establish myself in her good graces."

"I give you leave, my lord," that unusual lady said with an encouraging smile. "I am open to persuasion."

Philip sat back and laughed. "I begin to see why my Danila is not as other young schoolgirls. I am much impressed with your good standing, Miss Eddington, and I beg you to tell me the secret of your success."

"Love and friendship, Lord Oxborough. An irresistible combination."

"An admirable precept, Miss Eddington, and you may be sure I will take your advice to heart."

"I am sure you will, my lord. I am very pleased that you and Danila find each other so *sympatique*. I am happy for you both. While I had my doubts about the wisdom of sending her off with Mr. Devereaux, I see now that I must have been awarded some happy prescience since, as Danila has pronounced, 'things are working out so beautifully'."

Reluctantly the little party had to break up, but it was established that Miss Eddington would attend a wedding which would be performed sometime in the summer. Philip returned the girls to Portland Place, where they found a mound of calling cards left by a score of disappointed visitors.

Chapter
ELEVEN

After another week of this demanding social round, including obligatory attendance at two more debutante balls with the dismaying prospect of six more to go, Laurel was becoming thoroughly impatient. She complained one morning, when the four of them were riding in the park, "Jason, we have been here three weeks already, and we have yet to make a single trip to the auction houses unless," she added suspiciously, "you have been going alone."

With a sheepish expression he admitted, "You have caught me out, I'm afraid. I have made a couple of scouting excursions, but I haven't bought anything. I am waiting for your approval."

She looked at him resentfully but merely asked, "Have you found anything interesting?"

"Yes, and two pieces being held for me. Would you like to see them?"

"Yes!" she responded emphatically. "Can we go today?"

"Don't we have an afternoon commitment with Phil and Danila?"

"Oh, fiddle! We are all supposed to go on another picnic, but it sounds the greatest bore. I wish we could cry off."

"Perhaps we can, love, if you really wish to. Remember that part of Danila's plan was that I should become involved with my work and begin to throw her and Phil together."

"That's right," Laurel agreed with a laugh. "I have come to have a great deal of respect for her stratagems."

Jason grinned and quipped, "Perhaps we should ask her if it's time to take the next step. I wouldn't want to be accused of usurping the leadership."

"Actually I think she is more than ready. She has not been amused that Philip is constantly under attack since his supposed attachment to me has not served as much of a deterrent."

"Well then, let's catch up with them and tell her we wish to take a respite."

Their proposal met with not the least objection, "for," Danila conceded, "I have thought it was time myself but did not want to encourage you two to become caught up in your work again." And she looked at Jason accusingly.

"Don't scowl at me, you little termagant. I didn't bring up the subject, and I am in Laurel's black books for foraging on my own."

And so it was that Philip and Danila joined the party of young people on an excursion to Richmond, giving rise to whispers of prudery and speculation. Laurel and Jason went to Kensington to examine an exquisite china table of mahogany that was being offered for sale by a wealthy merchant who was redecorating his house in the more ostentatious Louis XIV period. The finish was marred by a few scratches and nicks, which showed the negligence of the unappreciative owners, but could easily be retouched by an expert craftsman. They decided it would look just the thing in the formal drawing room, so Jason bought it forthwith and directed that it be sent to Dismoreland.

They next went to the home of a young lord who was dangerously under the hatch from an overindulgence at the tables and was selling off some of the famliy heirlooms in an attempt to stay one step ahead of the dun collectors. Their eyes settled on an excellent eighteenth-century side table with a Grecian motif apron which echoed the frieze around the domed hall at Dismoreland and would be displayed not only as a treasure in itself but as a stand for a pair of Sèvres urns which Jason had sent back from France.

At both residences they had seen other objects that interested them, and they promised to return another day to inspect the available pieces more closely.

They went by Dismore House to inquire if Theo were home and so could qualify as chaperone because they realized that their habit of working in privacy would not conform to the mores of society. Fortunately the Muse was closeted in her room, resting from her morning exertions, when she has allowed herself to be coaxed into the role of celebrity by her publisher, and she amiably consented to lend her presence.

Jason had appropriated his cousin's library as a workroom and had spread the floor plans of Dismoreland on a large table. He and Laurel studied them, systematically making notations as to how the rooms would be used. When they had formed a general idea of what type of furniture would fit the purpose and the scale of the individual chambers, they felt they had prepared themselves to recognize the suitability of an object regardless of period, although for one room they did have a preconceived notion of a particular style, deciding that the elegantly simple, delicate Hepplewhite designs would be most suitable and comfortable in the new small family dining salon on the ground floor. There were numerous wall spaces that would accommodate the larger-scaled pieces of the pre-Georgian periods, and Jason decided to backtrack to purchase two of these for his dressing room, a William and Mary carved oak chest of drawers with a geometric pattern, mounted on a turned stand, and a large early-eighteenth-century carved oak armoire.

Theo came over to interrupt their deliberations, admonishing that they were not in Sussex and could not work into the night, and reminded them that they were all invited to attend a musical program and supper at Kenwood that evening.

Jason stood up, laughing, and said to Laurel, "Come on,

love. I'll take you home. I should not want to vex Maddy, for she might come to think I mean to take advantage of her sufferance."

With a resigned sigh Laurel rose also and observed wistfully, "I would not mind coming to London once in a while, for it is pleasant to go to the theatre, the galleries, the shops, and even some of the musical soirees and the smaller suppers where you can actually have agreeable conversations. But I would much prefer to come in the off-Season so that you could enjoy a more leisurely pace. This frantic rushing about from one engagement to the next is boring and fatiguing. I am ready to go home."

"Not yet, Laurel," Jason protested decidedly. "We have just started our rummaging. I hope you do not mean to desert me because I am becoming very enthused about this phase of our labours. We have a prodigious task before us, you know, since we have to choose not only furniture but draperies and carpets besides."

"Well, I should like to do *that*, but if you are going to be intimidated by those two scheming females, we will not get much accomplished," she said resentfully.

Jason laughed and promised, "I will talk to your mother and tell her I am being harassed by a dev'lish impatient taskmaster."

Laurel gave a satisfied smile and asked, "Where are we going tomorrow?"

Jason looked at her dubiously, charging, "I think that your association with that precocious child has had a surprising effect."

"At least she gets things done," Laurel replied, giving credit, as they stepped outside and turned to walk toward Portland Place.

"So Philip has observed. You both are obviously possessed."

"I didn't notice that you exactly stood fast yourself," she noted acerbically.

"You are really testing your wings, aren't you, you little minx? I can see that things will never be the same again—

not that I have any objection, you know," he owned with a mischievous grin.

Laurel lowered her eyes and tried not to show her pleasure, but Jason was well aware that she understood. He bent to kiss her forehead at the door of Schofield House, murmuring, "Wear your pale yellow gown, Laurel. I like that particularly."

She smiled happily and turned to go inside with a fluttering stomach and a singing heart but was soon brought to earth when Lady Madeline came to the top of the stairs and called down, "Laurel, you are so late. I should have known how it would be once you became involved in that business again. You will have to hurry, or we will be caught in the crush. Your bath has been ready for an hour, and we have been trying to keep it warm. I will have tea and some biscuits brought to you because we will likely not eat for hours."

"Mama, please calm yourself. I will be ready, I promise you, and I do not want anything to eat. Jason and Theo and I had a tea a little earlier."

Danila came to her room when Carrie was doing her hair, and Laurel confided that Jason had especially ordered her costume.

"That sounds promising," the younger girl approved.

Laurel smiled and turned to view herself in the cheval mirror as she pinned a small diamond clip in the twisted chignon at the back of her head.

"There! How do I look?"

"Like a ray of sunshine, Laurel," Danila said enviously, looking regretfully at her own dark cropped curls.

"You are a picture yourself, love. That emerald green is stunning with your colouring."

"Well," Danila proposed with a grin, "let us go to see if our gentlemen are as impressed with us as we are with ourselves."

The party all congregated at Scholfield House so that they might require only two carriages. The earl had agreed to escort the countess and Lady Madeline and Theo Dever-

179

eaux to the affair but would go on to his own engagement, though he committed himself to return for them at the end of the evening. The four young people followed in Jason's carriage.

The entertainment by an extremely talented string quartet proved to be one of the better musical programs of the Season, and it provided a pleasant relaxing interlude after some of the more hectic social affairs. The latter part of the evening was not as agreeable. Two gentlemen, one, Lord Orwell, a widower with three young children, who viewed Laurel as a likely candidate for the role of mother, and Lord James Pittman, a wealthy young lord, who had developed a genuine passion for her and desired her for his wife, both stepped up their pursuit, creating a considerable amount of tension. Laurel tried to discourage them categorically without being discourteous, and Jason held his temper with difficulty, casting baleful looks at his cousin, whose performance as a decoy was a good deal less than satisfactory. In the viscount's defense it must be noted that he was experiencing a little discomfiture himself, being the target of several ambitious young ladies and their mamas who still hoped to win his favour and were doing their best to circumvent his supposed *tendre* for Laurel.

Jason formed a firm resolution that his rivals would not be allowed to annoy her with their unwanted attentions, and he requested a private audience with Lady Madeline the next morning to explain that he had every intention of keeping Laurel very much occupied for several reasons.

She heard him out and did not raise any objections, merely asking him not to monopolize her time entirely, "for, you know, my dear, that I am so pleased to have her with me, and I cannot but wish to show her off."

"I understand, Maddy. She is the most beautiful lady in London, and I know you are extremely proud. But because she is so lovely, she is naturally sought after, and it really makes her deucedly uncomfortable. Another time it will be different and much less vexatious. She will come again, I promise you."

"I know, Jason, and I am very pleased that things are

finally falling into place. I will not interfere, but you had better talk to Danila because she may be a little less amenable."

"I think it is time I asserted my rights as guardian and demanded a little respect and obedience. She has had her day, but I have indulged her long enough," Jason said with a set expression.

He went in search of the others and found them sitting in the small interior garden court enjoying the lovely morning. He immediately told Danila forcefully, "My dear ward, I have come to give you notice that I withdraw my support of your little game and that I reject the idea of any 'understanding' or otherwise where we are concerned. I have other things to do than play a part in your scheme, and you may contrive your own explanation. Laurel and I need to devote most of our time and energy to the furnishing of Dismoreland while we are here, and in case you are contemplating any kind of objection, I will advise you that I have already cleared the intention with Lady Madeline. I will not countenance any more of your obtrusion."

"Well! I *do* think you are being unnecessarily contentious. I just might be of the same mind, you know," Danila retorted with an injured expression.

"It doesn't make any difference if you are or not, my dear girl," Jason stated emphatically, then turned to Laurel. "Come on, love, we have some very busy days ahead of us. Let us leave these children to work out their own problems."

"I say, Jase, what the devil put you in such a temper?" his cousin demanded testily. "I jolly well take exception to your damned condescending manner. You know I haven't been carried away with this setup myself."

"Sorry, Phil," Jason apologized ruefully. "I didn't mean to cut at you, but I have had enough of being obliged to promote these misconceptions, and I hereby resign my role. Why don't you announce your betrothal and have done with it?"

"That would certainly solve my problems," Philip remarked as he grinned at Danila, who was thinking furiously to fabricate a revised strategy. "But we may have to wait a week or so to make it more credible, although you would have been amused at the disapproving looks we received yesterday when we showed up without you."

"Well, you will just have to provide a little more fodder for the tattlemongers, and then, in a few days, you can set the record straight."

"But, Jason, even if we do that," Danila said dubiously, "that does not mean you should monopolize Laurel again as you have been wont to do in the past. Often we are engaged during the day when we do not require escorts."

Her guardian informed her blightingly, "If Laurel wished to accompany you to some of these affairs, it is for her to say so. But it is *her* choice, and you should not make demands any more than I. Is that clear?"

"That's not fair!" Danila protested petulantly. "You *know* she would rather go with you!"

"Well, I hope so anyway," a shameless gentleman acknowledged with a mischievous grin.

Laurel laughed and told him she would go get her bonnet and be ready to leave in a few minutes. Not wishing to listen to any more of his pesky ward's recriminations, Jason went inside to wait in the hall.

Danila placed her elbow on a marble pedestal, resting her chin on her fist with her lower lip thrust out belligerently. "Devil take it! Things were looking so promising, for he *has* been unsettled by the persistence of Laurel's suitors, and now he means to take her out of circulation!"

"Is that any less promising?" Philip asked.

"I don't know. He's such a deep one that it is hard to divine his intentions," Danila replied in frustration.

"My love, you are all about in the head if you think he does not mean to marry Laurel in the very near future. You are much too impatient. Now I want you to try to rid yourself of this obsession and turn your mind to our affairs. We will no longer require Jason and Laurel's presence and will appear everywhere together. I have not liked watching some of the loose fish hovering around you. I want them to know you belong to me."

"Well, I can tell you that I have not been all that pleased with things either, and those brass-faced hussies who are constantly hanging on you are asking for trouble," she admitted with a glowering expression. "I shall be happy to put their noses out of joint, so I am quite agreeable to the new arrangement. But I still mean to concern myself with Laurel's situation, for I do not trust Jason to come up to scratch without a shove. I shall just have to find another way."

Jason and Laurel happily went off to the City with the intent to concentrate on looking for Oriental carpets, and after examining the wares of several Turkish and Persian merchants who specialized in new imports, they chose two Persian carpets, a Feraghan for one of the smaller rooms and a large Kurdistan for the large first-floor drawing room, and an exquisite Hercke from Turkey, woven of silk pile with metal threads, that would be used in the formal dining room out of the main traffic aisles.

They were about to leave when Jason's attention was called to a new Persian hunting carpet that had just arrived. He and Laurel agreed that the size was perfect for the library, which also served as Jason's study, and they recklessly added it to their purchases.

Having spent such a profitable day, if such an extravagant spree could be so characterized, they stopped for a late luncheon and then browsed leisurely through some of the elegant shops on Oxford and Bond streets, occasionally considering some object that pleased them but deciding to limit their purchases on this trip to items that were of some priority.

When Jason returned her to Portland Place, Laurel told him she felt unusually done up after their full day of shopping and that she would prefer to remain at home that evening.

"We did overextend ourselves a bit, love, and it would probably do us both good to make an early night of it. Tomorrow, if you feel up to it, we will check out the drapers."

"All right. I'll be fine after a good night's sleep. These

183

late nights are what make me weary. I am glad we are not going to go out every evening."

"Well, do not get too spoiled, my dear. You shall certainly have to put in an appearance now and then," Jason teased.

"I know," Laurel bemoaned, "but I would like to avoid Almack's and some of the larger affairs when it is such a trial to pretend you are enjoying yourself."

Jason smiled at her indulgently and told her to think about colours and materials. He would come for her at ten o'clock in the morning.

Danila returned from her drive in the park with Philip a little while later and accepted Laurel's refusal to attend Almack's that evening without argument. "I am looking forward to appearing with Philip as my escort. I am tired of watching that odious Pamela Farrington fluttering her eyelashes at him."

"Is that—? Oh, yes, I know whom you mean. The copper-haired girl with the —uh—ample curves. I *have* noticed a little antagonism between the two of you. Did you have a problem at Miss Eddington's?"

"Not there," the girl replied hesitantly. "Actually it was at her home in Somerset. She invited me to spend two weeks there during one of the holidays. We had been friendly then. Everything went very well until her brother came home with Lord Robert Manion. And—well—I didn't try to attach him or anything, though you know I have this disposition to be friendly. I didn't even like him above half. But Lord Robert took a fancy to me, and Pamela was furious because she thought she had him in her pocket. If she would have just let the matter run its course, he probably would have returned to the fold. But she went out of her way to try to put me down, which of course I wouldn't stand for, and she finally fell into the most unladylike rage, cutting at me in pure spite. Lord Manion left the next day. Three months later we heard he was engaged to be married. Pamela holds me to blame for his desertion, and her family was furious with both of us because he was a good

184

catch, being heir to a marquess and plump in the pocket besides. It was as good as settled in their minds that he would offer for her. But I refuse to be the scapegoat because she behaved like a shrew. He probably counted himself well out of it."

"You are likely right, my love. But remember your assessment of her behaviour if you should be tempted to let fly. Let Philip handle it. He has been dodging eager young ladies for years, you know."

"I will try," Danila said resolutely, a posture considerably weakened by her subsequent remark. "But she had better not push me too far, though I will promise you I will not make a scene."

"Somehow I do not feel too reassured," Laurel observed doubtfully and judiciously went to alert her mother to keep an eye on things that evening.

"Well, if you really think there is trouble brewing, I will not go to the cardroom tonight. Surely they will not come to cuffs at Almack's. They would both be ostracized."

"Nothing so dramatic as that. But I *have* noticed that Miss Farrington has been flaunting her charms rather noticeably in Philip's direction, and if it appears in her superior little mind that Danila has cut her out again, she is apt to fly into the boughs."

Laurel also spoke to Philip. "Danila seems to have a particular antipathy toward someone called Odious Pamela Farrington, and I thought you should be aware."

"I am," the young man said with a rueful face. "When those two are together, you can almost see the sparks fly, but I must say that Danila has shown remarkable forbearance, considering the provocation. However, tonight I will demonstrate my partiality and hope it will stave off further advances."

Lady Clarinda agreed to join the party that evening when Lady Madeline informed her of the new complication and asked if she would keep her company since she meant to play the proper chaperone and would likely be bored all out of patience.

"Maddy," the countess said sympathetically, "I know you find the role extremely tiresome, being so popular yourself. Your admirers are not all that pleased either."

"Well, at least it has served to teach them where my priorities are, and they have resigned themselves to light flirtations, which I find much more comfortable."

"I don't think they are all exactly resigned, my dear. Lord Haskell is particularly frustrated. He is such an admirable gentleman and adores you. Don't you think you might deal very well with one another?"

"We could, I suppose. He is a dear man, but you know how it is with me. I just can't bring myself to accept another like that."

"I thought perhaps after seven years you might begin to feel differently," her friend ventured encouragingly.

"I doubt I ever will, Clarinda," Lady Madeline replied softly with a faraway look in her eye.

The countess had a fond memory of Lord Ingram herself, and she had always marveled at the unusually devoted relationship he enjoyed with his wife. She readily understood her friend's loyalty and did not press the issue, thinking that only time might turn the balance, yet having no great hope for it.

Philip escorted his three ladies to Almack's. In the carriage he told Danila that he meant to claim all the waltzes, even at the risk of scandalizing the assembly. He intended to assert his rights, for he did not propose to watch her swirling around the room in another man's arms.

Lady Clarinda protested, "My dear, that would be quite improper, for the waltz is played oftener now, and it would certainly be damaging to Danila's reputation."

"Then we will do as Jason suggested and put it about that she and I are bespoken and that an announcement will be sent to the *Gazette* tomorrow. I have tired of playing games."

"That would please me greatly, Philip," his mother approved, looking hopefully at Danila.

The girl smiled happily and confessed, "Actually it

would please me also. I am very proud to be Philip's choice, and Jason has upset my plans anyway." And she slid her small hand into Philip's large one as he gave a satisfied sigh that she showed herself so docile.

As soon as they entered the large ballroom, there was an immediate gravitation in their direction. Several gentlemen were disappointed that the group had lost two of its members, but many direct inquiries about the absentees were turned away easily. However, Pamela Farrington had no intention of being put off, and she asked with a contrived innocence, "Danila, my dear, where is your betrothed this evening?"

"Right—oh, you mean Jason? Well, actually, Pamela, I have to confess that was all a hum," Danila replied honestly. "You see, when he became my guardian, it was rather awkward, and we settled on that pretense before I went into society so that it would serve as something of a barrier to the fortune hunters. But he has tired of the charade and has abdicated his role in favour of his cousin. I must say I find the arrangement much more to my liking."

"Well!" spouted an outraged young lady, "I do think that is the most arrant cock-and-bull story I ever heard in my life. Obviously you cannot bear to see any man pay attention to another lady and must have them all dangling at your feet." Some of the group began to edge away in embarrassment, but the jealous girl continued the attack, accusing, "You are fair in the way to being a Jezebel!"

Philip knew that Danila could not be expected to take these animadversions submissively, and to ward off trouble, he protested, "Oh, surely not, Miss Farrington." He turned to Danila and admonished facetiously with a twinkle in his eye, "I absolutely forbid it! You are *not* to become a Jezebel, my love."

This flight of whimsey squelched Danila's anger. She burst out laughing, saying, "Philip, you are the most ridiculous man," and promptly found herself swung onto the floor in such a manner that it left no doubt as to the viscount's intentions and, for that matter, as to Danila's.

187

"Well, we got through that reasonably well," he gloated.

"*You* did, you mean. I was ready to scratch her eyes out."

"I know. I *do* think I handled it admirably," he congratulated himself with a smug expression.

Pamela flounced off to complain to her mother, who had witnessed the barbed interchange with apprehension, suddenly realizing that her ungovernable daughter had a deplorable tendency to lose her self-control and show her pettish nature. She hoped this last setdown would teach her a lesson. But in a losing battle with the willful girl she allowed herself to be persuaded to approach Lady Clarinda to discover if things were as they appeared and was lucklessly edified when the countess confirmed, "Oh, yes, Lady Farrington. It is perfectly true, and I am delighted. Danila is a lovely charming girl, and we all adore her. The earl and I are looking forward to claiming her as our daughter-in-law. A notice will be sent to the *Gazette* tomorrow."

Being completely flummoxed by this exuberant confidence, Lady Farrington returned to her daughter and told her that it was all settled and that she should stop making a cake of herself. Pamela was still in a rage that Danila was so well established and made several pithy comments throughout the evening about the shocking behaviour of some forward girls. She announced haughtily that she did not mean to associate with such brazen creatures, emphasizing her meaning by cutting Danila and Philip for the rest of the evening, a circumstance that they found extremely felicitous, especially when most of the other guests made a special point of seeking them out to offer congratulations.

Lady Clarinda and Lady Madeline decided the fence had been hurdled without undue aggravation, noting that Philip had everything under control. So they disappeared into the cardroom and, with their usual conservative play as partners at whist, managed to end the evening with a little extra pin money.

The next morning Philip went downstairs early to wait for his love. When she appeared a little after ten, he unceremoniously pulled her into the library. Reaching into his pocket, he produced a large diamond, surrounded by rubies, which he placed on her finger, pronouncing peremptorily, "That, my love, makes it official."

"Philip—it is beautiful. I am *so* happy." This artless declaration was followed by an impulsive embrace which naturally encouraged a willing gentleman to take advantage of his most favoured status, and he crushed her to him, kissing her passionately.

"Oh, my!" a breathless young lady observed with a bemused expression. "You never kissed me like that before!"

"Not because I haven't wanted to, my love. But you will admit the practice is rather exciting, and you were determined to put off our wedding, so I thought I had better exercise some discretion. However—" And he clearly demonstrated a definite revision in his strategy.

"Philip," a small voice asked shyly, "do you feel the earth shaking?"

"Is that what it is?" a deeply affected young man marveled. "I wondered why my knees were playing me tricks."

With a happy laugh Danila exclaimed startlingly, "Oh, I can't wait to tell Eddy!"

This questionable ambition caused her betrothed to lean back and look at her dubiously. "I do hope, my love, that you do not have some sort of compulsion to tell Miss Eddington everything. It could have a regrettably depressing effect on our relationship."

The girl blushed and sputtered, "Philip! You know I wouldn't—I mean—oh—what a disgraceful man you are!" And she hid her face against his chest in embarrassment.

He laughed and stroked her hair, teasing, "Well, I just thought I ought to clarify the matter, darling, but I'm sure you have some particular conceit that I will find comprehensible."

Danila recovered her composure and related her conversation with her friend about earthshaking love affairs and revealed the circumstances of Eddy's brief marriage. "I just want to tell her I know how she felt," she explained.

"Well, I can tell you, I am much relieved," Philip asserted with an exaggerated sigh, a continuing provocation that earned him an aggressive pummeling which naturally inspirited him to demonstrate his male superiority, which in this instance Danila did not have a mind to contest.

After several more minutes of this improper behaviour Danila realized that the fluttering in her stomach could be attributed, at least in part, to the fact that she had not eaten breakfast, and they went to the morning room to join the countess and Lady Madeline, who were entertaining Jason with an exposition of the evening's favourable outcome.

They looked up to greet the moonstruck pair, and Jason congratulated his cousin on his mastery, wishing him continued success.

Danila took up the gauntlet immediately, striking an unladylike aggressive position with one hand on her hip, vowing, "Jason, if I didn't know that contrary to appearances, you do like me and that you approve of me as Philip's choice, I could become very much at odds with you for your constant aggravations."

Jason laughed and bent to kiss her forehead affectionately, informing her reasonably, "But you do know it, so you have no cause to fly into a miff."

"But that's just it! You always think everybody should know everything when it would be more to your credit if you told somebody something," she expostulated in exasperation, coming perilously close to betraying her friend.

Lady Clarinda and Lady Madeline looked at each other in dismay, and Philip dissolved into a bout of laughter. Jason grinned at his attacker and said softly, "Point taken, my dear," just as Laurel entered the room, asking whatever had set Philip off.

"Just one of my bride-to-be's predictable solecisms, Laurel. I shall have to become accustomed," Philip told her, and Danila held out her hand, showing off her ring to ward off further questions.

"It is beautiful, Danila, and I am glad you have given up your dissimulation," Laurel approved. "Now you can truly enjoy the rest of the Season."

"Yes, it is going to be lovely," a happy girl agreed as she sat down to a huge breakfast, casting a bright look at her betrothed, who came to sit next to her with a frankly adoring expression.

Jason refrained from making a laconic remark since he knew that very shortly he would feel free to acknowledge his own infatuation. He envied his cousin's preferred status and determined to establish himself in the same fashion as soon as he returned from Dismoreland.

He announced, "Today and tomorrow, Laurel, we will go to the drapers and the auction houses, and then I must make a trip to Sussex. I received a message from Master Corcoran that he required my presence to approve a slight change in the conservatory, and I have one or two other things to add to his labours. I will come back as soon as I can."

Laurel tried to hide her disappointment and asked casually, "Did he say how far along he was?"

"No, so I am anxious to know myself. I will soon be able to give you a full report. Are you ready to tramp the streets again?"

"Yes. Are we still concentrating on the windows today?"

"I think we should. We have to make a start. Did you form any general idea?" he asked as he led her to his carriage.

"Well, I wondered, Jason, if you mean to decorate the rooms as separate entities. I mean—will there be a red room, a blue room, and a green room, and so on?"

"That sounds impressive," he said, not exactly committing himself. "Is that your concept of how it should be?"

"Perhaps, in a restrained manner. I thought, if the colours were not too bold, a single one could serve as an accent in each room and give it a special notice of its own."

"That sounds excellent, and I trust your instinct, for you know that you have a better eye for colour than I do."

"But I should like your approval, Jason. It is your house after all."

"I will tell you if I don't like something, love, but we are partners, remember, and that is your part."

With this assurance Laurel let herself be convinced and proceeded to choose colours and fabrics as she would for her very own, looking occasionally at Jason for approval, when he would feel an obligation at least to state a preference. But generally he stood back and watched in amusement as she sent the proprietors of several shops scurrying to their storerooms to find a particular shade or trimming. By the end of the day she had nearly completed the entire house, which spoke wonders for the amount of thought she had devoted to the matter, being so sure of the exact thing she was looking for.

That evening they accompanied Philip and Danila to the theatre and enjoyed a late supper but did not remain out too late since they intended to make an early visit to the auction houses to inspect the items which would be offered later in the day.

There were a number of elegant pieces, and Jason tried to read the expression on Laurel's face when she examined some of the things that were designed for a lady's boudoir. He imagined he detected a faint covetousness when her eyes fell on an exquisite Louis XV poudreuse, decorated with marquetry and gilded bronze, and a Sheraton lady's writing table with a sliding fire screen, both of which he determined to acquire for her because he knew she would not single them out herself.

She did remark on a mahogany architect's table with Chinese fretwork, and she announced *she* would bid on that. He made no objection and commented that *he* had rather a fancy for the impressive Louis XVI carved and gilt canopy bed, hung with faded tapestries.

Laurel privately thought it was a little ornate for a man's bedroom, but with new subdued drapery it might look less out of place. There were other pieces that also met their prerequisites, but once the bidding started, only these described were of enough interest that Jason stayed in the auction until he prevailed.

Laurel was disconcerted by certain of his purchases, and she realized that if things were going to work out as she hoped, he had bought them for her, a lovely thought which delighted her. But they were especially beautiful, and he could have meant them for one of the guest bedrooms. This dilemma of not knowing exactly how things stood was becoming oppressive, and she often had an attack of the nerves from the realization that she could no longer be satisfied with her old role.

Jason returned her to Portland Place and remained for dinner. When the others began to leave for their various engagements, he bade Laurel good night, warning her to beware of overeager suitors, promising to return posthaste to remain until the end of the Season.

Chapter
TWELVE

When Laurel wakened, she heard the patter of light rain, and she rose from her bed to look out the window. The skies were overcast, not with heavy black clouds, but with an almost uniform gray shroud that did not augur well for the enjoyment of outdoor activities. Often such an unfavourable weather condition could prevail for days, and she thought dismally that it properly suited her mood, remembering that Jason had gone. It dismayed her that just knowing she would not see him could be so depressing to her spirits. She had become snugly accustomed to enjoying his daily presence and, in her melancholy frame of mind, acutely recognized that she had become increasingly dependent on him for her happiness. She stood staring into the mist and considered how she had progressed to this fateful point, no longer having any illusions about how devastated she would be if she had to face a future without him. She knew that her attachment had reached dangerous proportions because one always had to acknowledge the conceivability of separation brought to pass by one of a number of unblessed circumstances. It seemed more important than ever that they should marry, for then there would be the happy prospect of children, who would be of great consolation to either of them if some dreadful calamity should beset them. After a few more moments of indulging in these dark contemplations she shook herself determinedly, trying to throw off her gloomy humour. The best cure she knew would be to seek out Danila, whose unfailingly cheerful disposition had a naturally inspiriting effect on her friends. Laurel dressed leisurely because the betrothed couple had attended a late party. The other ladies also had been engaged at another affair until the early morning, so she knew that the household would remain quiet for several more hours. But she had not eaten since last night's relatively early dinner, and she realized she was hungry. She went down to the small breakfast room that looked out onto the garden to find Lord Schofield just being served by the footman. He looked up with a smile of welcome.

"Good morning, Laurel. I hope you mean to brighten this day with your sunny presence," he greeted gallantly, bringing a smile to her face.

"My lord," she said primly, "it is early in the day to be playing the humbug. But you would be better served if Danila were here since I find myself in the doldrums this morning."

"My dear, I know you would prefer to have another gentleman in my place, but do you think you could make some effort to appear pleased?" the earl chided lightly with an understanding smile.

In embarrassment Laurel apologized, "Lord John, I am truly sorry to be so mumpish. You know very well you are one of my most favourite gentlemen, and I count myself extremely fortunate to have your exclusive company." Accepting a filled plate, she prompted, "I hope you will bring me up to date with all the latest happenings. These past few weeks I have been so caught up in frivolous pursuits, and even before, Jason and I were so involved in the Dismoreland project that I did not keep abreast of public events."

"Well, Laurel," the earl told her ruefully, "I don't think my expositions will lighten your mood, but I promise at least to distract you. I'm afraid that our royal family has been providing most of the table talk. Since the first of the year they have been served one affliction after another. First the Duke of Kent died, leaving his infant daughter, who will likely be queen one day. And then, a few days later, the old king finally gave up the ghost. As if that weren't enough, his heir nearly followed and in fact did not recover from his malady in time to attend his father's funeral."

"I *had* heard of the King's death, but not of the new King's illness. Was it really serious?" Laurel asked uncertainly since George IV had a history of alarming indispositions.

"Yes," the earl affirmed. "He almost died. It was a close thing. Fortunately he recovered because his politics are more acceptable than those of York. Then no sooner had the succession been resolved than we were unsettled by that madman Thistlewood."

"I have heard something about *that*, of course, since the trial was held since we came to town," Laurel said, "though I never quite understood what it was all about."

"It isn't easy to understand, Laurel. Thistlewood was a dedicated, somewhat naïve malcontent who was involved in a number of revolutionary demonstrations and was even arrested a few years ago after the Spa Field riots, but he was no match for the professional intriguers. The government has numerous spies who infiltrate the radical groups. I find myself more than a little at odds with the policies of the Home Office in using these rabble-rousers for their own purposes. I'm afraid some of our leaders have become rather overzealous in their desire to maintain the status quo of our social and political structures. Ever since the French and American revolutions we have had this ominous feeling of an impending uprising in England. The war with Napoleon served as a deterrent because the country had a common purpose, but afterwards, particularly when our economy suffered a postwar depression, the farmers and workers began to organize and cause minatory disturbances. So some misguided leaders conceived the plan of sending an *agent provocateur* among the plotters to encourage them to commit excesses which would turn the masses against them. I'm afraid Thistlewood and his companions were caught up in just such a scheme. One of their numbers was a certain Edwards who was a government spy, and when it became known that the group meant to plan and carry out some grand masterstroke, he urged them on until they conceived the appalling idea of assassinating the entire Cabinet on February twenty-third, when its members were to gather for dinner at Lord Harrowby's on Grosvenor Square. Can you imagine the disaster— Wellington, Castlereagh, Sidmouth, and the others all at one fell swoop?"

Laurel shuddered and dissented, "It doesn't bear thinking of. It's fortunate that the conspirators were apprehended before they could carry out their plan."

"Yes," Lord Schofield agreed with a wry expression. "They were captured at their meeting place on Cato Street, but the irony of it, my dear, is that they were bamboozled into the business, for there was never to be a Cabinet meeting in the first place."

Laurel looked at him in dismay and then said softly, "And some of them were hanged last week."

"Yes," the earl affirmed with a solemn face.

"What a dreadful story," Laurel denounced feelingly. "I suppose there was some purpose to it."

"Some thought so at any rate. There was to be a general election in March, you see, and the government wanted to discredit the radicals."

Laurel could not recover from the shock and lamented shakily, "I had no idea things like that went on."

"Politics, my dear, can be a very dirty business. It is incredible what power and privilege mean to some people and what they will do to keep it or get it. And for now it looks as though the Tories are safe. There have been a few other disturbances in the Midlands, but things seem to be settling down now that there is a promising improvement in the economy. And a good thing, too, because there will be enough of a donnybrook when the queen returns. One can only hope she will change her mind. Even Brougham is trying to dissuade her, but he should know she is not reasonable. I expect we will have to muddle through another royal scandal," he said with a deep sigh.

"Poor King George," Laurel sympathized. "He seems to have the most frightful luck in his private relationships, but I *do* wish he would contrive to *keep* them private."

"Well, with his lamentable lack of self-discipline he does rather bring a lot of the ridicule by the cartoonists on himself, although the disastrous marriage he made almost a quarter of a century ago—which likely accounts for many of the indiscretions that have made him seem the fool, for who knows what might have been if he could have married a woman he could like and respect—was forced on him by the old king, who seemed to have a regrettable compulsion to direct and so ruin the personal lives of nearly every one of his fifteen children. The poor princesses were always pitied for their rather dreary existences in what they themselves called their Nunnery."

Laurel sat back and smiled as she admonished, "Well, my lord, I can't say that your conversations have been particularly cheerful on this rather inauspicious day. But you did warn me, and I will admit that contemplating other people's misfortunes does at least serve to take you out of yourself."

The earl laughed and apologized. "I'm sorry, my dear. I should have tried to raise your spirits instead of relating all these depressing stories, but you are such a good listener that I let myself ramble on unforgivably."

"No, Lord John, I am glad you spoke as you did. It is not commendable that people should become so wrapped in cotton wool that they do not know what is going on in the world around them. I admit I have an unworthy impulse to leave town before the trial begins. But just closing one's eyes does not change things, and I suppose we all are going to have to bear the disgrace."

"Well, after it is all over, we will have a big celebration," the earl declared in an effort to look on a bright prospect. "One we have not had for sixty years, before either of us was born. I am sure the king will make it a spectacular show since he has been awaiting the day for a long time. I know that it galls him to have to postpone it, but he will not consider staging the coronation until this matter with the queen is resolved."

"There *is* that," Laurel agreed dubiously as she sat with her chin in her hand and a pensive look in her eye.

Philip entered to find two strangely quiet woolgatherers drinking their coffee, and he quizzed, "I know the weather is particularly inclement, but I do think your long faces rather exaggerate the point. You haven't come to cuffs, have you?"

Laurel and Lord Schofield looked up, a little startled by this unceremonious interruption, suggesting a totally improbable state of affairs, and they invited him to join them with smiles of reassurance.

"We have just taken the cares of the world on our shoulders and are finding them a heavy load," the earl told his son whimsically.

"My God! I hope you have it out of your systems," Philip exclaimed, staring at them disapprovingly. "I am feeling in especially high feather this morning and do not propose to be dashed down by depressing conversations."

Laurel giggled and charged, "You need not worry. I defy anyone to pose a serious mien when you are disposed to play the fool."

Philip grinned appreciatively and sat down with a heaping plate, remarking, "Danila and I were planning to go to Kew Gardens today and meant to claim your company, but that appears out of the question, so I am open to suggestions. What would you like to do?"

"Philip, you do not have to entertain me. I'm sure you and Danila would like some time alone."

"Laurel," the young man admonished with an air of impatience, "please do not be tiresome. I do not wish to debate the matter every time I ask you to accompany us. I insist that you just naturally presume that we wish you to join us. Do you think you could bring yourself to do that?"

"Well, that is my second setdown this morning," Laurel

said ruefully, "and I have to credit them to my ungracious manners, so I will try to put on a more pleasant face. Now. What does one do in London on such a beastly day?"

Lord Schofield rose and remarked dryly, "I don't know what you pleasure seekers can do, but I have to go listen to more arguments about the queen's return. The total immersion into the matter by the members has brought all other deliberations to a standstill, and it almost seems that the government is in abeyance. However, there is nothing for it but to get it over with, so I will leave you now. I would offer you orders of admission to the gallery, but the spectacle would only be dispiriting." And with a sigh of resignation he went to gather some papers from his study.

Laurel noted, "Lord John is really distressed about this grievous business, isn't he? I wouldn't have thought it would be that calamitous. There is a precedent after all."

"I expect he has received some intelligence about what evidence will be offered at the trial, and it offends his sense of dignity. He has become unhappily disenchanted with our outlandish royal family. Not to the point of being a republican, but he does think the crown should address itself to improving its image and so more solemnly represent the country."

"Yes, that would be more seemly, but one has to remember that despite their exalted station, they are only humans after all," Laurel said reasonably.

"So they are, my dear, though they are apt to have delusions of the old concept of divine right. It might take a few more generations to wipe that out entirely."

Danila came in on that last observation and asked curiously, as she noticed their serious faces, "What are you two talking about?"

Philip rose to kiss her good morning and advised, "We were just remarking the undignified picture our royal family presents to the public."

Danila wrinkled her nose and deplored, "I do think that is a particularly dreary subject, and it is enough that we should have to be subjected to Cruikshank's odiously coarse cartoons without bringing it up at the breakfast table. I hope you do not mean to pursue the matter."

Laurel and Philip looked at each other and burst into immoderate laughter until Danila stamped her foot and demanded that they cease immediately because what she said could not have been that funny and she meant to be let in on the joke.

Laurel informed her, wiping the tears from her face, "Oh, Danila, it *was* funny because Philip said much the same thing when he came in on Lord John and me discussing other infelicitous affairs. Being caught a second time, I confess myself the culprit."

"Well, we shall just have to find some pleasant activity that will divert you," Danila decided as she sat down to nibble on a biscuit. "What *are* we going to do today?"

"Couldn't we just stay home?" Laurel asked quizzically. "We will be drenched if we step outside the door. Don't you have some preparations to make for your wedding?"

"We do have some things to talk over, love," Philip told his betrothed. "I should like for us to be married as soon as the Season is over."

Danila gave him an approving smile and vowed, "Yes, I would like that also, darling. Philip, I wonder, since we have to postpone our visit to Kew, if we might not venture out to call on Mr. Halliburton. I think you should probably discuss my holdings with him so that we will have some idea of just what our responsibilities are. We may even want to dispose of some of the properties."

"Well, if you really want to brave the elements, we could do that," Philip agreed. "Do you want us to drop you off at the library, Laurel?"

"No, thank you. I have a number of things to keep me busy. Run along. I will be quite content left to my own devices."

After Philip and Danila left, Laurel went to the study and settled down to read *Ivanhoe*, which was almost always in someone's hands. Lady Clarinda and Lady Madeline looked in on her after an hour or so, and she joined them while they ate a light late breakfast. They were all appreciating the lazy day and presently wandered off to busy themselves with their own concerns.

The rain began to let up a little after noon, and about two o'clock the butler came to inform Laurel that Lord Orwell had called and requested a private audience.

She looked up in panic. Although she had been aware of the possibility that she would have to face up to refusing his offer, she had hoped he was astute enough to have devined her unreceptive attitude.

The butler suggested expressionlessly, "If you are not feeling good, Miss Laurel, I will so inform the gentleman."

Laurel smiled ruefully and bemoaned, "I wish it were that easy, Digby, but it would only put off the ordeal. I shall just have to bear up. Would you ask my mother to come to me? You may explain so she will understand."

"Yes, Miss Laurel."

A few moments later Lady Madeline entered to find her daughter battling her apprehensions. "My dear, do not be in such a taking. You have only to say no."

"But I hoped never to find myself in such a position that I should have to go through this, Mama. I *knew* I shouldn't have come to town."

"Laurel, don't be absurd. It is the natural order. Lord Orwell has been a widower for eight years and is considered a matrimonial prize of the first stare. Dozens of girls would envy you your position, not," Lady Madeline disclaimed as she noticed her daughter's shocked expression, "that I should wish you to consider his offer. You know I do not. But you should do him the courtesy to hear him out."

"But, Mama, he is so obtuse. I don't seem to be able to make him understand," Laurel wailed. "Would you—would you come with me?"

"It would not be seemly, my love. You are of age and must speak for yourself. However, I will come to your rescue in fifteen minutes if he is still here."

"Oh," Laurel said wrathfully, "how dare Jason leave me when he had to be aware that I would be approached! It was a dastardly thing to do, and so I shall tell him!"

"My dear, will you stop procrastinating? Raining animadversions on Jason's head will not resolve this particular matter."

"All right! I'm going. But I shall never forgive any of you for getting me into this," she announced dramatically and flounced out of the room, marching resolutely to the parlour, and, with only the slightest hesitation, opened the door to face a tall, slender black-browed gentleman with a long, solemn face.

She forced herself to remark pleasantly, "Good afternoon, Lord Orwell. I am surprised to see you on this extremely dismal day."

"Dismal it would seem, Miss Ingram, but for *my* purposes I find it entirely propitious, for I made sure you would be at home," a determined suitor told her blandly.

Laurel suddenly had an uncontrollable urge to babble and blurted out, "Yes, well, of course, like yourself, there are those who do not let such a little matter deter them. Philip and Danila were not at all daunted and kept an appointment. They asked me to join them, and so I should have, for one must learn to live with the unpredictable weather in London, don't you agree? It's just that I am not yet accustomed and I—well, you know what I mean. I do hope I don't become one of those die-away females who take cover at the slightest thing. Do you suppose I am so inclined? What a dreadful thing that would be—"

"Miss Ingram," Lord Orwell interrupted impatiently, not amused by this sudden loquacity, which he found most unbecoming. "I have come on a personal matter, and I beg you to attend me. First, however, there are some questions I should like to ask. Tell me, Miss Ingram, do you like children?"

Laurel was taken aback by this blunt approach and thought it a particularly nefarious strategy, for try as she might, she could not bring herself to say that she detested the little monsters, and she replied reluctantly, "Well, of course—what a poor female I should be if I did not."

He smiled approvingly and advised, "I assure you, Miss

Ingram, that being a female does not make that a natural outcome. My wife thoroughly disliked them."

"Even her own?" Laurel asked involuntarily.

"Yes. She never wished to be bothered with them. She was a very vain woman and was not satisfactory as a wife or a mother," he told her unemotionally.

"Oh, I'm sorry," Laurel said weakly, desperately wishing that fifteen minutes would pass before he got to the point.

"Yes, it was an unfortunate connection, which is what has discouraged me from considering marrying a second time. However, I am very fond of my children, and I have come to think that my daughters at least would be well served were I to provide them with a mother. In the coming years they will need a woman's guidance. My son, of course, will go to Eton. I have been very impressed with your maturity and your pleasant manner, Miss Ingram, and I am persuaded you have all the qualities that would become a wife and mother. So I have decided to offer you that role in my household. I hope you will accept."

Laurel stared at him incredulously, for she had never imagined a proposal of marriage would be so totally dispassionate. It was rather lowering actually, and she had the most absurd desire to burst out laughing. She had been dreading this moment, having visions of being embarrassed by a display of ardour or, at least, some tender feeling. But here was this man practically offering her an insult, and in her resentment she had no qualms about depressing his ambitions forthwith.

"Lord Orwell, I am honoured that you hold such a high opinion of me, but I am afraid you really do not know me very well. I do have a career, you know, which would keep me from being a full-time wife and mother. I work closely with Jason Devereaux, and I cannot believe a husband would countenance such a situation," she informed him deliberately.

"You may be sure I will not, Miss Ingram," a shocked gentleman declared forcefully. "I have not approved of that connection, but I decided to overlook it since once we are married, you will naturally disassociate yourself from such improper activities."

Beginning to bridle up, Laurel advised heatedly, "Lord Orwell, I wish you will not speak as though it were a settled thing. I have not said I would marry you. In fact, nothing is farther from my mind. I am sorry you insisted upon making me an offer. I have tried to make my position clear, but you paid no heed, and we are come to this!"

"Miss Ingram, I know it is often the case that a girl who is older—"

"I am only twenty-two!"

"—has accepted the fact that she may not marry, and no doubt you will need some time to accustom yourself to the happy prospect. I shall, of course, indulge you in this, but I would like to announce our engagement very shortly so that we might be married within the month. I have to return to my estate in Yorkshire and would see this settled."

"Lord Orwell," Laurel pleaded in exasperation, "you are not listening to me. I have refused you. I have no intention of giving up my work, and I will *not* change my mind."

A displeased gentleman looked at her frowningly, but before he could censure her, Lady Madeline knocked lightly and entered, saying pleasantly, "I apologize for intruding, Lord Orwell, but I am sure you understand that I have a concern for my daughter's reputation."

"Of course, Lady Madeline, you are quite right, and I confess that I did not think the matter would take so long to be resolved. I'm afraid Miss Ingram is showing herself to be deplorably willful. I hope you will be able to persuade her to be more reasonable." He turned to Laurel and told her condescendingly, "I will send for my children, who are staying with my sister in Kent, and bring them to meet you. I am sure you will find them charmingly behaved and not have reservations on that point. I leave you to reconsider and will return in a few days." And before Laurel and Lady Madeline could protest this intention, he had bowed out of the room, leaving two dismayed ladies looking at each other, totally at a loss for words.

Just as Lord Orwell was climbing into his carriage, Philip and Danila returned, and Danila demurred apprehensively, "Oh dear, do you suppose—?"

"Very likely," Philip confirmed. "And I suspect Laurel is regretting that she did not accompany us. She is probably in a devil of a temper."

They entered immediately to join mother and daughter, who had just begun to discuss the distressing interview. They were invited to come in and close the door.

"No doubt you observed the departure of our visitor," Laurel observed caustically.

"Yes, love," Danila said sympathetically. "Did he come up to scratch?"

"Do you know," Laurel deplored, looking at her friend with a baleful eye, "that I find that expression particularly offensive? It seems almost defamatory as a description of a proposal of marriage, not," she added acerbically, "that I find the experience of receiving one especially flattering." And then, suddenly being overcome with the absurdity of the affair, she put her hands over her mouth to keep from laughing but could not suppress her amusement, and she bemoaned, "Oh, dear, I fear I am totally depraved to show so little sensibility, but the whole thing is absolutely ridiculous." And she described Lord Orwell's proposal and his unshakable pomposity. "Now, even though I have said 'No!' and vexed him with references to my work, he has announced his intention of sending for his children to bring them to meet me!"

"What ails the man?" Danila spouted indignantly.

"I expect, my love," Philip surmised with a grin, "that my lord has become so toplofty after these several years of being considered a prime catch that it never once occurred to him that his suit could be refused."

"That was obvious," Laurel stated huffily. "He turned a deaf ear to my protests and proceeded to tell me how it would be. I was never so frustrated in my life. Can't we do something before he comes back with his children? Philip, can't you talk to him?"

"No hope there, I'm afraid. He would only suspect me

of ulterior motives since I had supposedly been one of your suitors myself."

"Well, we shall have to dissuade him somehow because I will not receive him when next he comes. How dreadful it would be to have to refuse him again with three pairs of trusting eyes looking at me hopefully. I couldn't possibly face it!"

"Of course not, love," Danila reassured her. "I must say, it is just like Jason to be unavailable when you need him. But don't worry. We will think of something," a predictable promise that made them all dissolve into laughter.

The following day the skies were still gray, but it was not raining, so the three friends decided to chance it and packed a picnic lunch, determined to enjoy their delayed excursion. After several pleasant hours they returned to prepare themselves for the evening's entertainment. Laurel once again refused to accompany the others, for she had no mind to risk the possibility of a confrontation with Lord Orwell.

In the morning Danila came to her room and informed her encouragingly that she did not need to play the hermit, "because I have discovered that your suitor has left town and is not expected back for three days. He has sent his regrets to several disappointed hostesses."

"Well, I suppose that much of a reprieve is a boon of sorts, but what will we do when he gets back?" Laurel said in relief.

"I'll—"

Laurel put up her hand and entreated, "Don't say it. I know. Just be sure you do."

They agreed to spend an afternoon at the shops, for Danila wished to choose some things for her trousseau. It was after four when they returned, and Digby immediately informed Laurel that Mr. Devereaux's man had delivered a message for her.

She took off her bonnet, threw it on a chair, and eagerly recovered the letter from the correspondence tray. Before she could open it, however, the knocker sounded, and both girls looked up to see Lord James Pittman being admitted.

His face lit up in a revealing smile as he saw Laurel, and he professed, "Miss Ingram, I hoped to find you at home. I have come to ask you to grant me a private interview."

Laurel looked at Danila miserably but resigned herself to her fate and decided to get it over with, so she responded, "Of course, Lord Pittman," and led the way to the parlour.

Danila hurried to report to Lady Madeline, who was sitting with Lady Clarinda in the drawing room, and an amused lady said whimsically, "Well, we will give him equal time. In fifteen minutes I will look in on them."

Downstairs an enamoured young man dropped to his knees by Laurel's side and vowed ardently, "Miss Ingram—Laurel—a beautiful name. It is ever in my mind, for so I think of you. I know you must realize how deeply affected I am. I'm afraid I have been rather obvious. And though I am aware that you have given me no encouragement, I could not but take heart when Lord Oxborough announced his engagement to Lady Danila. I had feared that you had a partiality for him, but you do not seem cut up, so I am persuaded that your attachment is not of a romantic nature."

"No, Lord Pittman, it was never that," Laurel said gently. "We have been good friends for many years, but—"

"Please, Laurel," the young lord interrupted pleadingly, "let me speak. I must tell you what is in my heart. I love you to distraction, and it is my greatest wish to have you by my side forever. My dearest Laurel, will you marry me?"

With a feeling of guilt at her unworthy reflection that "this is more like it" she found it much less comfortable to refuse him out of hand because this was the sort of thing she had been dreading. He was such a nice young man and so sincere and really had developed a passion for her. She felt truly unhappy to have to dash his hopes, and she searched her mind for a rejection that would not crush or humiliate him.

She reached out to take his hand, saying kindly, "Lord

Pittman, do come sit here on the couch, and we will speak frankly to one another," a suggestion which only half encouraged the young man as he looked at her with lovelorn eyes that made her wish to turn her head. She proceeded, "My lord, I am greatly honoured by your proposal, and it pains me to tell you that I cannot accept. But since you are such a superior gentleman, for whom I have much admiration, I will explain my refusal. I should not like you to think that I do not hold you in high regard. I must tell you, however, that I confide in you in the strictest confidence because it would be a embarrassment for me were my feelings to be known. You see, ever since I was a small child, I have had a special relationship with Jason Devereaux, and on my side at least it has become a deep and lasting love. I hope for an eventual marriage, but if it should never come to pass, I will just content myself with being his friend and assistant. It is important to me to continue our close association, and I could not do anything that would break my ties with him. I hope you will understand."

Even in his disappointment, Lord Pittman remained a considerate gentleman and he said gratefully, "Thank you for telling me, Miss Ingram—"

"—Laurel," she prompted.

"—Laurel. I did not realize, though perhaps I should have, for I have received more than one black look from him. If I had not been distracted by my preoccupation of Philip's status, I might have been more percipient. You need not be concerned, my dear. It is apparent to me now that Jason considers you his very own."

"I feel you are right, Lord Pittman—"

"James," he interposed with a wry smile.

"James—and I hope you will someday find a lovely girl who will love you as you deserve. We will remain friends, I hope."

"Of course. But I think now I will leave town to spend some time at my seat in Norfolk. I wish you every happiness, Laurel."

"Thank you, James, and I am truly sorry," she repeated with a sincere sympathy. "I never meant for you to be hurt."

"I know, my dear. You did not give me false hopes, but it was impossible not to fall in love with you. You are so very beautiful."

A few minutes after he left Lady Madeline entered the room to find her daughter alone with tears rolling down her face.

"My dear, was it very bad?"

"Dreadful," a miserable young lady confirmed. "Mama, he was so sweet and sincere, and I feel the veriest wretch."

"Yes, it is unfortunate that he fell deeply in love with you, for his mother wished for him to choose a bride this Season. Now I suspect it will be some time before he will listen to her importunities."

"Well, thank goodness that it is all over," Laurel said in relief.

"I think you are mistaken," her mother informed her enigmatically.

"What do you mean?" the girl asked uncertainly and then remembered, "Oh, of course, I shall have to find some way of avoiding Lord Orwell on his return."

"I wasn't considering him," her mother admitted.

"There are no others, Mama. There just couldn't be. I have not encouraged anyone."

"You do not have to, darling. You are so beautiful and charming that men can't help wanting you, and I have seen the signs of infatuation in at least two more cases."

"Who?" Laurel asked doubtfully.

"The Honourable Carlton Smythe—"

"He is just a baby!"

"He is twenty-three—and then there is that lecherous Duke of Yarwood, a notorious roué who is not to be trusted. You must refuse to see him alone—here or anywhere."

With a look of distaste Laurel deplored feelingly, "He is absolutely nauseating, and though I have noticed his leers, I never supposed he would make an honourable offer."

"I have a feeling he intends to, my love, so I beg you to beware," her mother warned again.

Suddenly Laurel remembered her letter, and she took it out of her pocket. "I have a message from Jason, Mama, but I have not had a chance to open it. Perhaps he is coming back, and I can rely on his protection." She read:

> *My dear Laurel,*
> *You are going to be very excited when you see how things are progressing here. Everything is shaping up excellently, although the artisans are a little behind schedule because of a delay in the delivery of some materials. I have decided to stay awhile longer to supervise the work while Master Corcoran makes a quick trip to Southampton to receive some more tiles from Portugal. I know you will be unhappy with me, but I have a particular interest that the work move as quickly as possible, so I will remain at least another week. If you have time and can persuade one of our members to accompany you, I wish you will choose wallpaper for the formal dining room, which is near completion. Jenkins will be returning to Sussex, and I hope you will send me a message. I will return as soon as I can. Tell Philip I count on his guardianship.*
> *With deepest affection,*
> *Jason*

This unpropitious communication sent an unhappy girl, already in a state of the dismals, into the depths once again, and she bemoaned with a hurt expression, "He promised he wouldn't leave me, but now he means to stay in Sussex another week or so. He probably won't come back at all!"

Lady Madeline asked curiously, "Has he met with some problem?"

"Nothing serious," Laurel denied resentfully. "He just wants to supervise the work while Master Corcoran is away for a few days."

"That sounds reasonable, my love," her mother admonished with an amused smile.

"At this point I don't feel like being reasonable. I wish I could go into seclusion like Theo." And in sudden inspiration Laurel exclaimed, "That's a famous idea! I will move in with Theo, and when Lord Orwell or anyone else inquires for me, you can say I have gone to visit a friend and do not plan to return for several days!"

"Laurel, that is a little drastic," her mother protested.

"No, it isn't. It's perfect," her daughter insisted. "I know Theo won't mind."

"Of course, she won't, love, and I suppose it would save you some embarrassing interviews," Lady Madeline conceded.

"Yes, I shall go tonight after dinner."

She hurried upstairs to her room to direct Carrie to pack some clothes for a week's absence and was soon disturbed by Danila, who cried in dismay, "What are you doing?"

"I am going to stay with Theo. I have had enough of refusing offers. Mama says I could expect two more, and I am crying craven."

"Surely Jason will be back in a day or so, and you need not go into hiding," Danila objected critically.

With an ironic look Laurel handed her the letter. When she finished reading, Danila expostulated, "Well, *that* is what one might have expected! Obviously he hasn't changed a bit. We should never have allowed him to leave town. When he returns—"

"If he does," Laurel said dubiously.

"He had better, or we will send Philip after him," her friend threatened darkly. "This is beyond anything, and we are going to have to take some drastic action. Your suitors don't seem to worry him in the least."

"Well, they worry me," Laurel attested, "and I don't mean to subject myself to any more overtures. I will send a message by Jenkins to tell Jason of my move and will make it seem that I decided to keep Theo company."

"You should tell him the truth. Perhaps he would return immediately."

"No. For while I am miffed because he broke his promise, I don't doubt he has a good reason for remaining."

The other members of the household were informed at dinner of Laurel's plans, and being sympathetic to her uneasiness, they did not try to dissuade her since she would be only a few blocks away. A note had been delivered to Theo Devereaux, and she had extended a warm welcome. So a trunk was sent ahead, and Philip and Danila dropped Laurel at Cavendish Square on their way to the theatre.

Chapter
THIRTEEN

Laurel settled in at Dismore House, feeling pleasantly relieved at having foiled her admirers. She happily set up a work area in the library, where Jason had spread out the plans for Dismoreland. Deciding to amuse herself by choosing not only the wallpaper for the dining room but for the bedchambers as well, she took the first step, planning colour schemes for all the rooms. Once again in her element, she lost herself in her labours, forgetting the pressures that had persuaded her to try to escape.

A few blocks away Danila was having a recurrence of her preoccupation with Jason's insensibility, and she was experiencing a feeling of urgency. By the time he came back to town, the Season would be almost over. She knew that Philip would likely forbid her to return to Sussex, as she would feel obliged to do if the matter were not resolved before it was time to leave. So Jason was just going to have to declare himself forthwith. She concentrated on inventing some diversion that would shock him out of his insufferable indifference. As she visualized possible courses of action, some of which approached the bizarre, she began to have reservations herself and decided it would be best not to discuss her options with Philip, who she suspected, with an understandable sense of guilt, would likely not approve of her somewhat drastic measures. For the moment, however, she held her schemes in abeyance since nothing could be done until Jason returned.

After several days of nonappearance by the object of their affections, His Grace the Duke of Yarwood and his young rival, the Honourable Carlton Smythe, were beginning to suspect that she might have left town, and they were obliged to resort to pressing the matter through an intermediary.

At the same time, not being aware that Laurel had withdrawn from the social scene, Lord Orwell, on his return, sent a message announcing his intention to call the following afternoon to acquaint Miss Ingram with his children. Though the letter was addressed to Laurel, Lady Madeline made free to open it. With a sense of culpability, attributable to her insistence that Laurel come to town, she felt obligated to checkmate the ambitious gentlemen who sought her daughter's hand in marriage.

She immediately penned a reply informing the presumptuous lord that Laurel was no longer in residence at Schofield House and that if he wished to pursue the matter, she would grant him an audience the next afternoon at two o'clock.

Before having properly primed herself for this confrontation, she was faced with yet another challenge. At eleven the following morning Mr. Smythe called. On being advised that Miss Ingram was away and was not expected back for several days, in desperation he asked if Lady Ingram would vouchsafe him an interview. The request was relayed, and with an air of martydom Lady Madeline descended to the parlour to hear the professions of a young man in the throes of his first serious infatuation.

With a somewhat flustered air he began, "Lady Madeline, you are very gracious to receive me. I had hoped particularly to see Miss Ingram and was disappointed to learn that she has left. I wonder if I might beg her direction."

"Mr. Smythe," Lady Madeline said gently, for this was an estimable young man who had a lot of promise, "at the risk of seeming unmannered, I must tell you, with the honourable intention to save you and Laurel an embarrassment, that she is aware of your aspirations and, with an excess of sensitivity, felt disinclined to have to refuse your offer, as she certainly must." Taking pity on him in his disappointment, she explained kindly, "It is nothing to do with you really, you know. Her affections have long been centered on another gentleman, and she could never entertain the thought of marrying anyone else."

The young man sighed in dejection and admitted, "I never really expected she would accept me. She has so many admirers and is so incredibly beautiful, but I had to put it to the touch. Hoping for a miracle, I suppose."

Lady Madeline smiled in sympathy and reassured him, "You are very young yet, Mr. Smythe, and have many admirable qualities. I am sure, when you bestow your affections again, you will not suffer another disappointment."

"You are very kind, Lady Ingram, and I appreciate your delicacy in this affair." He rose to leave and asked with an appealing sincerity, "You will tell Miss Ingram of my profound regret and that I wish her every happiness?"

"Of course, and I assure you she will count herself sincerely honoured that you wished to make her an offer."

Lady Madeline went upstairs to report to Lady Clarinda and remarked facetiously, "Well, two down and two to go—at least I hope it is only two."

"Well," her friend apprised, "you can be thankful that Philip has staked his claim, or we would be having the same trials with Danila. Our girls have created quite a stir."

"So they have. But as her guardian Jason would have had the responsibility to flummox Danila's suitors. Really, I am so put out with that young man. If he weren't such a slowtop, we would not be faced with these vexatious importunities."

"Maddy, I think you are trying to deceive yourself. I suspect you are reveling in turning away the moonstruck gentlemen, for you have long imagined Laurel as a belle."

With a sheepish face an unmasked lady confessed, "So I might have before we came to town, but I am come to find my role as mother protectress exceedingly cheerless."

Lady Clarinda laughed and wished her luck with her next interview, which promised to be a bit less amiable.

Promptly at two Lord Orwell was admitted to the elegant reception hall at Schofield House and was ushered to the parlour, where Lady Madeline awaited him. She felt an instant annoyance at his arrogant posture, but she said pleasantly, "Do come be seated, my lord."

"Thank you, but I prefer to stand," an obviously angry gentleman replied ungraciously.

"Well, if you insist, I will stand also because you are so very tall that it quite pains my neck to be looking up at you," Lady Madeline regretted and then waited expectantly for him to sit down.

Despite his intention to maintain a commanding presence, he was forced to bend to the point of showing his hostess due courtesy. So he sat stiffly on a chair and forthwith vented his displeasure. "Lady Ingram, I hope you mean to explain how it is that your daughter is absent when I specifically informed her that I meant to return in a few days with my children."

"Yes, well, you see, *that* is why, Lord Orwell," Lady Madeline told him bluntly. "Laurel does not wish to marry you, and since you ignored her refusal and seemed to feel that her acceptance was merely a matter of course, she withdrew so as not to have to refuse you again after she had met your children. She feared you would have given them to understand that she was to be their new mother, and when that proved to be a gross misrepresentation, she did not want it to appear that she had reversed herself because of them."

He remained silent with a forbidding expression, unwilling to believe that he was actually being rejected. In the realization that he found the possibility intolerable, he knew that he was actually more deeply affected than he wished to acknowledge and felt impelled to try to bring about a more favourable resolution. "Lady Ingram, perhaps I have been a little high-handed, but I am not a demonstrative man. Nevertheless, I assure you that I have a depth of feeling for your daughter and would treat her with honour and affection. I would bestow a handsome settlement, and she would have an important position as a marchioness. Surely as her mother you can see the advantages of such a connection. I would hope that you would use your influence to persuade Miss Ingram to take time to reconsider."

With this uncharacteristic relaxation of his arrogant posture Lady Madeline found it harder to treat him cavalierly, and she began to suspect that she was becoming uncommonly softhearted as she found herself explaining once again, "Lord Orwell, I am altogether prejudiced myself, so I can understand your regard. But in confidence I tell you that Laurel has been in love with Jason Devereaux forever, and though he has not yet declared himself, I am confident that they will soon be married. I have no wish to interfere. For that matter I could not. She is singularly self-possessed and means to direct her own destiny."

"I see," Lord Orwell said after a moment, when the futility of pursuing the matter became obvious. "It was not readily apparent, or I should not have allowed myself to entertain any aspirations," he attested almost resentfully, as though he had been taken in. "Of course, under those circumstances, I must consider myself well out of it, and you may assure Miss Ingram I will not repeat my offer."

In a benevolent manner, knowing he was genuinely disappointed, Lady Madeline allowed him his little delusion and merely remarked, "I am glad you understand, my lord," and courteously saw him to the door.

Once more she returned to her friend's boudoir to describe this latest hearing, bemoaning, "Really, Clarinda, that man is insufferably high in the instep. It was all I could do to behave with a proper degree of civility."

"I know. People like that, who are so impressed with their own consequence, are what give the nobility a bad name," the countess affirmed. "And it is regrettable because he is not really a bad sort and would make an admirable husband for some docile young lady."

"Perhaps, but he sets his sights too high," Lady Madeline deplored acerbically.

Lady Clarinda laughed and charged, "Maddy, you are a quiz. I hope you have your wits about you when Yarwood decides to put himself forward. He does not have the instincts of a gentleman."

"Well, with my experience I am sure I will handle him very creditably."

This confident posture was put to the test two evenings later, when Lady Madeline accompanied the earl and the countess to a reception for foreign dignitaries at Lord Castlereagh's. The duke, being a staunch Tory supporter, was also in attendance. After dinner His Grace approached Lady Madeline purposefully, inquiring, "I have missed the beauteous Laurel these last several days. Surely she has not left town already?"

"She has gone to stay with a friend, Your Grace. I do not know when she intends to return. I am afraid she is not enamoured with the London social whirl."

"You should have initiated her earlier," the duke chided blandly. "She would have found it easier."

"It was her choice to remain in the country," he was told tersely.

"I am very much attracted to her, I am sure you have observed," he continued, undeterred by her unfriendly manner.

"You and many others," Lady Madeline remarked indifferently.

"None of higher consequence, however. Eligible dukes are in short supply."

"Actually I know of no eligible dukes," an ill-disposed lady noted significantly.

"Maddy," His Grace admonished with an appreciative grin, "I hope you don't mean to throw a spoke in the wheel. My intentions are strictly honourable, you know."

"That is open to question," she replied caustically. "You forget I have known you for many years and am fully aware of your degenerate character."

"Surely you do not still hold it against me that I aspired to exalt our acquaintance, my dear. You were and still are an extremely beautiful woman, and but for your age I would certainly consider making you my duchess. However, if I marry again, I am resolved to choose a younger woman, for while I do have an heir, I think it would be prudent to provide insurance."

With an expression of revulsion Lady Madeline accused, "Arthur, you must be totally depraved to be so insensible. I do not mean to stand here to bandy words with you. I can assure you that Laurel would not for an instant consider your proposal. She has rather a low opinion of you, and," she emphasized, throwing caution to the winds in an effort to put him out of court, "when I told her I suspected you would make her an offer, she was appalled and decided to forgo the honour because she found the prospect nauseating."

"That is too bad," the duke regretted silkily, with a predatory glint in his eye, "though I have never found a woman's resistance particularly unmanning."

"My God!" Lady Madeline exclaimed apprehensively. "I warn you, Arthur, do not think to force yourself upon Laurel. She is not without her protectors, you know, and if it is in your mind to employ some nefarious means to gain your end, then I assure you you had better set your house in order," a threat that effectively rang a bell.

"Maddy! How bloodthirsty you have become," he protested in mock reproval. "You have certainly made your point, however, and I will assure you that my passion for your daughter is not so strong that I should wish to tempt Fate. I shall redirect my goals." With a leering grin he retreated to join a group of his cronies, whose reputations were not much better than his.

On the way home Lady Madeline regaled her companions with what she considered her coup de grâce. In a lighter mood, now that she had enacted her responsibilities in such a commendable fashion, she announced that she would consult Theo on the prospect of staging a grand assembly at Dismore House before they returned to Sussex, insisting, over her host's assurance that there was no reason to hold it there when Schofield House was at her disposal, "That is extremely kind of you, John. But I know you would not permit me to foot the bill, and I want to give one party myself, as I do every year. Besides, I wish to involve Theo," she said mischievously.

The next afternoon Lady Madeline presented herself at Cavendish Square and looked in on Laurel, who had just returned from the British Museum with Jason's mother.

"I came to report, my love, that the coast is clear and you may come out of hiding."

Laurel had to laugh and asked, "Did you have a frightful time of it?"

"It was not past bearing," Lady Madeline replied smugly, "but I confess I should not like to make it a regular thing. Anyway, you may now return to the fold."

"Do I have to? I am so well set up here, and it would be such a bother to pack up and move again," Laurel said ruefully.

"You might as well come now, for it would not be permissible for you to remain when Jason returns, as I do not think polite society would consider Theo a proper chaperone," her mother reminded.

"Well, he still does not say when that might be, but I suppose I must go on the presumption that he will," Laurel acknowledged skeptically. "I will gather up my things and move tomorrow."

"All right, darling. Is Theo in a benevolent mood? I have a proposition to put to her."

"Yes, she has been very amiable, and we have made several excursions," Laurel said encouragingly.

Lady Madeline went to her friend's room and announced peremptorily, "Theo, I have decided we should hold a ball here in a week or so to cap off a particularly successful Season."

"Why here?" the poetess asked inhospitably.

"Because I do not have my own establishment, and I would prefer not to impose on John and Clarinda."

"But you don't mind imposing on me?" an unreceptive lady asked caustically.

"Theo, don't be bearish. You won't have to do anything except attend the party, I promise you. And if Jason comes up to scratch, as I expect him to when he returns to town, we will have a long-awaited announcement to make."

"What makes you think he means to do so?" Theo asked alertly.

"Nothing specific actually. I just think he will."

"Well," a hopeful mother agreed grudgingly, "I suppose it would be a proper forum for that event if you are right. But do not think I mean to let you run tame here. I intend to have a great deal to say about the proceedings."

"Why, of course, Theo, if you wish," Lady Madeline said innocently.

Her friend looked at her suspiciously, suddenly realizing that she had fallen into the trap, and she admonished, shaking her head, "Maddy, you are positively the most unscrupulous creature," and then reluctantly burst out laughing.

Laurel entered on this cordial scene and asked indulgently, "Just what have you two trumped up to put you in such good humour?"

"Your shameless parent has gulled me again, and I find myself committed to cosponsoring a ball," Theo explained forbearingly.

"You should be on to her tricks by now," Laurel teased.

"One would think so, my dear, though, in this case, I find myself agreeable, so I will not make a piece of work of it."

"Well then, I will leave you to your deliberations. Did Mama tell you I am returning to Schofield House tomorrow?"

"No, and I shall be sorry to see you leave, my love, but perhaps Jason will condescend to rejoin us shortly."

"I hope so," Laurel said wistfully.

The next afternoon, once again established on Portland Place, Laurel was sitting at her desk, rearranging her notes, when Danila intruded with her usual lack of ceremony and, kicking her shoes off, curled up on the bed.

Tapping her pen on the table, Laurel looked at her with

raised brows and asked pungently, "Whose quarters did you invade in this brazen manner when I wasn't here?"

"No one's," came an immediate plaintive reply. "I am glad you're back!"

Giving up any attempt to hand the shameless girl a set-down, since it was obviously a hopeless proposition, Laurel laughed and remarked affably, "I haven't seen you for a couple of days. What have you been doing?"

"Oh, the same old thing," Danila said offhandedly, revealing her disenchantment with the demands of society. "I will be glad when the Season is over. I would much rather be alone with Philip and my good friends."

"Well, darling, very soon you will have your wish. Have you set a date for the wedding yet?"

"No, and I am in such a quandary about that because you know I have pledged to see you affianced also before I will leave you. And we are no nearer to settling things than we were when we first came to London!"

Laurel stared at the girl in disbelief. "Danila, I am persuaded you do actually have a maggot in your brain! I would have thought by now that Philip would have brought you to reason. You *must* rid yourself of this ridiculous obsession."

"Well, for a while I did give over, and look what happened!"

"What happened?" Laurel asked dryly.

"Nothing! That's just it!" Danila proclaimed triumphantly.

A hard-pressed young lady put her hands on her head and moaned, "Oh, why do I give you these openings? You are absolutely incorrigible!"

"Laurel, when *is* Jason coming back?"

"I don't know," she admitted reluctantly. "He just says in a few days, but he has been gone almost two weeks already."

"Yes, and do not tell me you have not been unhappy because it is plain as pikestaff. So we are going to have to bring about a denouement before the Season is over. It is just as important for me as for you because Philip will

223

raise the devil of a dust if I insist upon returning to Sussex with you."

"You would not go so far as to jeopardize your own happiness!" Laurel protested reprovingly.

"I might not be able to help myself because I hate to give up," Danila replied ruefully. "I thought we were so close, and then we let him escape the net."

"Danila, please—"

"Do not try to dissuade me," a stubborn, muddleheaded girl warned determinedly. "I have been thinking—"

"Oh, no—not again. I can't bear it," Laurel groaned apprehensively, imagining herself being drawn into another harebrained scheme.

"Yes. Now, Laurel, our next move must be dramatic so that Jason is struck all of a heap and compromises himself—"

"Danila," Laurel interrupted blightingly, "I have divined your problem. You obviously live in a fantasy world and should learn to express yourself in writing, as Theo does. It would be much easier on your friends."

The girl giggled but was not deterred and continued, "There are several possibilities, and I thought I would let you choose."

"Thank you," Laurel said with exaggeration.

"I suspect," Danila admitted, suddenly having reservations about revealing her inspirations, "that you may not like any of them."

"How could you think so, I wonder?"

Indignantly Danila proclaimed, "*I* do not hold it all that amusing. It is a very serious matter, and I should hope you would consider it so yourself."

"All right, love, I will hear you out. I expect I have no choice anyway," Laurel said in sufferance.

"Well, you know how upset Jason was when you were ill? I thought, if something happened to you . . ."

"I have to play the invalid again?" Laurel asked with obvious disfavour.

"Well, no, not exactly."

"*What*, exactly?"

224

"I thought—I thought that one day, when he was here, you—might fall down the stairs!"

"Fall down the stairs!" Laurel exploded, in horrified astonishment. "Danila, do you realize that people can get killed falling downstairs?"

"Laurel! What a gruesome thought!" a thoroughly discountenanced girl flared up reproachfully. "How could you say such a thing?"

"Because it's true, you miserable girl! Mama's Aunt Martha stumbled on stairs and broke her neck. Do you have a mind to do me in?"

"Oh. You couldn't be very careful?" Danila asked hopefully, reluctant to scotch this plan, failing to be properly impressed with Laurel's objections.

"No! And if your other suggestions are as outlandish as this one, you can save your breath!"

On reflection Danila agreed, "I suppose that idea *is* too risky, and I hope you will not take it into your head to try it after all."

"Danila," Laurel asked, suspecting she was being gammoned, "are you serious?"

The girl grinned and owned, "I am teasing, love. I know you will not be so imprudent. But—how about this? When Jason returns, we will go to Hyde Park to stroll around the grounds, and you can fall into the Serpentine!"

Envisioning this prospect was too much for Laurel, and she dissolved into a fit of laughter. "Danila, now I know you are gulling me. You little minx, how dare you be so outrageous?"

"But, Laurel, I am perfectly serious."

"No! I will not credit it."

"Yes. Just think of the possibilities. Jason will have to jump in to rescue you and, well—anything might happen."

"What might happen, my dear girl, is that my instinct for survival would no doubt rear its head, and I would save myself!"

"Do you mean to tell me you can *swim?*" Danila deplored with a dark frown.

"Yes, I'm afraid so," Laurel apologized, putting her hand over her mouth to hold back her laughter.

"Really, Laurel, you are the most unnatural girl. Can't you learn to use any wiles at all?"

"It appears not. I fear I am a hopeless case."

"I suppose that scheme won't do either. It would turn into a farce with you flailing about, looking the fool."

"Yes, so I think, too. I am sure I should make a hash of it."

Danila awarded her giddy friend a forbidding look and announced resolutely, "Then it shall have to be the third choice."

"Do you keep me in suspense. I am all atwitter."

"You must fall off your horse!"

"I have never fallen off a horse in my life!" Laurel protested indignantly.

"What has that to say to anything?"

"Actually, when I think of it," Laurel pronounced as she saw the flagrant flaws in this gamble, "I place that idea in the same category as your first suggestion. The results could be every bit as unacceptable."

"Not if you were riding slowly so that you would not be thrown for a loop," Danila explained reasonably.

"Wouldn't it be rather obvious?" Laurel asked dubiously.

"You could just sort of slide off when Jason wasn't looking, and then you could pretend you were hurt."

"Well, I must say, that is much less dismaying than your other brainstorms. But, Danila, I seem to have missed a point here. I *am* sorry to be such a dunderhead, but would you tell me just why it is that I must do something as madcap as this?"

"Oh, you *are* a goose! So that Jason will be alarmed and will take you in his arms and whisper soft words in your ear!"

"Why didn't you say so?" Laurel chided with a quivering lip. "Such an end result would certainly influence my decision."

"Laurel, you have been remarkably whimsical about this," Danila charged testily. "Will you do it?"

"I shall see how things work out the next few days. It might be entirely a wasted effort," Laurel replied unsatisfactorily. "Now let us speak of lighter matters. Did you know Mama and Theo were planning a ball?"

"Really? When?"

"In a week or so . . ."

Chapter
FOURTEEN

With the end of the Season in sight Laurel allowed herself to be persuaded to join her friends and Lady Madeline at a number of elegant affairs. She was particularly careful not to be too friendly towards eligible gentlemen, although it did appear that word had gotten around that she was adamant in her intention to remain unattached. One morning she asked Lady Madeline, "Mama, just what did you tell my admirers that I am no longer considered a prize?"

"I merely advised Mr. Smythe and Lord Orwell that your affections were already engaged. His Grace I threatened with bodily harm," her mother told her.

"It is no wonder you and Danila have such rapport," Laurel said, shaking her head. "She could have been your daughter. You are both past praying for."

Lady Madeline spent a lot of time with Theo Devereaux, planning their party, and the girls were occasionally called upon to break a deadlock. A message was sent to Jason demanding his presence, which he acknowledged promptly, advising that he would return immediately since he now had everything ordered to his satisfaction. This information was received with considerable expectation in the hearts and minds of several ladies, and Danila once again cornered Laurel in her room to encourage her to act out their little stratagem, "for we don't have much time."

"I didn't say I would do it, you know," Laurel reminded her.

"I know, but if he still has his head in the sand, will you then?" a plaguesome girl persisted.

"Maybe, if I feel the situation is desperate," Laurel replied, a less than enthusiastic, but, nonetheless, tolerably positive, response, which Danila found mildly hopeful.

That afternoon Laurel refused to ride with Danila and Philip because she did not want to be out when Jason called. Danila decided that they would return early as she meant to give her guardian a trimming for decamping in that unconscionable manner, a resolution that prompted her betrothed to warn, "My love, you had better show some restraint because you know you do not always come out too well when you pull caps with my cousin."

They had not been gone a quarter of an hour when Jason arrived. He was directed to the drawing room, where Laurel was waiting. If he had not already known how she felt about him, he would certainly have discerned it from the look of pure joy on her face when he walked into the door.

She stood and reached out her hands, welcoming him happily, "Jason, I am so glad to see you. I have been so impatient, wondering what you have been doing."

He grinned and pulled her into his arms as he said teasingly, "So you have missed me, too," and tightening his hold on her, he murmured hoarsely, "I can hardly bear it when I am away from you, darling. Did you know that?" He tilted her radiant face with his hand and kissed her with all the depth of passion he had been storing up all these years. "I love you, Laurel. I want very much to marry you."

"Oh, Jason, I have been waiting so long to hear you say that," Laurel confessed shakily. "I do love you so dreadfully."

He leaned back to look at her and said fiercely, "I have been the worst kind of fool. For a while I thought I should not press my suit because you were young and had not met

229

many other men. It wasn't always easy. I almost spoke when we were returning from Italy."

"I know, Jason. I have held that moment close to my heart and have chastised myself times out of mind for not encouraging you. I was afraid it might be just the mood of the moment. I was always afraid, you know, because," she confessed as she wrapped her arms tightly around his neck, "you see how it is with me. I could not bear it if you should be put off by my warmth of feeling."

"Yes, darling, I see how it is with you," he said softly. "So it is with me also, and I can assure you there is no possibility that I will ever have any objection to receiving constant reminders of your affections, especially since I propose to be very generous with mine." And he proceeded for the next several minutes to demonstrate his intentions, sending a willing Laurel into transports.

"Jason," Laurel said presently with a happy sigh, "I am so glad you have declared yourself before Danila lured me into another of her schemes."

"What is she up to now?" Jason asked quizzically.

Laurel laughed and described Danila's strategies for "striking him all of a heap." "I confess I wasn't too caught up with any of her ideas."

"I should hope not! That girl needs a firm hand. But," he conceded ruefully, "I can understand why she thought I needed a push, even though it was always my intention that we should marry. Everyone understood that, including Uncle George. He had a habit of speaking of us as a couple."

"What do you mean?"

"Oh, he would say things like 'When you and Laurel settle down . . .' I suspect he left Dismoreland to you as well as to me. I have thought on it, and I am convinced that you must have reminded him of his lost love. Anyway—I started to say—I did rather hang fire these past couple of years, still thinking you were not ready. Laurel, you little goose, why didn't you give me some sign? We have wasted so much time."

"I don't think so really, Jason," she said reflectively.

"We have already become so accustomed to each other and are such good friends that we will not have to go through a period of adjustment that most married couples, even Philip and Danila, have to experience. It will be just lovely."

The perfectly blissful look on her face encouraged her young man to resume his amorous activities, and he murmured in her ear, "Darling, I may have been a slowtop, but I suddenly find myself very impatient. Will you marry me very soon?"

"Of course, Jason. You know I wish to, but I *should* like it if we could move into Dismoreland," she said wistfully.

"And just what do you think I have been about these past two weeks?" he chided in mock indignation.

"Do you mean it *will* be ready?" she exclaimed happily.

"Most certainly, my love. I told you, remember, that I have given explicit orders that certain rooms be finished posthaste, and that included the most important one. I also have been working on plans to complete the other wing for a very special purpose," he remarked meaningfully, and then asked in a teasing voice, "Really, Laurel, did you actually think I meant to sleep in that big bed all by myself?"

"Well," she admitted unblushingly, "it did cross my mind that it was a bit sumptuous, and I *did* have hopes that you had bought the poudreuse and writing table for me."

Jason laughed and kissed her, remarking, "I know you will forgive me for staying away so long when you see how famously the work has progressed. I wanted the house ready for occupancy as soon as possible, so I have given Master Corcoran a deadline for finishing certain rooms."

"I can't wait to see it, Jason. And I have found wallpaper for some of the rooms. I have samples for you to approve. The rolls are being held for us for a few days."

"Good. And I have the plans to show you a couple of changes we made."

They spread their work on the card table and reported on their separate pursuits of the last two weeks, becoming fully preoccupied, as they usually did, which is how they were found by Danila and Philip an hour later.

Lighting upon this familiar and totally unwelcome scene, Danila came to stand over them and demanded ominously, *"What* are you *doing?"*

Jason turned a critical eye on his ward and said dryly, "It's nice to see you, too, Danila. Have you been behaving yourself?"

"Oh! You abominable man! Do not speak of me in such a fashion," the girl fumed predictably.

"It was not chivalrous, I admit. But you know, discourtesy breeds discourtesy," Jason told her.

Danila lowered her head and apologized, "I'm sorry, Jason. It's just that you have been gone so long, and it would seem that you could have put off working for one day at least."

"But I am very anxious that we make some decisions before we leave town," Jason explained provokingly, not being able to resist baiting her, knowing full well why she was so on her mettle.

"Is that *all* you ever think of? You might show Laurel a little sympathy. She has been having a perfectly awful time of it while you have been buried in your old Dismoreland!"

Jason raised an eyebrow and turned to Laurel, "Is that true, love? What happened?"

"Oh, nothing so dreadful," the pawn in these arguments demurred in embarrassment.

"She just had to turn away four suitors—that's all!" Danila announced dramatically.

"Only four?" Jason queried in amusement. "Let's see— that would have been Pittman and Orwell and—uh— Carlton Smythe and"—with a dark frown—"not Yarwood?"

"Mama warned me about that, Jason. That's one reason I went to stay with Theo. When he announced his intentions to my irrepressible mother, she made short work of him."

"Good! I'm sorry, Laurel. I wouldn't have left if I had

thought you would have been harassed by such a disreputable character," Jason apologized self-reproachfully.

"It's all right, Jason. Everything is fine now."

He leaned over to kiss her, causing Danila to sit up and take wide-eyed notice. She asked meaningfully, "Is there something you two should be telling us?"

"Yes, you saucy minx," Jason confirmed with a laugh. "Laurel and I are going to be married immediately and will go to Paris for our honeymoon, but we'll return in time for your wedding."

"And when will that be?" Philip asked with a deceptive calm.

"Oh—in five or six weeks."

"The devil it will! What makes you think I am going to await your pleasure?"

"Surely five or six weeks is not too long!" Jason protested in surprise.

"Wrong, my dear cousin. I am posting the banns Sunday, and Danila and I are going to be married in three weeks."

"When did you decide that?" Jason asked with suspicion.

"Just now!" Philip answered belligerently. "I'll be deuced if I am going to put off our wedding date to please you. *You* can wait!"

"It beats me why you are suddenly so unaccommodating," Jason said caustically. "You know the girls will want to attend each other, and I see no reason you should have precedence. Laurel and I have waited much longer than you and Danila—"

"That's not my fault. You're the one who couldn't see an inch beyond your nose," Philip noted unsympathetically.

Danila and Laurel were enjoying this surprising altercation, feeling a pleasurable excitement at their betrotheds' professed impatience, and they grinned at each other foolishly. But Danila suggested, "Perhaps we should put a stop to this before they come to dagger points."

Laurel nodded her agreement, so Danila marched over

to put her hand on Philip's arm. "Will you two stop battling like a couple of fighting cocks? There is a very simple solution to this dilemma, you know."

Both men eyed her balefully, not pleased with this unceremonious interruption just when they were warming to the battle, and she explained hurriedly, "We will have a double wedding."

Jason and Philip stared at her blankly, then looked at each other and burst out .laughing. Philip put his arms around her and apologized with a sheepish face, "I'm sorry, darling. We should have applied to you. I should have known you would think of something."

And so four happy friends settled themselves comfortably in pairs and began to make plans for the Grand Affair. It was agreed that at first they would go their separate ways but in a month would meet in Paris.

Lord Schofield came upon this harmonious scene, and he was immediately apprised of all the latest developments. He offered his congratulations, approved the arrangements, and promised that they would toast the couples before dinner that evening. Lady Madeline and Lady Clarinda also appeared and perceived the situation in a glance. Laurel confirmed their presumptions as she announced with a beatific expression, "It is all settled, Mama. Jason and I are to be married soon, and we will have a double wedding with Danila and Philip."

Lady Madeline smiled brilliantly and embraced her daughter and future son-in-law, declaring, "I am so pleased things have finally turned out as I hoped. It has been Theo's and my dearest wish. Oh dear! She should be here to join the celebration!"

"So she should, Maddy," Jason affirmed as he kissed Laurel lightly and rose from the couch. "I will go tell her the good news and bring her back for dinner."

So it was that a jubilant group gathered for a round of toasts and a sumptuous repast as the chef outdid himself, signifying the staff's approval of coming events.

The next day Lady Madeline, Danila, and Laurel hurried to the draper's to choose fabrics for two wedding dresses. Laurel chose an ivory lace over a satin petticoat that would look well with the ivory layered sheer silk organza that Danila had fancied. The dressmakers were sent for, and the next several mornings the girls were fully occupied preparing their bride clothes. The gentlemen themselves had their own wardrobes to order, a project that afforded some satisfaction to several bootmakers, tailors, and shirtmakers.

In a few days, on the first of June, a large assembly of close friends and special acquaintances gathered at Dismore House, on which happy occasion Lady Madeline and Theo Devereaux proudly announced Laurel and Jason's betrothal.

Jason kept Laurel to himself all evening, causing several to raise their brows, but he was not the least intimidated. Laurel found this wholly agreeable, for as she told her swain, "I do not much like to dance with anyone else," provoking him to lean over to kiss her lightly.

Laurel tried to hide her rosy cheeks as she remarked wonderingly, "I believe I am become quite the coquette, and I can't imagine how I managed to suppress my inclinations all these years when I am finding the role excessively easy."

"Darling, you had better behave yourself," Jason admonished, smiling with a particular warmth in his eyes, "or I shall whisk you off to some secluded corner and treat you as you deserve."

"Do not tempt me, Jason," Laurel told him impishly.

During the evening they were joined occasionally by other guests, and Philip and Danila gave them a cursory attention, "though," Danila observed with a self-satisfied smirk, "they are not the least aware that there is anyone else in the room. I never dreamed Jason would comport himself so admirably as a Romeo."

"To each his own, my love. Then it is the most natural thing," Philip commented wisely, and to prove his point, he tightened his arm around her waist and whispered seductively in her ear.

Preparing for two weddings was only slightly more complicated than preparing for one, and all projects went smoothly despite the numerous fingers in the pie. A carriage and escort were sent to Bath for Miss Eddington so that she would have the honour of participating in the prenuptial festivities, and she proved herself extremely helpful in keeping Danila on an even keel.

Finally, on a lovely summer morning, two ecstatic couples stood before the altar at St. Michael-in-the-Fields and spoke their vows, witnessed by members of their families and close friends. Lady Madeline was particularly moved, though even as she watched the ceremony with misty eyes, an unworthy thought intruded upon her consciousness. It suddenly occurred to her that a natural outcome of this day's work would place her in a not exactly desirable category, for the prospect of becoming a grandmother offended her precious vanity. With a deep sigh she reminded herself philosophically, "You, my dear Madeline, must accept the inevitable and resign yourself to middle age," and she consoled herself with the thought that she would, after all, just have to put it about that she had married very young.

Dell Bestsellers

- [ ] **SHOGUN** by James Clavell $3.50 (17800-2)
- [ ] **JUST ABOVE MY HEAD**
  by James Baldwin $3.50 (14777-8)
- [ ] **FIREBRAND'S WOMAN**
  by Vanessa Royall $2.95 (12597-9)
- [ ] **THE ESTABLISHMENT** by Howard Fast $3.25 (12296-1)
- [ ] **LOVING** by Danielle Steel $2.75 (14684-4)
- [ ] **THE TOP OF THE HILL** by Irwin Shaw $2.95 (18976-4)
- [ ] **JAILBIRD** by Kurt Vonnegut $3.25 (15447-2)
- [ ] **THE ENGLISH HEIRESS**
  by Roberta Gellis $2.50 (12141-8)
- [ ] **EFFIGIES** by William K. Wells $2.95 (12245-7)
- [ ] **FRENCHMAN'S MISTRESS**
  by Irene Michaels $2.75 (12545-6)
- [ ] **ALL WE KNOW OF HEAVEN**
  by Dore Mullen $2.50 (10178-6)
- [ ] **THE POWERS THAT BE**
  by David Halberstam $3.50 (16997-6)
- [ ] **THE LURE** by Felice Picano $2.75 (15081-7)
- [ ] **THE SETTLERS**
  by William Stuart Long $2.95 (15923-7)
- [ ] **CLASS REUNION** by Rona Jaffe $2.75 (11408-X)
- [ ] **TAI-PAN** by James Clavell $3.25 (18462-2)
- [ ] **KING RAT** by James Clavell $2.50 (14546-5)
- [ ] **RICH MAN, POOR MAN** by Irwin Shaw $2.95 (17424-4)
- [ ] **THE IMMIGRANTS** by Howard Fast $3.25 (14175-3)
- [ ] **TO LOVE AGAIN** by Danielle Steel $2.50 (18631-5)

At your local bookstore or use this handy coupon for ordering:

DELL BOOKS
P.O. BOX 1000, PINEBROOK, N.J. 07058

Please send me the books I have checked above. I am enclosing $ _____
(please add 75¢ per copy to cover postage and handling). Send check or money
order—no cash or C.O.D.'s. Please allow up to 8 weeks for shipment.

Mr/Mrs/Miss _____

Address _____

City _____ State/Zip _____